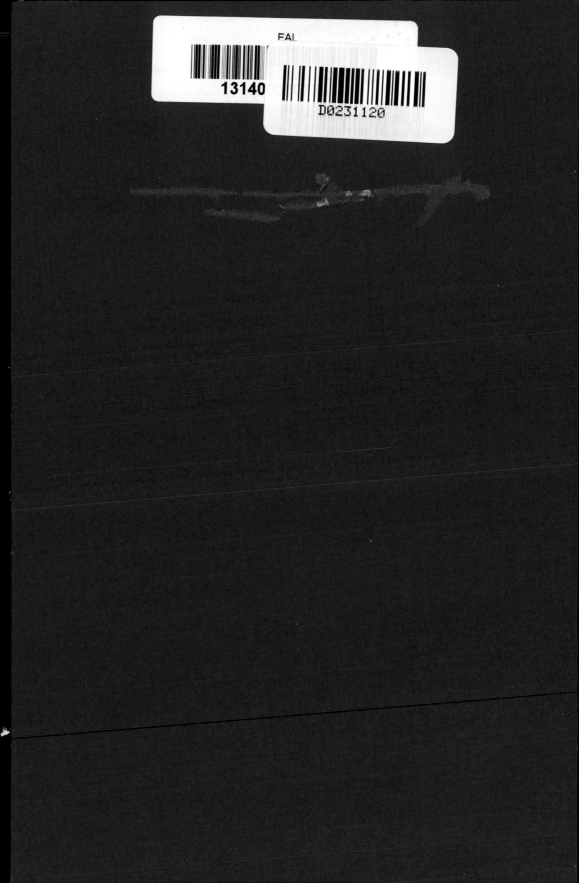

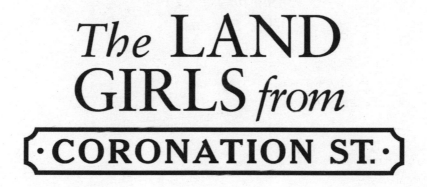

The LAND
GIRLS *from*
·CORONATION ST.·

Also by Maggie Sullivan

Christmas on Coronation Street
Mother's Day on Coronation Street
Snow on the Cobbles
The Postmistress

The LAND GIRLS *from*

·CORONATION ST.·

MAGGIE SULLIVAN

HarperCollins*Publishers*

HarperCollins*Publishers*
The News Building,
1 London Bridge Street,
London SE1 9GF

1

www.harpercollins.co.uk

HarperCollins*Publishers*
1st Floor, Watermarque Building, Ringsend Road
Dublin 4, Ireland

Coronation Street is an ITV Studios Production
Copyright © ITV Ventures Limited 2021

Maggie Sullivan asserts the moral right to
be identified as the author of this work

A catalogue record for this book
is available from the British Library

ISBN: 978-0-00-839396-0

Typeset in Sabon LT Std by Palimpsest Book Production Ltd, Falkirk, Stirlingshire

Printed and bound in Great Britain by CPI Group (UK) Ltd, Croydon CR0 4YY

MIX
Paper from
ponsible sources
C" C007454

:pendently certified FSC™ paper
forest management.

ww.harpercollins.co.uk/green

To Ann Parker and Jannet Wright

Part One

April 1943

Chapter 1

'Eeh, she's not got the sense she were born with, my Vera. Some of the things she says and does!' Ena Sharples gave an exaggerated sigh as she emptied the bottle of milk stout into her glass and looked in turn at each of her two companions. Ena got together with Martha Longhurst and Minnie Caldwell most nights at this hour in the snug at the Rovers Return in Coronation Street. It was Weatherfield's most popular local if you believed Annie Walker, the pub's landlady.

'It's the same with our Lily,' Martha said, matching Ena's sigh. 'I despair what she might be getting up to next.'

'If you don't mind my saying,' Minnie Caldwell cleared her throat though her voice was still muffled,

'Vera does have a few years on your lass, Martha. Such behaviour's more likely to be expected of Lily. How old is your Vera now, Ena?'

'She'll be 23 next March,' Ena said, staring straight ahead, her lips set tightly together. 'Though you wouldn't know it sometimes. I still maintain she's not been the same since she was dropped on her head when she was a kiddie.'

'True enough, my Lily's only 17.' Martha couldn't help a note of pride in her voice as her lips twitched into a smile. 'But the two of them get on well enough together,' she added quickly. 'It's quite surprising, really.'

'That's true. Vera always likes it whenever Lily comes over to the Mission when I have to go out for a long while. Though of course I never tell her the real reason Lily's there.'

'I was thinking more about the times Vera's been over at our place.' Martha stopped, aware that Ena had looked up sharply. 'Though it's only happened once or twice.'

'And when was that?' Ena demanded.

'I don't remember exactly.' Martha wished she'd never spoken. 'It was a while ago. And that reminds me,' she said quickly, 'do you still want Lily to come and sit with Vera tomorrow night?'

Ena pulled a creased cotton handkerchief from her handbag and wiped a dew drop from her nose. 'Yes, I do, as a matter of fact. I might be out late and I'll feel better in my mind if I know Vera's not on her own.'

'Of course.' Martha sat well back to avoid Ena's glare.

'It's because I've got to go and sort out the order of hymns for a marriage ceremony we've got on at the Mission next week,' Ena said.

'Oh, who's getting wed?' Martha asked, glad to break the tension.

'One of the young Joneses from Rosamund Street and I've to play the music for them. I need to find out what's what so's I can practise the accompaniment.'

Martha managed to suppress a giggle. Ena's harmonium playing was legendary in Coronation Street. She'd belt out tunes on her old harmonium at the Mission of Glad Tidings whether anyone wanted to be accompanied or not. 'All right,' Martha said, 'I'll ask her to come round straight from work, shall I? I'm sure she won't mind.'

'Aye,' Ena said, 'that way Vera'll think she's just stopping by for a chat.'

'Do you not think it might be time for you to leave Vera on her own more?' Minnie said suddenly, though her voice was barely above a whisper and her gaze didn't get beyond the top button of Ena's double-breasted coat. 'I know you leave her for the odd hour or so when you pop in to the Rovers, Ena, but don't you think you could start leaving her alone in the vestry for longer now?' Her voice trailed off and she stared down at her lap, almost overwhelmed that she'd dared to voice an opinion. She and Martha had often discussed the fact that Ena's protectiveness made Vera seem slower than perhaps she really was, but neither of them had ever plucked up the courage to say so.

For a moment Ena looked as if she was about to scold Minnie, and Minnie and Martha exchanged worried glances. But to their relief Ena merely shook her head. 'I don't want to leave her alone any longer than I have to. And neither would you. Not if you knew the kind of daft things she can get up to, even when I'm there.'

'Like what?' Martha asked.

'Never mind that!' Ena brushed her aside. 'She's weak and she's easily led. Just ripe for folk like that Elsie Tanner to tempt her into wicked ways. You've got to have eyes in the back of your head when you've got neighbours like her,' Ena went on, and she wagged her finger at no one in particular. 'I get worried every time I see her even talking to Vera. I swear I'll swing for that woman one day, but I'll not let her lead my daughter astray.' With that, she gulped down the last of her drink and hurriedly made her way out of the pub.

Elsie Tanner knocked on the door of the vestry and Vera Sharples opened it.

'Hello, love, it's good to see you. Are you all right?'

'Yes, thanks, Mrs Tanner, I'm fine,' Vera said. 'Ooh, you look nice.'

Elsie was wearing a snugly fitting dress with a low-cut bodice in a striking reddish print. It matched the red of her hair which had been piled up into stiff curls on top of her head as though she was ready for a special outing.

'Is your mam in?' Elsie asked with a smile, though she already knew the answer to her question.

'No, she's out,' Vera said. 'Lily's here with me.' She indicated the sitting room. 'She came round after work and I've made us a spam sandwich. Would you like one?' She opened the door wider to let Elsie in, and she couldn't help commenting on her silk stockings and high-heeled shoes.

'A present,' Elsie said, and to Vera's astonishment she winked. 'No thanks to the sandwich, but I might have a cup of summat if you can spare it.'

'We've got a bit of Camp left in the bottle – will that do?' Vera asked; she'd been given strict instructions not to offer tea to anyone without Ena's say so, as it was heavily rationed.

'That would be lovely. Thanks, love.' And Elsie carefully checked the street before she shut the door and followed Vera into the back room.

Vera and her mother had lived in the two-room living quarters behind the Mission of Glad Tidings for several years now, but they still didn't have much in the way of equipment or crockery. Vera took down the remaining cup from the dresser and put it on the freshly scrubbed table top. 'We have no more ration coupons till next week, I'm afraid,' Vera said.

'That's all right,' Elsie responded with a smile.

'Do you know Lily Longhurst?' Vera asked.

Elsie nodded towards Lily. 'Martha's lass? Of course. Hello chuck,' she said, 'and as a matter of fact I'm glad you're here, Lily. This could be your lucky night.' She turned to Vera. 'I was wondering if you knew anything about the GI barracks out at Burtonwood?' Elsie said.

'No.' Vera shook her head. 'What's that?'

'It's not far from here. It's the place where the American soldiers are based.'

Vera shrugged. She topped up a spoonful of the Camp coffee essence that she'd measured into the cup with boiling water from the pan that was hanging over the hearth and passed it to Elsie.

'Well, they've got a dance on there tonight at the barracks,' Elsie said. 'And I hear that they're looking for more girls to dance with the soldiers. They haven't got enough.'

Vera's eyes lit up and she looked at Lily. 'That sounds nice! What do you think, Lily?'

'Of course, you might have to ask your mother, before you can decide,' Elsie said before Lily could answer, 'but I did wonder if you might like to go?'

Vera's eyes widened.

'Is anyone else going from round here?' Lily wanted to know.

'Well, I'm going and I know there's at least a couple of other girls from Coronation Street and a couple from Rosamund Street who are keen to go,' Elsie said.

'I've never been to a proper dance,' Vera said and she clapped her hands like a little girl and looked at Elsie defiantly. 'But I can't ask my mother if she's not here, can I? And in any case, I know what she'll say.' For a moment she looked as if she might burst into tears. 'It's what she always says.' She took a deep breath and her expression brightened. 'But I want to go.'

'Then why don't we both go!' Lily said. 'I'd like to see *my* mam try and stop me.'

'You'd better leave a note for your mother, Vera,' Elsie suggested, 'or she'll be thinking you've gone missing or summat and get the police out.'

Vera giggled. 'How will we get there?' she asked.

'We don't have to worry about that. The American soldiers will send one of their trucks to pick us up,' Elsie said. 'If they want us, they have to fetch us, I always say.'

Now Vera hugged herself and giggled again. 'It's so exciting! But what should I wear?'

'Do we have to dress up, Mrs Tanner?' Lily asked. 'You look lovely if you don't mind my saying!'

Elsie laughed. 'I don't mind one little bit. Compliments are always welcome. Us girls have to take every opportunity to dress up, you know, Lily. We so rarely get the chance these days. Don't forget I've got little'uns at home, I'm not so footloose and fancy-free as you two. I've got to make the most of it.' Then she leaned across the table, her cleavage startlingly apparent. 'And I think you'd both better call me Elsie if we're going off to the dance together, don't you?'

'I'll have to go home and change,' Lily said.

'That's fine. If you could be back here in say, an hour?' Elsie said. 'Then we'll be in good time. I've got a sitter coming for little Linda and baby Dennis.'

'I can be ready in an hour,' Vera said. She looked really excited and, without heed, she stepped forward to make faces in the mirror that was over the mantelpiece.

'What are you doing? Be careful of the flames!' Elsie cried, and managed to haul her back in time, but Vera didn't seem to be aware of the danger. She was too busy pouting and running her fingers through her mousey-coloured hair, dragging it forwards across her right eye in the way she'd seen Veronica Lake do in the cinema. But Vera had a small, heart-shaped face that was almost completely covered by the lank curtain of hair, so that far from looking sexy, she hid most of her features and it was impossible to see her eyes at all.

'I don't care what my mother would say,' she said, giving up on her hair, but she knew her words sounded much bolder than she felt.

Lily ran all the way home. She was very excited and wanted to share her good news. She had made up her mind to go, whatever her mother said, though she hoped Martha wouldn't object to her going to a dance. After all, it wasn't every day she and Vera had the chance to go to a proper grown-up do with swing music and lots of men to dance with, though she thought it might be better not to say that they would be going with Elsie Tanner.

But when she arrived she found her father was home and she knew she would have a different kind of battle on her hands. Percy Longhurst was sitting at the dining table in his shirt sleeves, the morning's racing pages open in front of him, and he was shouting abuse at her mother who wasn't even in the room. As usual, Martha was in the kitchen where the banging of dishes and the rattling of pans threatened to drown out the abuse she was hurling back at her husband.

'And if you're not gambling it away, you lazy good-for-nothing, then you're pouring it down your throat!' It was not the first time Lily had heard Martha's accusations. She always tried to escape when they argued like this, but for a moment she was rooted to the spot.

'Don't you talk about me like that, when you spend every blooming night in the Rovers with your so-called pals.'

'You can't compare my two glasses of milk stout to what you manage to put away of a night. More than half of your wages' worth some nights, I reckon.'

'So what? I usually manage to win back most of what that costs by the next dinner time.'

Martha laughed. 'Are you kidding me? All I see is the money going out and staying out. How many times have I not had enough from you to put a decent meal on the table? If I wouldn't do my few hours in the corner shop I don't know where we'd be. Starving, most like.'

Neither of them seemed to notice Lily coming in and for several minutes she stood at the foot of the stairs in the living room, not wanting to draw attention to herself. They were trading the same old arguments and she had heard them all before so when she could stand it no longer she covered her ears with her hands and made her way up to her bedroom to change. The words were still flying freely when she came back down again, but Martha had moved into the living room.

Lily had settled for the pretty summer frock that Martha had made for her the previous summer that fortunately still fitted but she hesitated to show it off now, not sure whether she wanted them to notice her at all. The dress was in a heavy starched cotton and was covered with pink and blue flowers that she thought looked pretty against her pale complexion. At 17, she was very proud of her trim figure and the style of the dress was flattering with the shoulders widening out into puff sleeves and the bodice tapering towards her tiny waist that she liked to emphasize with a narrow belt. It was such a contrast to the shapeless overalls she had to wear at work when she had to make sure there was nothing that could catch in the sewing machine where she sat buttonholing and hemming all day. But if it was compliments she was hoping for she could see from the angry looks on their faces that she would have to wait a long time for either of her parents to actually notice she was there.

Lily crept down the stairs and was preparing to sneak across the room and out of the house when, to her horror, Percy suddenly reached out and caught hold of her wrist.

'And where do you think you're going, miss?' He pulled on her arm and she was forced to stop.

'Anywhere to get out of this madhouse!' Lily cried, but the grip tightened painfully. 'If you must know, I'm going to a dance,' she said.

'Let her go, Percy! You're as bad as Ena Sharples. You won't be back late, will you, love?' Martha said to Lily.

'Back from where? Where is this dance?' Percy pulled Lily towards him. 'Cos I say you're not going anywhere.'

'Oh yes I am. Let go of me!' Lily shouted, trying to free her arm. 'I'm going with Vera Sharples, as a matter of fact. As if you care,' she said. 'Her mother asked me to be with her tonight.' She dearly wanted to shout 'so there!' and to thumb her nose at her father but she didn't quite dare, though knowing that she had her mother's backing she did feel brave enough to tug her arm free from his grasp and immediately flee the house.

Vera was all ready and waiting when Lily returned. She was peeking through the net curtains of the parlour and she ran immediately to open the front door. 'I thought I'd wear my best dress,' she said, holding out the pink rayon and net skirt for Lily to admire. It had cap sleeves with little bows on the top and tiny frills that ran the whole way down the front. 'Mam says I look nice in this. And I like it too. Do you like it?' She did a twirl. 'It's got a belt – and see, it fastens at the front so that I don't need anyone to help button it up.'

'It looks really pretty,' Lily agreed, secretly thinking Vera had overdone it a bit.

'I wanted to look nice,' Vera said, with a sudden coyness. 'And you look nice too. I didn't want to let Elsie down,' she said and she gave a self-satisfied smile.

Burtonwood wasn't a long ride but by the time they arrived the dance was in full swing. The live music was blasting out through the loudspeakers and soldiers in their smart uniforms were clutching young girls in full-skirted dresses and whizzing them about the dancefloor.

From the moment they were helped down from the truck, all of the girls were whisked away to dance and Vera hardly saw Lily or Elsie again for the rest of the evening. Vera was not much of a dancer – she had never had any lessons – and she sometimes fell over her own feet, but none of her partners seemed to mind too much. She was willing and eager to try, and what they wanted was someone to swing, jive and jitterbug with across the dancefloor to the fast numbers or to put their arms around and hold closely during the slow numbers, and Vera never refused an offer.

By the time she had finished dancing the last waltz and the music had stopped, the crowd was beginning to thin and Vera had a sudden moment of panic, wondering what had happened to her friends and worrying about how she was going to get home. She had waved once to Elsie between dance sets when she had seen her at the bar, drinking and smoking with a particularly good-looking young man, and she had almost stepped on Lily's toes once during a slow foxtrot but hadn't seen either of them since so she was relieved to see Lily making her way across the dancefloor now.

'I thought I'd lost you,' Vera said, squeezing her friend's arm.

'That's not so easy,' Lily joked. 'Have you had a good time?'

'The best!' Vera's eyes shone as she wrapped her arms about her body in a huge hug. 'I lost count of how many different soldiers I've danced with. I feel quite giddy. It seemed like it was going on for ever. What time is it?'

'Dunno,' Lily replied. 'I suppose we better try and find Elsie.'

'I've got to take my shoes off – my feet are killing me,' Vera said.

'I'm sure no one will mind. Lots of them probably want to do the same thing! Are we going to get a ride home?'

'We most certainly are.' Elsie Tanner came up behind them and squeezed Vera's shoulder. 'In one of them army trucks like we came in. How are you doing, girls? Have you had a good time?'

Vera and Lily nodded enthusiastically.

At that moment a young soldier with two stripes on his sleeve waved a clipboard in the air and shouted, 'Anyone needing a ride back to Weatherfield please go to truck number two.' And he pointed to the yard where a truck already had the engine running.

'Come on, then, let's go,' Elsie said and, taking hold of Vera's arm, steered her in the right direction to where another soldier was helping the other Weatherfield girls into the truck. 'What do you think your mam will say when you get back?' Elsie asked Vera as the truck made its way down the bumpy dirt track. 'I bet she'll be waiting up with a rolling pin.'

Lily giggled but Vera frowned. 'I don't know and I almost don't care,' she said.

'Atta girl,' Elsie said. 'You make sure you keep your end up.'

'Honestly, I'm so tired right now I expect I'll fall straight into bed,' Vera said, 'though I must remember to get in on the right side this time. I did once forget and my mam got very cross with me.'

Lily looked puzzled. 'How do you mean? Don't tell me you still sleep in the same bed with your mam?'

Vera shrugged. 'Have done since me dad died. What's wrong with that?' she asked.

'Nowt,' Lily said quickly.

'Any road up, it's warmer that way.'

Elsie snorted but didn't say anything.

The truck turned onto a smoothly tarmacked road and, despite the dimness of the lighting, picked up speed as there were no other cars around. Lily sat back on the bench and stretched her slim legs in front of her.

'Are you glad you came?' she asked her friend.

Vera beamed. 'Course I am. I only hope I can get up in time for work in the morning. I can't afford for either me or me mam to have our wages docked.'

'Why should it affect your mam if you're late in at the factory?' Lily was curious.

'Cos we always go in together. We work on the same bench and she hates having to leave me to go to work on my own. She says she doesn't trust me to get dressed properly. Just because once I forgot to put on my liberty bodice and I had my jumper on inside out.'

Elsie sniggered. 'Why won't you be able to get up early?'

'Because I might still have a sore head,' Vera said, 'like I've got now.'

'Have you been drinking anything you shouldn't have?' Elsie wanted to know.

Vera looked uncertain. 'I suppose I might have in the stops in between the dancing. The soldiers always wanted to buy me a drink.'

'Like what? What were you drinking?'

'I've no idea. They were all so polite I left it up to them to choose, and that was a real treat. We never have anything to drink like that at home. I don't know where they got their coupons from. But it was just so wonderful to be free the whole night without me mother watching me all the time!' She made a sudden gesture, throwing her hands up in the air, palms open, shouting 'Wheeee!' and she was laughing suddenly, as if she really had been drinking.

'Next time make sure you ask for something like a lemonade or a Coca-Cola,' Elsie said, looking at the young woman carefully.

'Do you think there'll be a next time?' Vera asked.

'Why shouldn't there be?' Elsie said.

'Because Mam will probably try and stop me.'

'Then you remind her about tonight. You've come to no harm, have you? Now tell us more about who you were dancing with,' Elsie said.

'Yes, you said you danced with loads of GIs,' Lily said. 'Was there anyone special?'

Vera's eyes lit up and her cheeks reddened as she nodded. 'There was one special bloke, yes,' she said quietly.

'Ooh, go on, tell us more,' Elsie encouraged her. 'What was he like? How old was he? Was he good-looking?'

'He was lovely,' Vera said, and she closed her eyes and put her arms out as if she were dancing. 'He went with some other girls as well, but he kept coming back to dance with me and he bought me a lemonade shandy, I do remember that.'

'Where was he from? Anywhere we've heard of?' Lily asked. 'Only some of them seem to come from places I can't even pronounce.' She laughed.

'He comes from California. Imagine that!' Vera said.

'I think that sounds so romantic.' Lily clasped her hands together. 'Don't you, Elsie?'

'California's where they make all the films. Did you know that?' Elsie asked.

'I know, he told me,' Vera said with some pride, 'only he called them movies. Anyway, he's blond and very good-looking.'

'Better than any of the lads who hang around Coronation Street?' Lily's tone was disparaging.

'Oh yes, tons better,' Vera admitted.

'Are you going to see him again?' Elsie wanted to know.

'I hope so. He had to go off before the end tonight

so he couldn't see me home, but he said he'd come to Weatherfield as soon as he could get some time off. Isn't that wonderful?'

'I must admit it does sound pretty wonderful,' Lily agreed. 'You gave him your telephone number, I hope?'

'Good heavens, no!' Vera was horrified. 'Could you imagine my mother's face if she answered the phone to a Yank?'

'Well, how else is he going to find you?' Elsie said. 'Next time give him your number and then make sure you always answer the phone.'

'I told him I lived at the Mission of Glad Tidings. Surely everyone knows where that is?'

Elsie tried to hide a smile at Vera's naiveté. 'I expect he'll drop in as soon as he gets a chance,' she said. 'Will you tell your mam about him?'

'Not yet,' Vera said. 'Knowing her she won't believe me. She'll think I'm making it up.'

'So it'll be a surprise when he turns up on the doorstep, then?' Lily said.

'Yes!' Vera said emphatically. 'And then she'll see that I was right to go to the dance after all and there was nowt wrong in Elsie asking me.'

'Exactly.' Elsie smiled.

'So, what was his name, this good-looking GI?'

Vera suddenly looked coy. 'I don't know if I should tell you,' she teased. 'You might try to steal him.' Elsie and Lily both laughed.

'Oh, go on,' Lily said, 'I promise not to.'

'Well, he's called Ronald, that's nice, isn't it? It's my favourite name,' Vera said, not attempting to disguise the boastful note in her voice.

'I think that's a smashing name,' Elsie agreed.

'Ronald Reagan,' Vera said triumphantly. 'Now, how's that for a grand-sounding name?'

The cheek of the woman! Ena Sharples sat at the vestry table letting anger fire her blood as she fingered the note she had just picked up, though she had no idea what time it had been written. All she knew was that when she came home Vera was out and Lily had gone too. The note had been scribbled on a piece of card torn from the last box of Weetabix breakfast cereal that had been in their almost-bare food cupboard and she recognized Vera's scrawl and dreadful spelling, immediately. *'Gone to a danse at the solgers base,'* she read. *'Don't wory, I'm with Elsie Tanner. Might be home late. See you later. V.'*

She'd read it so many times she knew it by heart and she tore it into shreds that she fed into the dying embers of the fire that smouldered in the grate. With Elsie Tanner indeed! The gall of that woman to entice my daughter away from her own home, when I bet she knew I'd be out, Ena thought, her rage exploding once more.

Ena's first reaction was that she should wait up until

they got home and confront Elsie, while at the same time banning Vera from ever speaking to the wretched woman again. But the more she thought about it the more she realized that that would probably make matters worse. Despite her age, Vera was obviously going through the rebellious stage that affected most girls when they hit adolescence. But as Vera was no longer an adolescent, to keep opposing her directly as she had done in the past was probably not a good idea.

Right now, what Vera needed was to be distracted, her attention diverted to other things, and there was only one way to deal with the problem. What better way than to find her a husband? Someone she could marry quickly, who would give her babies. *That* would keep her occupied and Ena would no longer have to worry. Marriage would not only keep her out of trouble but would remove her from the influence of the Elsie Tanners of this world.

The more Ena thought about it, the more she liked the idea and she began thinking about the men she knew who might make a suitable husband. It didn't take her too long to settle on Eric Bowman and she smiled with satisfaction. Then she switched off the light and went to bed; it might be best to let Vera think she had won this round.

Vera wasn't sure what kind of a welcome she expected when the truck dropped her off outside the Mission, for Ena always had something to say by way of a greeting whenever Vera went out, but she wasn't expecting the silence that she did find. She had, at the least, expected her mother to be sitting at the table, looking grim, her face buried in a newspaper. But there was nothing. No shouting, no angry face.

She still felt buoyed up by the excitement of the evening and it had temporarily made her lose her fear, for all she could think about was telling her mother about the people she'd met and the wonderful time she had had. But now, all that would have to wait until morning. Vera crept around the vestry as quietly as she could and, undressing quickly, crawled into bed. She could hear the deep breathing noises coming from Ena's side and thought about the considerable victory she had won tonight.

It would never have occurred to her to think that the snores might not be genuine. . . .

Vera was disappointed when more than a week went by and there was still no sign of Private Ronald Reagan. Ena had never asked her whether she'd enjoyed the dance and she hadn't managed to pluck up the courage to tell her about it. It had all seemed so different by the next morning and her bravado had evaporated. But now, when her mother repeatedly asked her what was wrong and why she was looking down in the dumps, she eventually ventured to tell her about the soldier she'd met and how it now looked like he had let her down. But if she had hoped for some sympathy she was to be even more disappointed, for Ena's first response was to hoot with laughter. She then proceeded to shout at her daughter, like she usually did, and hit her about the head with a rolled-up newspaper.

'You're soft in the head, you, just like I've always said,' Ena sneered. 'How could you be so stupid as to believe him, a GI? Ronald Reagan, indeed! Pah! And I thought you were supposed to be a cinemagoer.' But she didn't bother to explain what she meant by that.

'Maybe he's ill. Or maybe he couldn't find the Mission,' Vera whimpered, all bravado gone.

'If you believe that you'll believe anything!' Ena tossed her head angrily. 'I've told you before not to trust folk so easily.'

'Maybe I should try to go to his barracks. I could ask Elsie how to get there. She'll know how I can find him.'

Now Ena raised her hand in the threatening gesture Vera was used to. She took a step forwards and Vera instinctively jumped out of the way though she knew Ena was unlikely to actually strike her.

'Don't you let me hear you talk about that barracks ever again!' Ena shouted. 'And if I catch you going anywhere near that floozy of an Elsie Tanner, I swear I'll—' She clenched her fists in frustration though she didn't finish the sentence, but Vera's behaviour had made her more determined than ever to seek out Eric Bowman.

Vera was astonished at the strength of feeling behind Ena's outburst about Elsie and could only stare at her mother, open-mouthed.

'It's not Elsie's fault he's not shown up,' she said eventually, though so softly she couldn't be sure that Ena had heard. 'And I had a lovely time at the dance,' she said more boldly, though Ena's stern glare made her stand well back. 'I thought you'd be pleased for me. It's not as though it's my fault that it's not turned out well – I wasn't to know.' Then she turned and ran, shutting the bedroom door before she let the pent-up tears of frustration and humiliation cascade down her cheeks.

Chapter 2

'I hear you're on the lookout for a fella.' Elsie Tanner approached Ena Sharples with a cheeky sparkle in her eye when they were in the Rovers Return one night, several days after the dance fiasco. 'Looking for some poor sucker you can trick into becoming an unsuspecting bridegroom, are you?'

Ena had, of course, confided her plans to her cronies, and they'd relished spreading the gossip.

Ena's brow wrinkled and she opened her mouth to protest but Elsie got in first. 'Not for yourself, of course; I realize you're a bit long in the tooth for that.' Elsie fingered her own low-cut blouse to reveal even more cleavage than usual and patted her heavily reddened curls. She paused long enough to giggle at Ena's outraged expression but not long enough to let Ena get a word in. 'You want someone for your poor lass who you've tried to keep hidden away all this time, wrapped up in cotton wool. God knows you've done your best to protect her from the world, all these years, like some kind of sleeping beauty.' Elsie was gratified to see Ena's face blush scarlet and her eyes practically bulge out of their sockets. 'I suppose you think that getting her married off will keep her out of harm's way?' she said with a laugh. 'But first you've got to find a Prince Charming who's willing to take her on. Not that there's owt wrong with Vera, she's a good lass. It's you he'd be wanting to steer clear of.'

'I'll thank you to keep your nose out of our family business, Elsie Tanner!' Ena snapped, and she stood up to confront Elsie, stretching to her full height. 'Haven't you done enough harm already?'

Elsie's eyes widened for a moment in feigned innocence then glinted as her brow furrowed. 'And I'll thank you to keep a civil tongue in your head, Mrs Sharples. Though I doubt you'll find a prince hanging around Weatherfield these days, certainly not one willing to wake your daughter up with a kiss. Not that the poor girl will know which end is up by the time you've done with her.' She gave a short laugh. 'You'll have sucked all the life out of her so that she won't know how to have a good time. I feel sorry for the lass, is all I can say, and the sooner she gets out of your clutches the better.'

'Your sympathy is wasted, Elsie Tanner.' Ena practically spat the name out. 'My daughter's perfectly capable of having a good time – in her own way.'

'What, like she did at the dance I took her to at the American base?' Elsie emphasized the words tauntingly. 'From the way she behaved I reckon it's the first grown-up treat she's ever had, but do you know what? She was no different from any of the other young lasses there. It's only a pity you weren't there to see it, but I made sure she had a good time.' Elsie fumbled in her handbag and turned away to light a cigarette, then she turned back to face Ena one more time, almost puffing the smoke in her face. 'Although I say it myself, I think it was the best night of her young life.'

Elsie was gratified when Ena's cheeks puffed out, displaying her obvious anger. 'And I'll tell you something else for nothing,' Elsie said, with a satisfied smile, 'your Vera's not half the dimwit you like to make her out to be. All she needs is the chance to have a bit of fun with friends of her own age, not live gathering dust in a mission hall.'

Elsie picked up her port and lemon and started to walk away, but Ena prodded Elsie's shoulder sharply with her finger. 'How dare you!' Ena raised her voice

'Oh, I dare, all right.' Elsie cut off her words with a grin. 'It's just a pity Vera doesn't dare a bit more.' And Elsie laughed out loud. 'I tell you what,' she went on, not trying to stop the smoke from her cigarette from curling in Ena's direction, 'Why don't you leave it to me? I'll find her a suitable lad.' She said the words scornfully. 'Though I don't know how he'll feel about having to take on her mother as well.'

'You've no need to bother, thank you very much,' Ena all but shouted. 'There are some very eligible young lads come to the Mission of a Sunday, who could do far worse than our Vera.'

'A mission boy, is that right?' Elsie scoffed. 'And what would he be doing in the Glad Tidings hall when there's a war on?' She winked and watched with satisfaction as Ena clenched and unclenched her fists, her chest heaving.

'I'll have you know I've already got my eye on someone who's just the ticket.' Ena attempted to end the conversation.

'And what does Vera think of him?' Elsie asked. 'Or do you not care?'

'My Vera doesn't think owt without my say so. She'll do as she's told.'

'Is that right? Well, you might be in for a nasty shock, Ena Sharples. Believe you me, there's more to that girl than meets the eye.' Elsie's tone had an exultant ring.

She leaned forwards and wagged her finger close to Ena's face. 'I reckon that daughter of yours will surprise you one of these days, you mark my words.'

Chapter 3

Vera was sitting on the edge of her bed and she couldn't stop crying. Ena had already left in disgust, but Vera didn't know how she was going to face the girls at the factory where they worked together. How could she, once the story of Ena's barney with Elsie in the Rovers Return had done the rounds? Now everyone would know that Ena was on the lookout for a nice Christian boy so that she could marry Vera off as soon as possible. The story had already whipped round Coronation Street, so the factory girls were bound to have heard it too. The trouble was that in Weatherfield everyone knew everyone else's business, sometimes before they had time to know their own.

'Surely she wouldn't do that to me?' Vera sobbed

out loud. She thought back to all the times she had let her mother take charge of things. It had always been easier that way, but did Ena really think Vera would let her choose a husband for her?

As soon as Vera clocked on at the factory and hung up her coat she doubled over, pretending she badly needed to go to the lav, and she begged her supervisor to allow her five minutes' special time. What she really needed was some cold water to splash on her face before anyone saw her puffy eyes because she'd cried all the way as she ran to get to work on time. Her supervisor tapped her watch and held up her hand – five minutes and no more – so Vera disappeared down the stairs and into the basement as quickly as she could before anyone else could see her go. Vera hated working on the same factory bench as Ena; she felt as if she was under constant scrutiny but that was something she'd had no choice about.

It was cold and dark in the basement and there was a lingering smell of disinfectant on the damp air so she had to take a deep breath to avoid losing her breakfast. But at least down there the racket of the machinery was nothing more than a distant hum. Vera leaned up against the cold damp wall, taking no heed of the condensation. She turned on the solitary tap in the sink in the corridor and wiped her eyes and nose with the piece of flimsy cotton from her pocket that served as a handkerchief.

Fancy my own mother talking about me in public like that – Vera's thoughts were screaming in her head – as if I had no feelings? She wants to find me a husband but what about what *I* want? She sat down heavily on a nearby carton. I can't let her take over my life like that. The words were swimming silently in her head because she didn't say them out loud for fear she might start crying again. She took a deep breath. I'll show her, she thought. I might have made a mistake with one American soldier but there are plenty more fish in the sea. I'll find my own husband, thank you very much.

Suddenly feeling full of defiance and with a new determination, she stood up abruptly, but just as quickly sat down again. The story was bound to be all around the factory floor by now and really she just wanted to go home.

Vera didn't realize she'd made any kind of noise until she heard a reedy, high-pitched male voice call out, 'Who's there? What are you doing down here? Show yourself, now.' And the next minute a flashlight was shining directly into her eyes.

She lifted her hands to fend off the glare. 'It's me,' she said, unhelpfully.

'Yer what?'

'I said it's me,' she repeated.

'And who's me when you're at home? Say your name.' The voice struck a deeper note as if trying to sound more authoritative. 'What are you doing down here? It's not time for a lav break yet.'

'It's Vera Sharples.' Her voice trembled. 'I work upstairs in the factory and I got special permission to use the lav. I've not been feeling well and I won't be long.'

The beam of the torch flashed to the side and was no longer directed onto her face. Vera blinked, trying to refocus to the dim, shadowy light. It took a few moments but she could eventually see that the young man standing in front of her was considerably taller than she was and that he was slim, even skinny, like a matchstick man. His face seemed to be in even darker shadow, as if he hadn't shaved. He was wearing dark overalls, probably regulation brown, she guessed, with Earnshaw embroidered on the left-hand breast pocket. He looked familiar and she was sure she had seen him hanging around the factory.

'Was it the lav you was wanting?' he asked, not unkindly.

'I did, but I'm all right now, thanks. I'm ready to go back up.'

'Here, I'll put the light on for you,' he said. 'Them stairs can be dangerous in the dark.'

She heard the click of a light switch but nothing happened.

'Don't worry, I've got my torch here,' he said. 'Come on, then, I'll take you back upstairs.' And he flashed the light in front of him.

'Thanks,' she said again.

'It's pretty gloomy down here in the best of times, never mind when the lights are not working. It's a good job I've got a torch,' he said, and he offered her his arm. 'I'm Bob, by the way. Bob Lomax. I'm one of the maintenance men,' he added proudly.

'Thanks very much, Bob,' Vera said and she clung on to his arm. As they climbed the stairs the heat of the factory hit her forcibly, as did the light, and she glanced across to look more closely at his face. He was quite handsome, she decided, though his needing-a-shave look was made all the more obvious by a slanting white scar that slashed across his upper lip. The dark brown of his hair was emphasized by the paleness of his skin, in particular the boyish cowlick that fell across his forehead. He looked at her as she regarded him and smiled.

He looked like a dark-haired version of her favourite film star, Alan Ladd, Vera thought as she let go of his arm. 'Thanks, Bob.' She made exaggerated lip movements since she knew her words would be swallowed up by the racket of the machinery as they emerged once more onto the factory floor and she gave a little wave as she hurried towards her bench. Bob stood watching her for a moment before turning away and she didn't realize she was grinning as she took her place on the workbench until she saw her mother scowling at her.

'Are you wanting to get your wages docked, or get

35

thrown out of here altogether, grinning like the Cheshire cat?' Ena barked. 'Where the heck have you been?'

Vera drew her lips into a straight line and chose not to answer. She caught sight of the supervisor making sure that she was returning to her work and tried her best to look as if she really had been ill.

Chapter 4

Ena stood in front of the mirror over the hearth and dropped her felt hat onto the hairnet that covered her hair. She patted it down without looking. She didn't really need to use the mirror as she had long since mastered the feel of the movements involved and she knew just where to position her arms so that the hat fell more or less accurately into place.

'Are you ready, Vera? We haven't got all day!' she shouted in the general direction of the bedroom. 'I hope you've put on the blue skirt with the buttons down the front like I told you. It looks nice with your best white blouse. Here, I'll button it for you, you do want to look good.'

Vera came out of the bedroom, scowling. She hated

the blue skirt Martha Longhurst had made for her before the war had even started and she'd been tempted to ignore her mother's instructions and put on something else.

'You should wear that more often, there's nowt wrong with it,' Ena said as Vera stood sullenly in front of her. 'I don't know what you're fussing about. Now fetch your coat and let's be having you.'

'I still don't know why we're going to the Bowmans,' Vera complained as she trailed down the street after her mother. 'Why would we want to visit the rag-and-bone man? Shouldn't he be calling on us?'

'Course he should, and Mr Bowman does, in his line of work, but this is not about his work, you daft ha'p'orth. I've been trying to tell you, only you seem determined not to listen, it's about you getting a chance to meet his son.'

'You mean Eric the Bogeyman? Cos that's what the kids around here call him, you know.' Vera giggled. 'Why would I want to meet him again?'

'You should know better than to call people names,' Ena said sternly. 'He does well now that he's working with his father and I bet he's very nice if you'd take the time to get to know him.'

'But I already know him. We were in the same class at school for a bit,' Vera said.

'That's as maybe, but you don't really *know* him. You've never actually had a conversation with him, have you?'

'What about?'

'About anything. Whatever it is you young people like to talk about,' Ena said and, setting her lips in a tight, determined line, she speeded up her pace as they turned into Inkerman Street and stopped at the corner before they reached the old chapel. She banged the knocker of the first house in the terraced row and before the door was opened she leaned across to adjust Vera's collar.

'Stand up straight, girl, and remember to be polite. You want them all to like you, don't you?'

'How do you mean?' Vera was genuinely puzzled, not putting Eric the Bogeyman together with her mother's plans to find her a husband. 'The Bowmans? Why do they have to like me?'

'Because it would help, if you're going to be their daughter-in-law,' Ena said.

Vera stared at her as if she had spoken a foreign language, but at that moment the door was opened by a small, round woman with a grease-spotted apron tied across her large stomach.

'Mrs Sharples! So pleased you both could come. This is such a good idea of yours, we're all very excited. You must be Vera and I bet you're excited too.' She put out her hand. 'I'm Aggie Bowman.'

Vera ignored the hand and merely stood on the door-step, staring.

'You've probably seen me before, at the Mission,'

Aggie said to Vera. 'The whole family's occasionally been there to worship of a Sunday. He's a good Christian, is my Eric.'

When Vera didn't respond Ena hurriedly filled the silence. 'Vera was only saying how she remembers Eric from school.'

'Of course,' Aggie said. 'Well, him and Wilf is waiting for you. Do come in.' And she led the way down the dimly lit, busily wallpapered corridor. She showed them into the back room and indicated they should sit at the dark wood table that was covered with a white lacy tablecloth. Then she disappeared. Eric was already sitting next to his father at the other end of the table and they both nodded to the visitors. Some thick cups and saucers like the ones in the factory cafeteria had been laid out at one end of the table and in the centre stood a single plate stand with half a dozen pink wafer biscuits.

When Aggie Bowman came back with a teapot in one hand and a jug of hot water in the other, she solemnly began to fill the cups.

'Pass them round, Eric, dear,' she said.

Vera stared down into her lap, trying not to look at him. When Vera had last seen him he had been sitting up high on the rag-and-bone cart next to his father as he steered the horses through the cobbled streets and she was surprised to see, close to, how small and skinny he was when he stood up, though he still seemed to have the runny nose he'd been known for at school. He didn't look as if he'd made any effort to dress for the occasion, Vera thought, looking down at her hated blue skirt. His crumpled shirt was collarless and hung from his scrawny neck as if it was several sizes too big and his shirt sleeves, scruffily rolled up to the elbows, revealed two stick-like arms. He grinned as he put a cup with a cracked saucer down on the table in front of Vera and sniffed into his cuff. But she couldn't smile back. She looked away.

'I've seen you before, haven't I?' he said, peering at her over his beaklike nose, 'not just when I've been on the cart with Dad.'

Vera nodded. 'We were both in Mrs Angel's class for a bit,' she said, 'at Bessie Street school.'

Eric glanced at his mother before looking back at Vera. 'And I've seen you in the Mission Hall,' he said.

As he spoke, Vera could see that his top teeth stuck out over the bottom ones. She shrugged without answering and the room fell to silence.'

'I'm sure you've not spoken to each other since you were at school and Vera's mother thought it would be a nice idea for you two to meet properly,' Aggie said to Eric when a few uncomfortable moments had elapsed in which the grandfather clock in the hallway could be heard ticking loudly. 'So you could get to know one another.' There was a pause. 'You might find you want to arrange to go to the flicks together or something,'

41

she said, trying to sound hearty. 'And. . . . well, who knows after that? You're both of an age to be making up your own minds about these things, I'm sure.' She cleared her throat and sat back in her chair, staring at the plate of biscuits that no one had touched. Meanwhile Wilf Bowman never said a word.

Vera looked at her mother and from the stern look on Ena's face she could see that leaving her daughter to make her own mind up about anything was not what Ena had in mind. Suddenly Vera felt as if her throat was being squeezed and she wanted to cry. Is this really what her mother had been planning for her? She looked across the table again at Eric and saw his damp chin where a faint trace of tea seemed to have dribbled from the corner of his mouth. No, no, no! This was definitely not what she wanted. She would not be marrying Eric Bowman no matter what her mother thought. Somehow Vera would have to show Ena that she was capable of making her own decisions.

'Lily will be here shortly.' Ena raised her voice so that Vera would be sure to hear her over the top of the motley choir that were singing on the wireless. She raised it another notch so that she was almost shouting. 'Martha said Lily would be popping in some time though I told her there was no need as I shouldn't be back too late,' Ena bellowed.

'I don't mind her coming. She's good company. And you don't have to shout, I can hear, you know,' Vera said, though she pitched her own voice louder. She was curled up on the overstuffed couch in the living area, leafing slowly through a cinema stars' magazine that Elsie Tanner had given her. Elsie gave her all her old magazines as she finished with them and Vera was delighted because she had no money to buy things like that and she was glad her mother no longer tried to put a stop to Elsie passing them on. She was looking to see if she could find any of Alan Ladd to check that Bob Lomax really did look like him. Some of the pictures had been cut out, but Vera didn't mind. There were still plenty left, even if there were none of Clark Gable, another favourite, who was now serving with the US Air Force. Not that she had anywhere to put them. She didn't have a wall of her own to pin pictures on like Elsie had once shown Vera in her bedroom at number 11. But if she did find any while Ena was out, she intended to stick them into the scrapbook she kept hidden under their bed. So far she'd had no luck.

Vera shrugged and glanced up. 'You don't have to wait till Lily comes, you know. I'll be perfectly all right until she gets here,' Vera said. 'And even if she doesn't come. . . .' she dared to add. She looked at her mother's face to check her reaction, but Ena didn't seem to have heard.

All Ena said was, 'Well, I'll be off then. Tar-rah.' And, surprisingly, for once she left without a backward glance.

As soon as she heard the door shut Vera jumped up, stretched out her arms and walked slowly round the room, skipping on every other step. She was actually glad to be on her own for a bit and she began to hum along to 'That Old Black Magic' that the choir was singing on the wireless and doing little dance steps in time to Glenn Miller's well-known dance band. She'd meant what she'd said. She was perfectly capable of being on her own in the flat. She was more than able to look after herself if only her mother would give her a chance. She didn't know why she always made such a fuss. Did Ena think she had to ask Lily to come over to sit with her every time she went out? Did she think Vera wouldn't notice? Fortunately, Vera really enjoyed Lily's company. She hummed and tapped her feet some more as the music switched to the Benny Goodman band playing 'Taking a Chance on Love'. She smiled each time she caught her image in the mirror and, as she twirled by, she held up her arms as if she was dancing with Alan Ladd and tilted her head to rest on his imaginary shoulder. Only this time the face she saw was Bob Lomax. She paused while she parted her hair as if she was drawing back curtains and pulled forward the hair from one side of her centre parting to cover one eye, in her favourite Veronica Lake pose, and practised the famous film star's pout that the magazines always called 'sexy' as she stared into Bob's brown eyes. After a while she tired of playing film stars and sat down with what was left of the magazine and she began to wonder just how much longer Lily was going to be.

A loud bang made her jump and at first she wasn't sure if it had come from the front of the Mission where the hall and the vestry flat opened onto Viaduct Street, or from the side alley that backed onto Hardcastle's old mill, which was now Elliston's factory. The curtains were still open and she peered out of the front window. Dusk was beginning to fall and she didn't see anyone. Then there was another loud bang that felt close to her face and she hopped backwards as she saw the shape of a fist hammering on the glass. It gave her the fright of her life. She still couldn't see a face and her heart was pounding as a man's voice shouted at her to close the curtains immediately or she would be reported for failing to keep the blackout. She quickly drew them together and had to wait for her breathing to calm down and her hands to stop trembling before she turned out the lights and opened the side door of the vestry. She slid cautiously out into the alley. Her eyes strained in the descending dark but she still couldn't see anything and walked forward a few steps until she heard strange noises coming from somewhere ahead.

Vera stood rooted to the spot, not sure what to make

of the soft moans and heavy breathing followed by the occasional grunt that floated towards her on the evening air. She saw a young girl somehow entangled with a young lad, but she couldn't make out their faces and she didn't know what on earth was going on. The girl's long fair hair had fanned out as she was being pressed up against the wall by the boy, who seemed to have his trousers gathered round his ankles. Her first impression was that it looked like a scene from a Laurel and Hardy film and she wanted to laugh and call out, 'This is another fine mess you've got me in.' But then she remembered the things she'd seen some of the young girls and the soldiers doing in the murky shadows on the night of the dance and, as another thought struck her, Vera took a step backwards, involuntarily shrieking, 'Oh my goodness!' and ran back towards the door.

As she did so, she thought she heard Lily's voice shout, 'What the hell. . . .?' and became aware of the pounding footsteps of someone following her down the alley. Before Vera could do anything, the figure behind her bundled her through the side entrance and into the vestry. Vera made a startled noise and turned as quickly as she could to slam the door and shoot the bolt. But it was too late. She came face to face with Lily, who was hastily buttoning her blouse and tucking it back into her skirt.

'Who on earth was that? What's going on?' Vera

sounded worried. 'He's not going to follow you in here, is he?' Her voice expressed genuine concern.

Lily gave a rueful laugh, a resigned look on her face. 'I shouldn't think so, not after being so rudely interrupted, so you can calm down. He's probably running as fast as he can right now in the opposite direction.' She put her hands on Vera's shoulders, alarmed that the older girl looked so distressed. 'What did you see that's upset you so much?'

Vera put her hands up to her face and shook her head. 'Nothing!' she said emphatically. 'I didn't see nothing.'

'Well, that's all right, then.' Lily stepped closer to Vera and gently pulled her hands away from her face. 'And I hope it will stay that way. You must promise to say nothing to my mam, or to yours if it comes to that, about. . . . whatever it was that you didn't see. You won't say anything, will you?' she repeated, sounding suddenly anxious.

'Cross my heart and hope to die – but how can I say owt about summat I didn't see?' Vera sounded genuinely puzzled.

Lily grinned.

'I don't understand what the problem is,' Vera said.

'The problem is that I told my mam that I was going to see Peter tonight before I came here. She likes Peter.'

'And wasn't that Peter?' Vera asked innocently.

'No, it wasn't.'

'Who is this Peter anyway?'

'Pete Mason, the boy she thinks I'm stepping out with.'

'And aren't you?' Vera looked confused.

Lily tilted her head first to one side and then to the other. 'It's hard to explain. I know you're 22, five years older than me, but you've never really courted anyone have you?' Lily said, not unkindly.

Vera shook her head. 'No, not yet.'

'The thing is, sometimes I think we are together and sometimes we're not. It might not be easy for you to understand. I do see him occasionally to please my mam because for some reason she trusts him and she doesn't mind me being with him.'

'But you don't like this Peter?'

'It's not that I don't like him, it's just that. . . . well, honestly, he's dull as dishwater.'

'Can't you tell your mam that?'

Lily laughed. 'I've tried but she won't listen. I said to her once, "Why don't you go out with him if you think he's so great?"'

Vera snorted with laughter. 'You never!'

'Honest to God, I did, though she didn't think it was funny and she went on and on about Peter, like he's the best boy in town and I should be grateful he even looks at me. I don't know what she'd say if she knew about Johnny.'

'So is Johnny the one who. . . .?'

'Yes,' Lily said quickly. 'He's the one you didn't see.' She giggled.

'And why does your mam not like him?'

'She's never met him, but she knows his mother and his grandmother and you should hear how she slags them off. She says he's not fit to shine my shoes.'

Vera shrugged. 'Sticks and stones. . . .' she said.

'You what?'

'You know, "sticks and stones can break my bones but names can never hurt me". That's what my mam taught me to say when the kids at school got nasty.'

'Yes, well, but we're not at school any more, are we?' Lily was somewhat exasperated. 'I like to think I've grown out of all that,' she said, trying not to sound superior.

'What's his other name, this Johnny?' Vera asked.

'Why do you want to know?' Lily frowned.

'Because then it'll be a proper secret.'

Lily rolled her eyes.

'But I promise I'll not tell a soul,' Vera said earnestly.

Lily sighed. 'It's Johnny Bradwell, if you must know. He lives at the other end of Viaduct Street. Satisfied?'

Vera nodded.

'But now you've really got to promise me you won't tell,' Lily said. 'If my mam hears that I've been stepping out with one of the Bradwells she'll go spare. Promise me, Vera, that you won't say owt.'

'Course I won't. I've said so, haven't I? I'll swear to

that on the Holy Bible if you want, there's plenty of them lying about.' She made a move towards a tattered book stuffed into the corner of the pew bench that took up a quarter of the kitchen.

Lily couldn't help laughing. 'Na, there's really no need for that. I trust you.'

'I'm glad about that.' Vera sounded relieved. 'Do you want some coffee? My mam left some water boiling, though there's no milk.'

Vera made the ersatz coffee from the bottle of Camp that was standing on the table. Most people grumbled that Camp was nothing like coffee, but beggars couldn't be choosers, she thought. She glanced up when Lily went to take a look in the mirror and watched as the younger girl began to comb out her tangled blonde curls, winding them round her fingers into sausage-shaped rolls and pinning them back from her face with giant kirby grips. She had a pretty, oval-shaped face which, for a moment, looked clownish as she dabbed some lipstick from her handbag onto her high cheek-bones, but she blended the redness into her pale skin as if it were rouge. She then drew the bright red stick across her lips making them suddenly as crimson as the Mission doorstep and it was as if her whole face came alive.

'Can I have some of that?' Vera asked.

Lily shook her head. 'Best not right now. You don't want your mam stopping me from coming here, do you? Though I promise you can have some if we go out anywhere.'

'Did you know that Elsie Tanner gave me some lipstick to put on when we went to the dance?' Vera said proudly, rubbing her lips with her finger. 'But it had all come off by the time I got home so Mam never knew.'

Lily laughed. 'Just as well. She'd have had your guts for garters if she'd have caught you. No doubt she'd have said it was the work of the devil.'

'The devil? You mean Elsie Tanner? They're all the same in Mam's book,' Vera said, and they both chuckled. Vera waited until they had settled on the couch before she asked, 'Are you going to marry this Johnny?'

Lily spluttered, spraying the hot liquid she'd been sipping across the stone floor. 'Marry him? Good gracious, we're a long ways off thinking about things like that. It was only a bit of slap and tickle out there. Nothing more serious than that.'

'Then why would your mam be so upset if she knew about it?'

'Because she'd assume it was more serious than it really was. She forgets what she got up to when she was my age. Though as I say, I don't think she'd mind so much if it had been Peter Mason out there.'

'Would she really want you to get married now?' Vera asked.

Lily shrugged. 'I think if I told her Peter and I were

seriously courting she'd have me down that church before any of us could say Jack Robinson.'

'Really?' Vera was surprised. 'Why does she want you to get married so quick?' She sounded perplexed. 'You're not even as old as me and I'd have thought she'd be pleased you were popular and had lots of boyfriends, right now.'

'My mam doesn't think like that. She doesn't mind me going out and having a bit of fun, but she's not happy with me going out with a load of different lads. She's of a mind that only marriage can keep me out of harm's way, if you know what I mean.'

Vera began to shake her head, so Lily added, 'Put it this way, she doesn't want me getting up the duff before I've had a chance to say "I do".'

Vera frowned. 'I thought you had to be married before you could actually have a baby?' Vera had been trying to piece together things she had overheard the girls at work giggling about and she'd thought she understood, but now she wasn't so sure.

'I'm afraid it's not that simple.' Lily couldn't believe Vera's ignorance. She felt embarrassed having to explain to her things she and her friends had taken for granted. 'Once you've started – you know, once you're getting your monthlies,' Lily began, 'you can have a baby any time if you're fooling around with a bloke; if you're unlucky, that is, and can't get him to marry you in time.' Lily was doing her best. 'I'm surprised your mam's not told you about that,' she said.

'I have tried to ask her but she's always putting me off. She says she'll tell me some other time and then she never does.'

'You need to be careful is what I'm saying. Don't let him go too far. You don't want to get caught out getting pregnant before you get wed.'

'And you get pregnant by sleeping in the same bed with your husband?' Vera asked innocently.

'Well. . . . yes, basically.' Lily felt a little flustered. 'Though he doesn't have to be your husband, that's what I've been trying to tell you. And you don't actually have to be in bed.'

Vera suddenly giggled and Lily was thankful because it relieved the tension. 'You mean you could be in an alley?' Vera asked for it was as if the light had suddenly dawned.

Lily let out a sigh of relief and hoped she wouldn't have to go into any more details. 'You could be in an alley,' she agreed. 'And that's when you don't tell your mother about what you've been up to. But I'll tell you something for nothing, Vera, I'm not in any rush to get married. That hanky-panky is not all it's cracked up to be. In fact, it can be a right pain.'

'It sounded as though it was painful,' Vera said innocently. 'And is that what you have to do when you're married?'

Lily nodded, trying not to show her impatience.

'Is that what makes babies?' Vera asked. Lily nodded again and Vera thought she finally understood.

'And was it not fun?'

'It was a bit of both, if I'm honest. But my argument is: if I don't try it out with more than one boy before I get married, how can I be sure I'll be marrying the right one?'

'The one you really love, you mean?'

'Aye. Otherwise you could get stuck for life with someone you don't even like and believe me that can be dreadful. You only have to look at my mam and dad.' Lily saw a surprised look cross Vera's face, so she smiled and said, 'But the thing I'm saying is: I don't need my mother to know every time I want to try someone out.'

'I wonder how many my mam tried out before she got wed?' Vera said suddenly.

'I don't know and I don't suggest you ask her.' Lily giggled. 'But I do know that before I get married I intend to try out a lot more than one.'

Vera frowned. 'But my mam says that going with lots of men means you're dirty; like Elsie Tanner. Only *I* don't think she's dirty. I think she's nice,' she added with a wistful look.

'Our mams don't always think like we do,' Lily said, 'and my dad certainly doesn't, so sometimes we have to do what we think is right, whether they agree or not.'

'Do you think you'd be rowing all the time if you married Johnny?' Vera asked.

'I can't rightly say. I don't hardly know him.' Lily sat back and sipped what remained of her cup of Camp coffee though it was cold by now.

'That's funny. It looked like you did, from what you were doing in the alley,' Vera said innocently.

'I thought you didn't see anything?' Lily turned on her in a flash.

'No, I didn't. Not really,' Vera responded quickly. 'I just meant—'

'Well, anyway, whatever you think you saw, it was all sort of . . . Well, I was just trying to get to know him a bit better.' Lily did her best to sound dismissive.

They sat in silence for a few moments then Vera said, 'I've decided I'm going to marry Bob.'

'Who's Bob?' Lily said, surprised.

'Bob Lomax. You know, the maintenance man I told you about. He found me downstairs at work by the toilets that day I wasn't feeling so good at the factory when there'd been all that fuss between my mam and Elsie Tanner. Dead nice, he was.' Her voice sounded dreamlike. 'He waited until I was ready and then shone his torch all the way up the stairs.'

'Oh yes, I remember. He certainly sounded very

decent. But to think of marrying him, isn't that being a bit hasty?'

'No more hasty than my mam thinking she can marry me off to Eric Bowman.'

'You what? Whoa! Hang on a minute, who's he when he's at home? And how come you've never mentioned him before?'

Vera shrugged. 'Eric Rag-and-bone-man, I call him,' she said miserably, her eyes suddenly brimming.

Lily stared at her in astonishment. 'You've never mentioned him before. Where's he suddenly sprung from, then?'

'I've been wanting to tell you ever since my mam decided to fix me up with a husband, but I can't bear to talk about him. I feel too embarrassed even to think about him.' Vera lifted her shoulders than slumped back against the lumpy cushions on the couch. 'I was in the same class at school with him for a bit and Mam kept saying how she'd do anything to stop Elsie Tanner from leading me astray and then suddenly she's dragging me off to the Rag-and-Bones' house, saying we'd been asked to tea. Ha! Hot water and wafer biscuits more like, with him and his mam and his dad, though he never said owt all afternoon.'

'And what did the rest of you talk about?' Lily asked.

'I didn't say anything. They talked about Eric and me going off to the pictures together, getting to know each other,' Vera said miserably.

'And Eric? Did he really not say anything?'

Vera shook her head. 'Hardly a word, just kept sniffing his horrible runny nose. And all the way home Mam kept talking about how he'd be just right for me.' Vera swiped at her eyes angrily with the back of her hand as the tears began to fall.

'And I presume you haven't been out with him?' Lily asked.

Vera shuddered. 'No, I have not.' She was quite emphatic. 'And I never will.'

'Why? What's he like?' Lily said.

'You must have seen him,' Vera said. 'He comes to Coronation Street most weeks with his dad, with the rag-and-bone cart. He's dead skinny, with a nose like a bird that leaks like a tap and oh, he's horrible! He looks like rags and bones himself. Mam seems to think they're a decent churchgoing family and that's all she cares about. But I won't marry him, no matter what she says,' she said defiantly. She began to sob.

'I suppose your mam wants you to get married so that you can't get caught having babies without being wed, like we were talking about before,' Lily said.

Vera sat up suddenly, a determined look on her face. 'I don't care. I'll choose my own husband, thank you very much, no matter what my mam says.' Her voice was strong again. 'And now that I've met Bob, that settles it. It'll be like it is in the films.' She put her hand up to her hair and patted it as though she was striking a pose.

'I suppose marrying Bob would be one way to get you out of being trapped into something with this awful-sounding Eric bloke, but it would be a good idea to get to know Bob a bit better before you go making any announcements, don't you think?'

'Why, when I'm sure he's the one?'

'That's as maybe, but are you sure *he* wants to marry *you*? You don't want any let-downs later. And once you're married you'd be stuck. Wouldn't you like to have some fun first? You know, like you did that night at the dance?'

Vera suddenly looked frightened and her neck and cheeks went pink. 'I didn't do anything wrong, did I? What would my ma—'

'Oh, bugger your mam!' Lily burst out and that made Vera scream with laughter and put her fingers over her lips, but at that moment there was a knock on the door and both girls froze. When Vera ventured to answer it, she was relieved to see it was Elsie Tanner. Elsie stubbed out her cigarette as she accepted Vera's invitation into the vestry.

'Hello, girls,' she said cheerily. 'Having a bit of fun while your mam's out?'

Vera smiled coyly. 'Shall we tell her, Lily?' she said and when Lily nodded she outlined the gist of their earlier conversation.

'You won't tell my mam or Mrs Sharples, will you?' Lily said.

'No, of course not, don't look so worried,' Elsie said. 'Your secret's safe with me. Though I must tell you I was wed at your age, Lily. Not that I'm suggesting you do that, but you can see why Mrs Sharples thinks it might be a good idea.'

'We want to enjoy ourselves first, don't we, Vera?' Lily said, 'not get tied down with babies. But the thing is, we both want to get away from home. And marriage seems to be the only way out . . .'

Chapter 5

Lily came out of Earnshaw's Clothing factory only minutes after the klaxon sounded announcing the changeover from the morning to the evening shift. The noise of the horn blasted around the old factory walls and filled the air between the tightly packed houses in the surrounding streets. Before the war the factory had employed cheap labour from the villages beyond Weatherfield and they had made all types of clothing. Now the workers were mainly local women and girls, the machines had been converted and they manufactured forces' uniforms only. But Lily wasn't thinking about the yards of heavy duty fabrics she had to haul about most mornings, or the hours she spent hunched over the large industrial sewing machines she had been trained to operate; tonight, as she set off in the direction of home, her head was filled with thoughts of Johnny Bradwell. She hadn't seen him since he had run away the night Vera had caught the two of them in the alley. She hoped that the incident hadn't put him off completely and she kept wondering where she could go and what she might do to bump into him again.

Lily had first met Johnny on a summer's evening not unlike this one when she had been in the midst of the jostling crowds emerging from the factory. She had been walking, head bowed against the strong wind, and hadn't seen him in her path until it was too late. Afterwards he admitted that he had spotted her and that he'd deliberately woven his way across the crowded pavement in order to get a closer look. He had nearly knocked her down in his eagerness, but she had grabbed hold of his arm to prevent herself from falling. When she'd looked up, she'd immediately been struck by his good looks, the smoothness of his sleeked-back hair and his cheeky grin. Her legs had felt like jelly when she'd realized that his hand was still clasped around hers.

'I'm so sorry,' she said, 'I wasn't looking where I was going. I hope I didn't hurt you.' She tried to withdraw her hand.

'Not at all, it was my fault,' he'd said immediately. 'Are you all right?'

'I'm fine,' she said, not wanting to admit that she was shaken.

'No, you're not,' he contradicted. 'Look, your hand's trembling.' He lifted her fingers gently and held her open hand, palm up. 'I'm really sorry, I wasn't looking where I was going. My name's Johnny, by the way.'

'Lily,' she said, feeling the blood rushing to her cheeks.

'Here, let me carry that bag for you, Lily.'

She couldn't resist his ready smile.

'Where do you live?' he'd asked. 'The least I can do is to walk you home.'

Lily thought of home and the angry, oppressive atmosphere she had left behind that morning, the same tensions she could be walking into this evening if her father was still at home. Long ago she had found to her cost that it was not a good idea to take strangers there, unannounced.

'No, thank you all the same but there's no need . . .' she began.

But before she could say anything further he had put a protective arm around her and was guiding her in the direction she had originally been heading. Lily had stopped protesting and walked meekly by his side. It felt nice being escorted and she was happy to walk with him for a little way. However, when they reached the Rovers Return in Coronation Street, Lily suddenly woke up to the fact that being so close to home she could easily come across someone she knew and she stopped walking and turned to face him. She was surprised to find him gazing directly at her and she had to avert her eyes.

'Thanks so much, Johnny,' she said. 'I do appreciate you bringing me this far, but I'm very close to home now so it's fine if you leave me here.' The Longhursts didn't live on Coronation Street itself but on Mawdsley Street; the two streets shared a back alley, whereby the houses on each side could be accessed through their back yards.

He put his finger under her chin and tilted her face slightly so that she was forced to look up at him.

'That's OK, I understand,' he said, and there was a knowing look on his face. 'Maybe we'll meet up again some time,' he said. 'The name's Johnny Bradwell. Lily . . .?' he asked as he stuffed his hands deep into his pockets.

Lily stiffened when she heard the name. 'Longhurst,' she said, somewhat reluctantly, though nothing registered on his face.

He'd merely nodded and given her a wink before he began to walk back the way they had come, whistling 'As Time Goes By' under his breath, while Lily had stood frozen.

Johnny Bradwell was not a name she dared to mention at home, even though since meeting him he had filled her thoughts, for as she'd told Vera, she'd heard her mother on several occasions speaking ill of his entire family. But now that she had met him she realized that a badly behaved family didn't make him any less attractive. On the contrary, as far as she was concerned he was far too good-looking to ignore and his family's reputation made him all the more exciting to pursue.

Chapter 6

'Well, look at you, all dressed up like a dog's dinner,' Ena said, eyeing Vera's dirndl skirt and Ceylonese blouse that she usually saved for the weekends. 'And where would you be off to at this hour?'

'I'm going to the pictures, if you must know,' Vera said, brightly. 'The new Will Hay film, *It Ain't Hay*, is on at the Rex.'

'More to the point, who are you going with?' A slight smile played on Ena's lips. 'I trust he's coming to pick you up?'

Vera had been trying to fix her hair in the mirror, rolling it round her fingers the way she'd seen Lily do, but each time she tried to pin the sausage curls they fell about her face again and hung limply.

'Here, let me!' Ena snatched the hairbrush from Vera's hands and began to line up the curls across her forehead.

'I'm going with Lily,' Vera said, handing Ena the clips.

'Oh, I thought you were going with Eric,' Ena said, her voice suddenly tight.

'What made you think that?' Vera tried to sound matter-of-fact.

'Didn't he ask you?' Ena said.

'Yes, you know very well that that was why he telephoned, but I told him no,' Vera said, holding up the next kirby grip.

Ena stopped what she was doing. 'What do you mean you said no?' she positively snapped.

'Don't worry, I was polite. But I told you I didn't want anything to do with him when we went there and I meant it.' Vera's voice began to quiver and she took a deep breath. She kept her eyes down, staring into her lap. She was determined not to give in even though she could sense that her mother was glaring at her.

At that moment Vera thought she heard a knock at the front door of the vestry flat but she couldn't be sure as the air-raid siren started whining at the same time.

'Hm. It doesn't look like you'll be going anywhere,' Ena sneered.

The remainder of the clips dropped from Vera's lap

as she hurried to answer the door, and when she opened it the siren's wail seemed to fill the entire flat. She ushered Lily inside while in the street people were fleeing in all directions as the drone of the enemy aircraft grew louder too. They hadn't had an air raid for some time but everyone seemed to have remembered the drill as streams of people were heading towards the main entrance of the Mission to seek shelter in the ample basement. Intent on their purpose, they mostly kept their heads down, not even looking to see whether any fire bombs had already landed.

'Am I relieved to have made it in time!' Lily said. 'I'd not long since set off when the sirens sounded but I thought I'd better keep going and get here as fast as possible rather than going back. Besides, my mam and dad always hide in the cupboard under the stairs and there's never enough room for me. It's the one place they don't row.' She giggled.

'Well, I'm glad to see you,' Vera said. 'But do come in quickly or Mam will start start yelling at us about the light,' she said, and, opening the door wide, she grabbed Lily's arm and pulled her across the threshold.

Ena had already gone downstairs and Vera picked up the torch that was lying on the table in the hall and shone it in the direction of the stairs that led down into the basement. She guided Lily through the hall and down the familiar cellar steps into the semi-darkness.

They were greeted by the warm waves that were

coming off the crowds as the cellar was already half-full. The blackout blinds, permanently drawn over the basement half-windows, made it difficult to see in the weak lighting coming off the lamps that were spread around the large room, and it took a few moments for Vera's eyes to adjust, but there was no mistaking her mother already sitting at the piano trying to lead a sing-song of her favourite hymns, while others were trying to drown her out and to raise their spirits with old songs from the Great War like 'Pack Up Your Troubles', and 'Keep the Home Fires Burning'. It was often where she could be found when she wasn't on her warden duties of an evening.

'It's a shame we're going to miss out going to the pictures,' Vera said. 'I was looking forward to it.'

'Maybe they'll keep the film on for a few extra days so we can go later in the week,' Lily said. 'Although if the all-clear sounds there might still be time for them to show the whole film through tonight.'

It was less than half an hour before the all-clear sounded and, after waiting a few extra minutes in case there was another wave of danger, people began to emerge once more into what was left of the evening sunshine. Vera had to blink hard in order for her eyes to adjust after the murkiness of the basement as they came back up the stairs.

'Do you think they might show the film tonight now that the danger's passed?' Vera said. 'It's not that late.'

'True, we weren't down there very long,' Lily said. 'So maybe no harm done. Perhaps we should take a stroll down to the cinema and see what's happening. I don't know about you, but I could do with some fresh air after that musty cellar.'

Vera glanced back into the hall towards the piano where her mother looked almost disappointed as she gathered together her sheets of music. Vera waved at her and indicated she and Lily were going out. Ena glared and gave a brief nod of acknowledgement, the distance too far for her to shout, her arms too full to wave back.

'I'm ready and Mam knows we're leaving,' Vera said.

'Let's go then,' Lily said. 'The evening might not end up as bad as we thought.'

They walked down to the centre of Weatherfield and found a notice had been pinned up at the box office confirming that there would be one showing of the programme tonight instead of the usual two. It would begin shortly and it would include the B film, the thriller with Jack Palance that had previously been billed, and an extended Pathé newsreel with an update on the progress of the war, as well as the main feature, *It Ain't Hay*. Vera was listening as Lily read it out and it took her a few moments to realize that she was standing next to Bob Lomax. No longer in his work overalls, he looked very different in his button-down shirt and snug-fitting home-knit pullover under a shabby tweed jacket, a cowlick of hair managing to escape from under his flat cap.

'Hello, Bob,' she said. 'How are you?' Her pulse was suddenly racing and she knew her cheeks must have reddened beyond the rouge she had applied quickly before she left the house.

Bob stared at her blankly.

'It's Vera Sharples,' she said. 'Do you remember? We met in the basement at the factory when I wasn't feeling very well and you kindly helped me back up the stairs to my bench.' She cleared her throat in embarrassment.

Bob still looked puzzled and he stared at her for a few moments more before his face cleared and to her relief he said, 'Oh yes, I remember.'

'I've been looking out for you at the factory,' she said, with a sudden burst of confidence.

'Why was that?' He sounded surprised.

'So that I could thank you properly for rescuing me,' Vera said.

'No need,' Bob said. He touched the edge of his cap and was about to hurry away but Lily suddenly stepped in.

'I don't think we've been introduced,' she said.

Vera could feel the warmth from her cheeks slowly spread down her neck and up into the roots of her hair. 'Bob, this is Lily Longhurst, my friend. Lily, this is Bob Lomax from work.'

'Pleased to meet you, Bob, I'm sure,' Lily said and she nodded her head towards him and smiled. 'I take it you've not seen this film, then?'

'Er, no, not yet,' he stammered.

'Then maybe we could all go together?' Lily said.

'Well, yes I suppose we could . . .' Bob started to say.

'That's wonderful,' Lily said and she steered them towards the queue for the cheaper tickets that was now forming down the side of the cinema.

Vera was delighted by her friend's boldness and she hung back to walk alongside Bob. Seconds later she could see that Lily had stopped to talk to a lad already in the queue that she didn't recognize. As they drew level, Lily grabbed Vera's arm.

'Vera, I want you to meet a friend of mine. This is Johnny Bradwell,' she said, her face flushed with obvious excitement. A tall, good-looking boy stepped away from the queue, and, without speaking, nodded towards Vera and Bob. 'Johnny wants me to go and sit in the more expensive seats with him,' Lily said, pointing to the queue for the one and sixes on the opposite side of the box office. 'You don't mind, do you? Then you two can sit together,' she said. She bent close to Vera's ear. 'Johnny wants to sit on the back row,' she whispered and she elbowed Vera playfully in the ribs. She smiled at Bob and before Vera could say more than, 'Well, I suppose . . .' Lily and Johnny had moved away, leaving Vera and Bob, bemused, looking tight-lipped and tense in the middle of the queue.

'Is your friend courting then?' Bob said when they had stood in silence for several minutes.

'She's not really . . .' Vera began, though she realized she didn't know how to continue. Fortunately there was no time to say anything further as they had reached the box-office window where Bob paid for his ticket and Vera scrabbled through the change in her pocket to pay for her own.

The cinema was filling up quickly and they took two of the few remaining seats on the second row where they were close to where the organ emerged in the interval between performances. Neither spoke, but as the lights dimmed Vera took several sideways glances at Bob and inched over closer to him, willing him to put his arm around her, or to make some friendly gesture instead of keeping his hands firmly tucked away in his jacket pockets.

When the film was over Vera was pleased to see Lily waiting for her by the ticket window in the foyer. She was with Johnny and they were holding hands and staring into each other's eyes.

'Johnny's offered to walk me home,' Lily said quickly as Vera and Bob approached. 'But I don't want to leave you in the lurch, Vera.' She turned to Bob. 'The thing is, Vera's mam sort of expects me to see her safely home and I was wondering whether you might like to do that tonight, Bob?'

Bob looked surprised and opened his mouth to speak but Lily didn't give him a chance to refuse. Instead, she put her hand out and patted his arm. 'Thanks so much, that's a real weight off my mind. I appreciate it,' she said, as she glanced at Vera, 'and I know Vera will too. Be seeing you then, Vera. Enjoy the walk home,' she added and, with a little wave of her hand, Lily looped her arm through Johnny's as they walked away from the cinema and in the direction of Mawdsley Street.

Vera stood and watched her go, her mind in turmoil. She knew she should have been pleased that Bob would be seeing her home but she wished that he'd offered or that she'd had the courage to ask him herself. More importantly, what would her mother say to her coming home with a lad? And Bob didn't look pleased either. As he kicked loose stones into the road he had a sullen look on his face.

'I suppose we'd best be off then,' he said eventually. 'Which way?'

Vera pointed, and he set off in the direction of the Mission at such a pace that Vera had to practically run to keep up with him.

When they arrived, the Mission Hall and the vestry

were in darkness like all the surrounding houses in the neighbourhood and Bob flashed the diffused light of his torch quickly in an effort to seek out the front door. The brief illumination of the familiar porch gave Vera a false kind of courage; the evening was almost ending, Bob would be leaving her alone, so without giving herself time to think she pulled him into the doorway and kissed him on the lips as she had seen the film stars do. She wasn't sure who was the more astonished, but she knew she had done the right thing when Bob responded immediately, shocking her into silence as he pushed her lips apart with his tongue. She didn't object, she barely moved, letting him press up against her while laying his hand tentatively on her coat across her chest. But then they both sprang apart when there was the sudden noise of loud footsteps coming from inside the flat and by the time Ena opened the front door they were standing on opposite sides of the door mat.

'What's he doing here?' Ena looked Bob up and down, the expression on her face looking like she had something nasty on her shoe.

'Bob very kindly offered to walk me home, to save Lily the bother,' Vera said, quickly, not wanting to get her friend into trouble. 'Wasn't that nice of him?' She cleared her throat, worried that she could feel her voice weakening.

'Yes, very nice,' was Ena's clipped response. 'Ta very

much.' She grabbed hold of Vera's arm to pull her indoors and with her free hand made a shooing gesture towards Bob. 'Now be off with you,' she shouted, 'that's quite enough excitement for one night. It's time this one was off to bed.'

This last comment incensed Vera. How dare her mother humiliate her like that in front of Bob? She felt a sudden renewed burst of energy and she pulled her arm roughly out of her mother's grip. 'Thanks Bob, for a lovely evening,' she called after him, and she blew him a kiss as if Ena hadn't spoken.

Meanwhile Ena grabbed hold of Vera's arm and spun her round to face her.

'So Lily had other fish to fry, did she?' She wagged her finger in Vera's face. 'If you'd have listened to me in the first place and gone to the pictures with Eric there'd have been no need for Lily to be put out or for this Bob character to poke his nose in at all.'

'There's nowt wrong with Bob!' Vera said vehemently. 'He's very nice. And as a matter of fact I'm going to . . .' But remembering something Lily had said, she pulled up short of making an announcement.

'As a matter of fact . . . what?' Ena imitated Vera's voice.

'Nothing.' Vera sounded suddenly subdued. 'But don't think you can ever get me to go out with that Eric. I won't, not ever.' She rallied. 'In fact, Elsie says . . .' No, she shouldn't say anything about Elsie.

There was a sudden silence. Vera could see her mother's face twitching and she worried that she might have gone too far.

'Elsie says what?' Ena's voice was menacing.

'Nothing,' Vera said, and fast as she could she went into the bedroom and, in a moment of pique, she dared to slam the door.

If Vera thought she was the only one suffering the anger of her mother she was wrong, for Lily fared no better when she arrived home only a few streets away from the Mission. She hadn't expected her mother to be waiting up for her and that could only mean one thing – her father was at home and had been lashing out with his tongue.

'What time do you call this?' Martha Longhurst was waiting by the front door as Lily inserted her key in the lock.

'What do you mean? I told you I was going out.' Lily did her best to sound offhand.

'Yes, but the pictures don't end this late.'

Lily explained about the late start. 'Did you not hear the siren go off?' she asked innocently.

'Of course we did, but that didn't make you this late. What did Ena say when you dropped Vera off?'

That was a question Lily hadn't anticipated and there was an awkward silence before she confessed. 'Actually, I didn't.'

'What do you mean, you didn't? Where is she?' Momentarily, fear flashed across Martha's face.

'We bumped into a friend of hers.'

'What do you mean? Vera doesn't have any friends. Ena's always seen to that.'

Lily didn't respond.

'Who is she, this friend?'

'It's not a she . . . it was a bloke she knew from work.'

Martha's eyes opened wide. 'Are you mad, girl? Ena will kill Vera and then she'll be on the warpath coming after you and I won't blame her.' She shook her head in disbelief until the next thought struck her. 'Who saw you home, then?' she suddenly asked.

'I met someone I knew as well.' Lily felt her face redden and she had to take a deep breath.

'Some coincidence!' Martha's tone was sarcastic.

'Yes, it really was.' It might have been true but even as she said it Lily realized how flimsy it sounded.

'What's his name?' This time Martha cut to the chase.

'Johnny,' Lily said quietly as if that would make a difference.

'Johnny what?' Martha persisted.

Lily kept the fingers of both hands crossed behind her back. 'I don't know his second name,' she lied.

'You mean you let any boy you met in the street see you home? What were you thinking about?'

'No, it wasn't like that. I knew him from before.'

'I don't know what your father's gonna say when he finds out,' Martha said, and she shook her head.

'Why does he have to find out?' Lily threw down the challenge. 'You don't have to tell him.'

Martha's shoulders slumped and she suddenly looked defeated. 'He'll find out one way or another, you know he always does.' She sighed. 'I don't know why you didn't you go out with Peter like you said you probably would, then none of this would have happened.' She sounded exhausted but Lily didn't like the way the conversation was heading and she grabbed at the chance to turn things around.

'Honestly!' she said in as cross a voice as she dared muster, and she suddenly stamped her foot. 'Always throwing Peter in my face, as if he's the best catch in the world. You're as bad as Mrs Sharples. She expects Vera to go out with that dreadful Eric the Bogeyman chap and she won't hear a word against him.'

'I'm nothing like Ena Sharples and don't you ever dare to say that I am! And I don't know how you could compare yourself to Vera. When have we ever kept you prisoner like Ena keeps that poor girl? You have lots of freedom for someone your age. Your father's always telling me I spoil you, letting you get up to all sorts. In fact, if he knew the half of this . . . It's lucky for you he got drunk for a change and fell asleep.'

'Well, this time he doesn't have to know, does he? There's certainly no reason for you to tell him.'

'What? You think I'll tell lies for you?' Martha looked horrified. 'I have no wish to become anyone's punching bag.'

'Then you don't want to go upsetting him now, do you?'

Martha hesitated for a second too long and Lily grinned. 'Thanks, Ma,' she said, though she couldn't help wondering how long her movements would stay a secret in that house.

'I don't know what I'm going to do with you.' Martha shook her head again.

'Nothing . . .' Lily whispered the word. 'For once, do nothing. Just don't go telling tales about me to my dad. Then there's really no need for either of us to get into trouble.' And before her mother could respond, Lily ran upstairs, breathing hard at the thought of her narrow escape.

Chapter 7

Vera had never had a friend like Lily before and far from being cross with her about the incident at the cinema Vera wished she could be more like her. She would love to be so relaxed and carefree with boys as Lily appeared to be. Lily always seemed to be able to make up her own mind and to know how to behave. But mostly Vera envied the younger girl her freedom. Lily seemed to go where she wanted, whenever she wanted, without her mother constantly watching and questioning her every move. The brief moment of independence Vera had experienced with Elsie Tanner when they had gone off to the dance in the Burtonwood barracks had left her wanting more and made her determined to seek out a way to have it. It wouldn't be easy, but there had to be a way. She clenched her fist and suddenly thumped the scratched wooden tabletop so that the plates on the dresser behind it rattled and Lily jumped.

'I'm sorry I left you in the lurch like that,' Lily said as if reading Vera's mind. The two girls were sitting together in the vestry at the Mission and they could hear Ena in the background, belting out one of her favourite hymns on the piano. 'Well, perhaps not exactly in the lurch; at least Bob saw you safely home.'

'Yes, of course he did.' Vera laughed.

'Was your mother cross?' Lily wanted to know. 'I know mine was when I had to admit I hadn't seen you all the way home.'

Vera looked at her in surprise. 'I don't care what my mother thinks!' She suddenly raised her voice, though as she said the words she realized that she'd spoken with far more courage than she felt.

'I presume you didn't tell her you plan to marry Bob?' Lily said with a laugh. 'Do you still fancy him now that you've had a chance to talk to him a bit?'

Vera felt her cheeks burn. 'Yes, of course I do.' She paused. 'And I fully intend to see him again soon. But somehow I've got to get my mother used to the idea and then she'll realize that she can forget about anyone else she's been trying to line up.' Vera frowned. 'I'm going to marry the man I want to marry and not some old rag-and-bone man that my mother has decided will do.'

'Is she still keen on the idea of that Eric bloke?'

'I'm afraid she is. She still throws up his name every time I mention the idea of going out. I honestly don't know what she thinks is so special about him. To hear her talk, you'd think he was the only lad in the world.'

'Did Bob ask you out, then?'

'Not yet,' Vera admitted. 'But I'm sure he will.'

Lily laughed. 'Well, if he hasn't asked by Christmas, next year's a leap year so you can ask him. You can even ask him to marry you if you still fancy that idea.'

'I very much fancy that idea,' Vera said. 'It's the only way I can think of to get out of this house.'

'I know what you mean,' Lily sighed. 'I feel the same way. I'm tired of the constant rows and me being piggy in the middle. I want to live my own life.'

Vera stared into space, locked in her own thoughts. 'Somehow I've got to get my mother to like Bob.'

Chapter 8

July 1943

Vera might have spoken bold words with a newfound confidence when she was talking to Lily, but when Ena began to give her the cold shoulder following her evening with Bob, Vera was more upset at first than she wanted to admit. She wasn't used to Ena speaking only when it was absolutely necessary and she found herself telling Elsie Tanner about it when she happened to meet her at the corner shop.

'What's up with you, love? You look proper down in the dumps,' Elsie said.

'That's because I am,' Vera replied and she couldn't stop spilling out the whole story from the night Bob had walked her home from the cinema to her mother punishing her with silence.

Elsie laughed at first at the thought of Ena having nothing to say, but that reduced Vera to tears and she quickly saw it was sympathy that was needed.

'It must be really hard because you're in each other's pockets all the time,' Elsie said, as Vera gradually calmed down. 'Do you ever have any time to yourself?'

'Only when I see Lily.' Vera sniffled into her handkerchief. 'And I don't see so much of her now because she's got her own . . .' She stopped and put her hand to her mouth.

'Boyfriend?' Elsie supplied the word and she smiled broadly. 'Good for her!'

'Oh dear. I'm not supposed to say. Her mam doesn't know.' Vera wiped away the stray tears that were still on her cheeks.

'Don't worry. I shan't snitch,' Elsie said. 'But the point is, apart from when Ena spends an hour or so in the Rovers it means that you're with her for all the rest of the time?'

Vera nodded miserably. 'We go to work together of a morning, work all day on the same bench, and then walk home together at the end of the day. That's why I want to get married. So that I can get away.'

Elsie stopped for a moment to light a cigarette. They were by a wall where she cupped her hands as she struck a match, trying to find sufficient shelter from the wind. Vera looked up as they paused and noticed two posters that had recently been pasted there. They each showed a smiling young girl in uniform. One had aeroplanes flying in the background and it said they were looking for recruits for the Women's Royal Air Force, the other was an advertisement for the WRENS and showed a girl with a packed suitcase ready to go to relieve any man who might want to join the navy and go to sea. Elsie glanced up and suddenly smiled. 'Now, there's another way you could leave home,' she said. 'Ever thought of joining up?'

'Do you think they'd take me?' Vera looked doubtful.

'You never know till you try,' Elsie said. They carried on walking, Elsie blowing smoke rings into the wind. 'But if that's a bit too drastic for you, then why don't you try to avoid Ena by changing your routine?'

'How do you mean?'

'I mean like change your shift or summat so that you're not both doing everything at the same time.'

Vera stared gloomily down at the cobbles beneath her feet. 'I suppose I could ask to work a different shift,' she said thoughtfully. 'Or I could put in for overtime,' she said. 'That's something my mam wouldn't want to be doing, though I don't know what she'll say if I suggest it.'

Elsie whipped the cigarette from her mouth, removing a grain of tobacco from the tip of her tongue with her brightly painted fingernail. 'Then don't suggest it, just do it!' she said triumphantly. 'Don't keep fighting her all the time. Tell her after you've done it. After all, she can hardly complain if it brings in extra money.'

'No, she can't.' Vera smiled at last. 'I'll do that. Thank you, Elsie.'

Elsie grinned. 'And whatever you do don't tell Ena it was my idea.'

But Ena didn't bother to ask whose idea it was, all she did was to pour scorn on the whole notion when Vera made her announcement.

'You doing overtime?' she scoffed. 'Don't be so daft. Do you want to kill yourself, girl? You haven't got the stamina apart from anything else.' And Vera felt as if she was six years old.

But she tried to remember what Elsie had said: 'Don't ask, just do it', and she had been right. The very thought of Vera having done something off her own bat had forced Ena out of her silence, although Vera was shocked by the strength of her mother's reaction.

'You'll tell them tomorrow you've made a mistake and you'll be doing no such thing.' Ena was determined to have the last word as usual, but for once Vera wouldn't let her.

'It's too late for that,' Vera said with a smile of satisfaction, 'I've already signed up and I start tomorrow,' though as she said the words she couldn't help wondering, what if her mother was right?

The next evening as she came out of work after her

extra shift, Vera recognized that Ena had definitely been right about her being exhausted at the end of the day; but one thing she hadn't thought about was that she would be walking home on her own in the dark.

She left the building by the side entrance and was walking slowly towards the gates when she thought she recognized the figure a little way ahead of her and she hurried her steps as much as she could to catch him up.

'Bob! Bob Lomax!' she called into the night and she was pleased when he stopped and turned.

'Well, if it isn't Vera Sharples,' he said, and Vera glowed that this time he had remembered her name.

'I didn't think we'd be bumping into each other this soon,' he said.

Vera explained that she'd volunteered for overtime, and he said that he had too. 'Does your mother not mind you walking home in the dark?' Bob said, and Vera shrugged. 'What would she say if I walked you home as I'm going that way?'

'I don't think she'd be able to say anything, do you?' Vera giggled. 'But I'd say that it would be very nice, thank you, Bob.' Vera felt extremely grateful and she smiled as they fell into step.

But if Bob hoped for the same reward as last time with a kiss from Vera when they reached the Mission, he was to be disappointed, for as they approached the vestry they could see that Ena was standing on the doorstep with her chin set and her arms folded firmly across her chest.

'Hmph!' she grunted as she glared at Bob before turning on Vera. 'I was wondering how you'd manage. I hope you've said thank you,' she said and she turned on her heel and went indoors.

For the next few days Vera didn't know how long she would be able to continue working the extra hours, for by the end of each one she was exhausted and she had difficulty getting up each morning, but she was determined to continue as long as she could. And then, as Elsie had predicted, by the end of the week things had begun to change. A new routine was established. Bob walked her home every night and Ena was no longer waiting on the doorstep or shooing Bob away when they arrived.

It seemed natural, then, for Vera to accept when Bob asked her to go the cinema with him at the weekend. Ena tossed her head and made disparaging noises when Vera told her he had asked her and when Bob arrived to pick Vera up she didn't have much to say to him but she didn't even try to stop them going.

As they made their way to join the queue for the film *This Land Is Mine*, starring Charles Laughton and Maureen O'Hara, one of Vera's favourite actresses, Vera saw Lily lining up for the more expensive seats on the other side of the box office and, as she might have expected, Lily was with Johnny.

'Oh, Lily, it's been ages!' Vera said and the two girls embraced.

'I heard you've been too busy working overtime to see your friends!' Lily joked.

'Oh, no, not too busy for you, Lily,' Vera said seriously. 'I *have* been working extra hours but I don't know how much longer I'll be able to keep it up,' she admitted. Then she nodded towards Johnny. 'But I can see you've been pretty busy too.' The words popped out without thought. Lily blushed and linked her arm more tightly through Johnny's but he merely grinned and patted her hand.

Without joining in the conversation, Bob pulled Vera away to join the queue for the cheaper seats, and all Vera could do was to wave. 'Come round and see me again,' she called and Lily called back, 'I will, really soon. Enjoy the film.'

Vera and Bob sat as they had done before, close to the front, where the cigarette smoke didn't seem to be quite so dense and, as the projectors began to roll with the latest newsreel footage following the progress of the war, Vera closed her eyes to avoid seeing the military action caught by the cameras. She couldn't believe that when she opened them again the words The End were flashing on the screen and Charles Laughton's name was heading up the cast list for the main feature.

'Oh dear, I'm so sorry. Have I really slept through it all?'

Vera was mortified when Bob nodded. 'I'm afraid so,' he said, 'you missed a good film.'

'I really am sorry for wasting the ticket,' Vera said.

'You didn't waste it, you sat in the seat all the time, didn't you?' Bob said with a chuckle. 'You looked very comfortable. But I tell you what, you can pay for the tickets next time.'

Vera felt a rush of warmth to her cheeks. 'If you would really like there to be a next time, Bob,' she said coyly, and while the theatre was still dark she leaned over and kissed him lightly on the lips. When the main lights came up she could see that he was blushing too.

'I would like there to be a next time,' he said, 'only I don't know what your mother would have to say about that. I feel like she's always trying to get rid of me.'

Vera giggled. 'Well, I'm not going to let her do that any more,' she said. 'In fact, why don't you come in for a cup of tea when we get back to the Mission tonight. She can't shoo you away if I've invited you,' she said remembering Elsie Tanner's advice once more.

'I've asked Bob to come in for a drink.' Vera spoke up as soon as she put her foot inside the vestry door. 'I want to thank him for all the times he's walked me home from work.'

Bob followed her inside, and Vera could see Ena's

startled face. 'He can have my tea ration, so you don't have to worry,' Vera said, 'and I think we might have a couple of biscuits left in the box.' Vera immediately began to busy herself with the hot water before Ena could protest. 'Shall I make one for you, Mam?' she asked.

Ena looked at Vera and then frowned at their visitor. Whatever diversions for Vera she had been planning while they were out certainly hadn't involved Bob Lomax. She could see that she would have to get a move on, but there was nothing she could do about it right now.

Lily was pleased to see Vera at the cinema as she hadn't seen her for some time and she was surprised how much she had missed her friend. I'm sure Vera understands that I've been very busy, she thought with a grin, and she snuggled down in the back row on the seat next to Johnny. She always tried to get as close as she could under the cover of the coat he threw over the two of them. She and Johnny went to the cinema regularly, though neither of them knew much about the films that had been showing as they always sat on the back row and Johnny only seemed to be interested in one thing. She had quickly learned what to expect, though she felt safe in the knowledge that in such a public place he could only go so far. It had been fun at first although she now feared the novelty was wearing off, for Johnny was demanding more. She was worried that he seemed to be losing interest and she was desperately trying to work out what she could do to win him back. The more she hated the situation at home, the more she had seen Johnny as her ticket out of Weatherfield and she couldn't afford to lose him, even if that meant that she had to give in to him completely.

Ena was relieved when Vera finally announced that she was ready to give up working overtime because she was too exhausted to continue, though she stopped short of reminding Vera that that was what she had predicted. But she was alarmed to see that by then Vera and Bob had established a new routine. Almost without her realizing how it had happened, Bob had become a frequent visitor to the Mission and Ena no longer seemed able to scare him away. Vera would regularly invite him in to the flat to share her tea ration or a cup of Camp coffee, without so much as a by-your-leave. Ena knew she had to act fast and do something drastic if she wanted to assert her power and reintroduce Eric Bowman into Vera's life and not allow her to refuse. She was pondering her options when Vera announced that she and Bob wished to talk to her – together.

Vera had unsuccessfully confronted Ena in the caretaker's flat at the Mission of Glad Tidings on many occasions, but this was different. Now she felt there was even more at stake as they came together face to face one more time. She had never felt quite so intimidated, but having Bob beside her gave her courage. She glanced at him standing beside her and saw that his cheeks had reddened. He squeezed her hand, though he refused to look at her directly. She squeezed his cold fingers back and then spoke up as they'd agreed.

'Mam, we've got something to tell you, Bob and me,' she said with a slight quaver in her voice.

Ena was at the belfast sink and was wiping her hands on a flimsy looking towel. She threw it over her shoulder and turned to face the young couple.

She took up a frightening stance with her legs apart and her arms akimbo and glared at her daughter. For a moment Vera was tongue-tied.

'Bob's asked me to marry him,' Vera said eventually. She saw Ena's eyebrows shoot up, then was unable to hold her gaze and she had to work hard in order to keep her voice steady.

'Have you now?' Ena had been startled but now she looked at Bob sceptically. 'And whatever happened to "asking my permission", eh?'

Vera felt another squeeze from Bob's cold hand. 'I'm over 21, Mam,' she felt emboldened to say, though her voice lacked confidence and the words came out in a rush.

'That's as may be in the eyes of the law,' Ena snarled, 'but you're my daughter.'

Vera shrank back for a moment. 'Naturally we're

hoping we'll have your blessing,' she said, and this time she turned to Bob and grinned.

'What you're hoping for and what you get might be two different things,' Ena said. 'Ever think of that?'

'Yes, we realize . . .' Vera began, momentarily deflated, though determined not to show it, but Ena cut across her and addressed Bob. 'What does your mam think?' She shot the question at him.

Bob spent so long gazing down at the boots he'd spent half of the previous evening polishing that Ena turned to Vera.

'Have you told his mam yet?'

Vera shook her head. 'Not yet. We wanted to tell you first.'

'And what have you got to offer my daughter if I was to say yes?' Ena turned again to Bob. 'As you know, she's used to a decent home and she needs looking after. What can you provide for her? Have you thought about that?'

Finally Bob opened his mouth. 'Of course I have,' he said defensively. 'I – I earn a steady wage as you know,' he stammered, 'and I'm sure we could live with my parents until we find somewhere to rent.'

'If you live anywhere you'll live here at the Mission. There's plenty of room!' Ena snapped at him, and Vera gasped but she knew better than to intervene at this point. 'And if you ever do get wed I trust you realize that the ceremony will be here too.'

'Oh, but I'm not sure my folks would want to come to a service in—' Bob began, but Ena cut him off.

'It'll be that or nothing, laddie,' Ena said, thinking how much easier the Bowmans would have been to deal with. 'That won't be up for discussion,' she said firmly and she glared at him until he had to look away.

Vera's head was beginning to ache and she wished that they had sat down before they had begun to talk as she was beginning to feel uncomfortable.

'So, let's talk weddings,' Ena said, suddenly sitting down at the table. Vera took the opportunity and grabbed a chair, indicating Bob should do so too. 'Can I ask who's going to pay for this wedding, should it ever go ahead?' Ena looked from one to the other.

Vera couldn't avoid a sigh escaping. She knew that now was the time to ask about what had happened to the pay packets she'd given up to her mother so readily every week on the understanding that Ena would save for Vera's future. But her bravery didn't stretch that far, and she didn't dare to ask.

'We – we haven't got that far as to talk about payment,' Bob said uncertainly, 'but I did get a ring and now might be as good a time as any to give it to you, Vera.' And he brought out from his breast pocket what looked like a brass curtain ring with a claw in the middle holding a small piece of colourless glass in place. He turned to Vera now and she beamed back at him, but before he could put it on her finger, Ena seized it out of his hand and held it up, making a show of briefly examining it.

'Whatever you paid for it, it was too much,' she said scornfully, then she looked at Vera.

'You wouldn't want to be wearing something that would turn your finger green, now would you?' she said. 'She wants something she can show off, don't you, love?'

'But it would do,' Vera began, 'till I can get a proper one.' And she reached out for it, but Ena tossed it onto the table.

'Have you told him what kind of a ring you'd really like?' Ena asked Vera.

'Well, no . . .'

'Then I suggest that you do. Then we'll see how good his intentions are. I tell you what, laddie,' Ena said, her voice suddenly sounding reasonable, 'why don't you come back with a proper ring, and then maybe we can talk again?' she said, though her mind was already working on other ways that she could use the situation to nip this unwelcome development in the bud.

Ena banged the brass knocker louder than was necessary and was about to knock again when she heard the sound of slippers shuffling towards the door.

'Mrs Sharples?' a small voice asked as the door was opened a crack.

'Aye, Pat Lomax, I presume. I think you're expecting

me.' Ena put out her foot to widen the gap and pushed her way inside.

'I'm in the kitchen,' Pat Lomax said, pointing to the open door at the end of the narrow hallway. The small voice belonged to a small woman with sparse, mousey-coloured hair and a slight stoop who barely came up to Ena's shoulder. 'I hope that's all right?'

Ena sat down at the kitchen table without waiting to be asked and looked around the small room, taking in the pans suspended from hooks on the ceiling and the blackened kettle that was hanging over the hearth. She folded her arms across her chest.

'Is our Bob your Vera's first boyfriend?' Pat Lomax asked timidly as she sat down opposite.

'Of course he is,' Ena all but snorted. 'You don't think I'd let her go courting just anyone who happened to turn up on the doorstep, do you? At least she knows him from work.'

'Then you know she could go further and fare far worse,' Pat said. 'My lad comes from a very respectable home, as you can see. He's a good lad and a good worker and we have high hopes for him. Do you know, he practically runs that repair shop down at the factory?'

She half rose as she spoke, leaning forward, and she punctuated her words by prodding the well-marked wooden table with her finger. Then she seemed to deflate as she sat down again.

'I don't reckon she's his first girlfriend,' Ena said.

'Happen not, but there's nowt wrong with that. He's a healthy young lad and I don't always make it my business to know what he gets up to. Lads have to do what lads have to do and I say it's best for them to do it as well away from home as possible. His dad's always told him: you don't want to be messing about on your own doorstep.'

'Aye and if you had a daughter I can tell you that you wouldn't want her messing about on anyone else's doorstep either! Now, I suppose you know that they're talking about getting wed?'

'Well, yes, so they said, though I did think as much. Vera's the first girl he's brought home,' Pat said, 'so he must think a lot of her.'

'That's as maybe, but we need to get down to business,' Ena said. 'For whatever reason, my Vera seems keen to marry your Bob and no matter what I say I can't shake her off it.'

Pat looked taken aback. 'Why would you want to do that?' she asked. 'Are you not keen then?' Pat frowned and looked confused. She stiffened slightly as she said, 'What seems to be the problem?'

'My problem is how can either of them really know what they want? I mean, what does your Bob know of the world?'

'Or your Vera for that matter!' Pat retorted quickly, and Ena pounced.

'That's exactly my point,' Ena said with a satisfied

smile. 'I think they need a chance to get to know each other. They need to take their time and not rush into anything.'

'Hmm . . . I suppose waiting a bit would do no harm,' Pat said.

'There's no real hurry now, is there? It's not as though he's waiting to be sent off to the front line or anything. He's not even on the list waiting for his call-up papers, as I understand,' Ena said.

'No, well, that's unfortunate.' Pat looked embarrassed. 'That's on account of his . . . er . . . medical problems.'

'That he's a bit deaf you mean? And his flat feet?' Ena said and she couldn't resist a slight sneer. 'I want you to know that I've told them they'll have to wait to get engaged at least till they can afford to get a decent ring. Summat Vera can show off.' She paused and leaned forward across the table. 'But then I would suggest that we both encourage them to have a long engagement.' She sat back with a self-satisfied smile.

'If you really think that's for the best, I suppose it wouldn't do any harm,' Pat said, though she did feel a little bemused.

'Good, then that's sorted.' And Ena scraped her chair back on the tiles as she prepared to leave. 'Oh, and just so's you know, if and when they do eventually tie the knot,' she said, 'it will be at the Mission of Glad Tidings down by the viaduct.'

Pat's hand fluttered to her cheeks which suddenly looked as if they had been smeared with lipstick.

'Oh dear, no, I don't think so,' she said apologetically but firmly. 'We regularly attend our own church down the road here and that's where we'd like our son to be married.'

Ena glared. 'The Mission is not only our church but it's home to me and Vera as well – and we can have it for free,' she said and she set her face into a determined expression and looked Pat straight in the eye.

Pat slowly got out of the chair but Ena was already standing. 'Thank you for coming, it's been nice to meet you,' Pat said rather formally and she put out her hand, but Ena looked distracted as she shook it limply. She was already planning how she might use a lengthy engagement to prove to Vera that she could do far better in the matrimonial market than Bob Lomax.

'And where do you think you're going, miss, all done up like a dog's dinner?'

Lily shook her hand free of her father's grasp with more than her usual irritation, for she was keen to get off.

'If you must know I'm going to see Vera. I've not been there for ages,' she replied.

'That's good,' Martha intervened, 'because I'm going to meet Ena in the Rovers shortly and she always likes it when she knows you're with Vera.' Lily was surprised when her mother backed her up. Then, 'Between you and me, Vera should have lots to tell you,' she said, though she didn't elaborate.

'If she's only going to Vera's, then why is she all got up like that, eh?' Percy Longhurst barked at Martha as if Lily wasn't there. 'All that black stuff round her eyes?' He came closer to Lily to get a good look at her make-up.

Lily took a step back. She hadn't been feeling well all day so she had added a touch of rouge to her pale cheeks in an attempt to look brighter and she'd been experimenting on her eyes with the kohl Elsie Tanner had given her. Johnny always seemed to be attracted to girls who wore it and Lily wanted to see if Vera thought it had the right effect on her. It was too bad her father had noticed it first.

Lily sighed. She knew better than to bring Johnny's name into this conversation. 'It's what everybody's wearing,' she said. 'You're out of touch.'

'Really?' Martha joined in again. 'The only person I've seen wearing it is Elsie Tanner – and we all know what kind of a woman *she* is. Are you fooling around with someone we don't know about?'

'No, I'm not,' Lily lied, 'but it would serve you right if I was.'

'What did you say?' Percy squared up to confront her and Lily could feel her anger beginning to flare, all this because her mother thought the Bradwell family was beneath her.

'Oh, Lily, it's not as though we've kept you on a chain like poor Vera,' Martha appealed to her. 'We only want what's best for you, you know that; we worry about you.'

'Well you won't have to worry about me much longer cos I intend to be off and out of your hair as soon as I possibly can!' Lily's temper snapped and the words slipped out before she could stop them though she wished she could claw them back as soon as they were out of her mouth. The irony was, they were true. With any luck she'd be able to leave home sooner than planned. Hadn't Johnny promised to marry her when she'd finally given in to him in the deserted Anderson shelter near the Field, the recreation ground where they often liked to go. The only problem was that she hadn't meant to share her secret so soon. Her words were met by a moment of stunned silence. Then both her parents spoke at once.

'And where do you think you'll be going?' Martha cried.

'Why, you ungrateful little madam!' Percy said.

Lily was scared for a moment when she saw their faces and wondered what they'd say when she told them the whole truth. Taking a deep breath she turned to run out of the house. She had no intentions of telling them more right now, at least not until she had seen Johnny.

'I believe you've got lots to tell me! Are you and Bob stepping out or something? Don't tell me your mother's agreed to let him come near?' Lily came bursting into the kitchen as soon as Vera opened the front door and both girls fell upon each other with screams of delight.

Vera giggled. 'It's more than that,' she said and Lily's eyes opened wide.

'My mam's been hinting,' Lily said, 'though she hasn't gone into details, 'but she's off to meet your mam in the Rovers right now. So, what's the latest?'

'We started stepping out soon after he was seeing me home when we were both working overtime. She couldn't very well turn him away at the door and it wasn't long before we were like – courting.'

'What did your mother say to that?' Lily wanted to know.

Vera was excitedly about to close the door when she spotted Elsie Tanner on the other side of the street.

'Hey, Vera!' Elsie called. 'Do I gather that congratulations are in order? There's rumours flying around that you're getting hitched – are you, Vera?' Elsie crossed the road and came to the door. 'If that's right then we need to crack open the Christmas sherry.'

'I don't know about the sherry,' Vera said and laughed, 'my mam keeps it under lock and key, but you can come and join us in a cup of tea at least. Mam's not in and she'll be gone a couple of hours, I reckon.'

'I'd guess as much. I saw her settling in at the Rovers not ten minutes since,' Elsie said with a grin.

'No doubt she's telling my mam and her cronies the same story,' Lily said, 'so come on, Vera, and tell us all about it.' She looked even more excited than Vera as she led the way through to the kitchen. 'Are you and Bob really going to get wed?'

'Yes, we are,' Vera said, her eyes wide. 'Bob asked me to marry him – well, I asked him really, but he agreed and then we talked to my mam, together, Bob and me,' Vera said and she clapped her hands together like an excited child.

'And what did Ena say to that? Was she surprised?' Elsie wanted to know.

'You won't believe it, but she didn't object,' Vera said. 'I was worried that she didn't really like Bob but for once she was on my side, and we're going to get engaged; it's all fixed,' Vera said excitedly.

'When? Have you got a ring?' Lily picked up Vera's hand but let it go again with a disappointed look when she saw the ring finger was empty.

'Not yet.' Vera hesitated then said, 'We haven't decided exactly when. Mam thought Bob should buy me something really decent before we make the announcement and he'll have to save up for that. He had bought me some cheap thing that I thought would have been all right, but she said it looked like a curtain ring and she made him take it back.'

'Typical Ena.' Elsie rolled her eyes, but Vera ignored her. 'She wants to make sure I get a really nice ring that I can show off,' she said and she held up her hand as if to admire her wedding finger even though it was bare. 'Now wasn't that lovely of her, for once?'

Elsie and Lily exchanged glances but neither said anything.

'And have you met Bob's mam?' Lily asked. 'What does Mrs Lomax think of it all?'

'I'd have thought she'd be pleased to get Bob off her hands,' Elsie said with a grin.

'Yes, she's very nice and she did seem quite happy with it all,' Vera said. 'Though when Mam went to see her they couldn't agree about where the wedding should be. But I'm not going to worry about that yet. I'm happy that we're engaged. Well, *almost* engaged.'

There was an awkward few moments of silence after Vera said that; even Lily looked subdued. Then Elsie said, 'I'm sure you'll be engaged soon, though you might have to accept waiting a little while before it actually happens. It could take some time for Bob to save up for a ring and then for your mam to decide whether she likes it or not.'

Vera frowned, not quite understanding the implications behind Elsie's words.

'Did your mam say how long she'd expect you to be engaged once you got the ring?' Lily asked. Vera shook her head. 'I was wondering if you might end up having to wait again till they agree on a church?'

'That's true,' Elsie said. 'You know, Vera love, it's best to be prepared that you might not be able to get away from this place for quite some time yet,' Elsie went on. 'You know how your mam can be. She might have led you into thinking you're going to get married soon and then she'll keep on finding different things to put in your way.'

Vera pulled a long face. It was true. Now that she thought about it her mother had often done that. 'We didn't talk about how long it all might take before I could leave,' she said, and for a moment her lower lip quivered.

'No, I don't suppose you did,' Elsie said, her tone gentler now. 'But she might be hoping you'll get fed up waiting for Bob and then you'll be glad to accept someone else instead, someone of your mam's choosing.'

Vera looked horrified. 'Do you really think she'd do that?'

Lily went to sit beside Vera on the couch and she put her arm round her friend while Vera used the back of her hand to swipe away a tear that had escaped down her cheek.

Suddenly Lily giggled in an attempt to lighten the mood. 'Of course, you could always run away and get married,' she said. 'Elope. Isn't that the word, Elsie?'

'Why? Is that what you and your young man are thinking of doing?' Elsie laughed too.

'His name's Johnny,' Lily said, then her face paled. 'Yes, I'd love to be able to do that. To go and get married somewhere dead romantic, just the two of us.' For a moment she looked as if she was going to be sick, though she continued to smile. 'I bet that would be the cheapest option as well. Imagine, the two of you on your own, Vera, with no one else telling you what to do. Wouldn't that be wonderful?'

Vera laughed. 'Where could I go that my mother wouldn't find me and drag me back?'

Lily shrugged her shoulders. 'You're probably right,' she said.

'And what would we live on? I've got no money. Mam takes my wage packet every week and only gives me back some spending money.'

'What about Bob?' Lily said. 'I presume he must be earning enough to keep you both once you're married.'

Vera looked up. 'I thought Mam had been saving my wages for a wedding,' she said, her voice cracking and she began to cry softly.

'Maybe she has,' Elsie said, 'because I'm sure she'd like you to get married. But the question is, does she really want you to marry Bob?'

Vera had a sudden picture in her mind of Eric. 'But if I don't marry Bob then I might never really get away from here,' she said in a shocked voice.

'Oh, I think you will,' Elsie said, 'but you're going to have to be very strong and stand up to your mother if you want your husband to be someone of your own choosing.'

Vera stared up at her and this time she didn't even try to catch the tears that had begun to stream down her face.

Chapter 9

Lily was really upset by the time she left Vera's. She felt sorry for her friend that she was so restricted by her mother, always having to do her bidding, never doing anything that she wanted to do, but now she was beginning to feel even more sorry for herself. She wished she had listened more carefully to some of the things her mother had tried to talk to her about after she had started her monthlies, but it had been easier to dismiss Martha Longhurst as being out of touch and too set in her ways to know anything about being in love. Even the thought of talking to her mother about it made Lily blush. How could old-fashioned Martha understand the ways of modern young girls?

Instead, Lily had chosen to be guided by Johnny

Bradwell. She had listened to him, convincing herself that she could trust him, but now she was left wondering if that trust had been misplaced. She'd believed him when he'd promised to 'take care of things' even though, she now had to admit, she didn't know exactly what that had meant. She'd told him that she loved him and he'd claimed that he loved her and had promised to look after her. Well, now that she was going to have to put that love to the test, she had to admit she was afraid. But she could hardly own up to her mother that she wished she had taken notice of her warnings, because it was probably too late.

When she had woken up that morning, Lily had been sick several times although she had managed to get out of the house without her mother noticing. She had felt light-headed by the time she got to work and when she had fainted the section supervisor had actually wanted to send her home. But Lily had refused, passing it off as something she had eaten that had disagreed with her and she had almost believed her own story; but 'almost' was the best she could do. She had managed to set her feelings aside while she and Elsie had tried to encourage Vera in her battle against Ena, but now that she was back outside in the fresh air she could feel the bile once more rising in her throat.

Lily kicked out angrily, disturbing some of the loose stones that lay in the cracks on the pavement, and she didn't care that she sent them flying into the roadway in all directions. 'It isn't fair,' she said over and over, and she really believed it wasn't fair if what she most feared was true. She curled her fists into the pockets of her home-knitted cardigan, thinking about what she was going to say to her parents. She had already boasted to them that she would be leaving home soon but before that could happen she would have to talk to Johnny.

They met as they usually did outside the cinema and Lily was pleased that it was a mild summer's night.

'Can we skip the film tonight?' Lily said as soon as she saw him. 'I'd rather go for a walk.'

Johnny grinned. 'Great, I know the perfect place, it's not far.'

'No, Johnny. When I say a walk I mean a walk. Not a—' But she never finished her sentence because he stood in front of her, preventing her from moving, and sealed his lips on hers. As soon as she felt his tongue touch hers, for once she pushed him away. 'No, Johnny!' she said. 'Can we carry on walking, please? There's something I have to talk to you about.'

'Gosh, this does sound serious,' Johnny said, though the smile hadn't left his lips.

'It is.' Suddenly she stopped. 'It has something to do with the Anderson shelter on the Field,' she said.

A look flashed across his eyes that she couldn't quite read, and then she saw all the colour drain from his face. At least she finally had his attention.

He pushed his hands deep into his trouser pockets. 'The Anderson shelter? You mean where we were fooling around?' he mumbled.

'Come on, Johnny. We did a lot more than fool around, we both know that, and you said you'd take care of everything.'

'And I did,' he snapped. She could see anger flare in his eyes and she suddenly felt afraid. 'You know I did so you can't blame me for any—'

But she didn't let him finish. 'Who else can I blame? I think I'm pregnant,' Lily said simply. She had been determined not to lose her temper, or to cry, though she knew she was dangerously on the verge of both but she tried not to let her panic show.

'You can't be. It's not possible,' he fired at her and she so wanted to believe him that for a moment his bluster caught her on the hop. But fear clutched at her when she realized he was refusing to accept any responsibility.

'You can't possibly be pregnant from that night,' he repeated. 'It's too soon. How could you possibly know?'

'Because my monthlies are normally regular as clockwork.' She hung her head, ashamed to have to talk about something so deeply personal. 'I knew straight away.'

He hesitated no more than a beat before he looked up and smiled directly at her as he said, 'You can't prove that it's mine. How do I know how many other lads you've been with?'

Lily drew in breath sharply, incredulous at his accusations. How dare he!

But he wouldn't let it go. 'This is typical of you,' he said, 'trying to trap me. I must admit I'd been warned, though I didn't want to believe it, but you women are all the same.'

Now Lily looked up at him but her shocked stare seemed to give him more courage.

'The trouble with you young girls is that you don't know the difference between having a bit of fun and thinking you can trap a lad for life.' He wagged his finger inches from her face. 'Well, let me tell you this is one lad who won't be caught up in your lies like that.'

Lily's eyes widened. 'But Johnny, you said that—'

'And if you believed that then you'll believe anything. Don't you know all lads say that?'

'But I – I thought you said we'd get married soon anyway. You *promised*.'

'How could I have promised marriage when you know very well I'll be called up to the army very soon and the last thing I need is to have a nagging wife and a brat hanging from my neck?' And to Lily's horror he actually laughed. She stared at him in disbelief as he took a step away then turned back to look at her, his eyes filled with nothing but scorn and contempt. 'You must be dafter than you look, Lily,' he said and he strode away from her quickly and didn't look back.

*

Vera, mindful of Elsie's warning, took every opportunity to invite Bob into the Mission, determined to show Ena that they were a happy courting couple even without a ring and that nothing she could say would keep them apart for long.

One night she and Bob came back from the cinema early as the main feature film had been interrupted by an air-raid siren. It had taken a while before it was established that it was a false alarm and by this time the rest of the cinema performance had been abandoned for the night. Bob and Vera were sitting in the vestry sharing what was left of the tea in the teapot when Ena arrived with Albert Tatlock, one of their Coronation Street neighbours; they both sported their ARP warden's armbands and Albert was swinging his ARP helmet in his hand.

'Owt left in the pot?' Ena asked and she glared accusingly at Bob.

'Not much,' Vera said. 'We didn't know you'd be coming back so soon. But I can top up what's left with some more water if you hang on a minute.' And she rushed to heat up the pan over the hearth.

'Our lovely quiet evening at the Rovers was ruined when that thing went off and folk went rushing down to the basement for shelter. Albert and me decided we'd take a chance on getting safely back here and sure enough when we were halfway down Coronation Street the hooter went off for the all-clear. One of the firewatchers tipped us off that it had been a false alarm but we didn't bother going back. I thought we could catch a cup of tea here.'

Albert Tatlock sat down at the table and shook his head. 'I felt sorry for that fire watcher. He said it was the third false alarm they'd had this week. I'd frankly lost count, but false or not, they have to go out and check, just in case. They've really got their hands full.'

'Are they still looking for volunteers?' Ena suddenly said.

'Aye, they're always on the lookout for new blood as you might say,' Albert said. 'Anyone with a bit of time on their hands who's willing to do their bit.'

'Well, I reckon there's one willing volunteer sitting right here.' She stared at Bob across the table and his brow furrowed as he glared back. 'What do you say, Bob?' she challenged him. 'You could do worse than to offer to join the defence team.'

'That sounds like a good idea, Bob.' Vera sounded naively enthusiastic as she tended to the hot water.

'You tell him, Vera,' Ena encouraged her. 'Sounds like the position's made for him.' She patted Bob's hand and he recoiled, startled. 'There you are then, Bob,' she goaded him, 'you couldn't get a better endorsement than that,' and she smiled.

'You can go down to the town hall any time, lad, there'll always be someone there pleased to sign you up.' Albert joined in the conversation innocently before Bob had had a chance to say anything. 'I know they'll always welcome an extra pair of hands on the team; or should I say, extra pair of eyes?' He chuckled. 'They're especially keen to recruit young eyes. Spotting a fire in good time before it takes hold can really save a lot of lives.'

'He could become quite the local hero,' Ena said, looking directly at Vera as she chose her words carefully.

Vera frowned. 'How come? He'll not be in any danger, will he? What exactly does a fire watcher do?'

'Exactly that,' Ena said and sighed. 'He watches for fires that start up from them incendiary things the Jerries chuck down at us from them planes. He either puts them out before they can get going properly, or he calls in the rest of the team if there's a fire needs fighting. It's a very important job – next best thing to being a soldier,' she added cruelly. The blood rose from Bob's neck upwards and he refused to look at her, but she couldn't let it go. 'Of course, if it was your ears or your feet that were required it might be a different story,' she said tartly.

'There's nowt wrong with his eyes.' Vera rushed to defend him. She put her arms across his shoulders and gave him an awkward sideways hug but he didn't respond.

'Imagine how important you'll look with your own stirrup pump and your bucket and shovel,' Ena went on as if Vera hadn't spoken. 'Oh yes, and your tin hat and armband. Those in themselves will make you look important. I think being a fire watcher would suit you down to the ground.'

'You've already reported a couple of fires you spotted,' Vera said with pride, 'haven't you, Bob? He managed to shout to one of the wardens in time for them to get it under control before it flared up into something big,' she said, her eyes glowing.

She'd have no opposition there, Ena could see; Vera already liked the idea of hanging on to the arm of a local hero and Bob had been too surprised by her suggestion to refuse. She sat back in her chair with a satisfied smile.

Chapter 10

At first Vera was thrilled by Bob's new duties and she proudly boasted to anyone who would listen that Bob had now been inaugurated as a valuable young member of the local fire watch team. It took a while until she began to realize that, in practice, this meant that they now had less time than ever to spend together. If Bob wasn't working he was out watching for incendiary bombs or any hint of a flame that could expand quickly into a full-blown fire. Vera now had to spend most evenings and large chunks of the weekends either on her own or trailing in her mother's wake, much as she had before, as Bob fulfilled his role on the fire watch rota; and she began to wonder if the marriage that she had so longed for as a way of escaping from her mother and the Mission would ever really take place.

'Honestly, we see more of each other at work than we do during our so-called time off. I'm lucky if I see Bob once a week outside work these days,' she moaned to Lily one evening when the two girls had come home from the cinema together. The programme, thankfully, had run through from beginning to end without interruption though *For Whom the Bell Tolls* had done nothing to lighten their mood.

'I still don't have a ring to show that we are properly engaged and we're still no nearer setting a date for the wedding,' Vera complained. 'I only ever get to go out with you and I'm still sharing a bed with my mother. Honestly!' she almost shouted in frustration. 'I'm getting fed up. I want to do something different for a change. I may as well not be courting Bob at all!'

To her surprise, instead of mumbling agreement as she usually did, Lily merely flared at her. 'At least you know that you're going to be married one day,' Lily burst out, then she gasped and choked back a sob.

Vera automatically put her hand out to touch her friend's arm. 'Lily? What do you mean?' But Lily pulled her arm away abruptly and burst into tears. 'Lily? What's wrong?' Vera asked gently. 'You'll be married one day, an' all.'

Lily shook her head and for a moment she sobbed

quietly without looking at Vera. 'No, I won't.' She sounded angry.

'Don't be so daft,' Vera insisted, 'of course you will. Johnny and you will—'

'No, we won't!' Lily all but shouted. 'There *is* no "Johnny and me". As far as I'm concerned he doesn't exist.'

Vera was shocked. 'Why? What's happened?' she asked, but she had to wait several minutes for the sobbing to subside and for Lily to find her voice once more.

'You mustn't tell anyone, Vera, you must swear.'

Vera suddenly looked alarmed. 'I won't tell,' she promised. 'I'm your friend. But you're scaring me, Lily. What is it I mustn't tell?'

'I thought I was pregnant,' Lily said simply, 'and I told Johnny.' Vera sat back and put her hands to her mouth. The colour had drained from Lily's face. 'I expected him to . . .' Lily began again. 'I assumed . . .' She drew in a deep breath. 'But I was wrong. He didn't want to know.'

Vera's eyes narrowed. 'You mean you – you know – you . . . with Johnny?' She waved her fingers vaguely in the air.

'You mustn't tell anyone, Vera,' Lily said again, grasping hold of Vera's hand.

'You mean you *did*? Oh!'

'I'd promised myself I wasn't going to let him until we were married, but then . . . well, I suppose it just happened and the next thing I knew my monthlies were late. So much for him taking care of things!' she said with disgust.

Vera gasped again and put her hand to her mouth.

'I told Johnny because I thought that if you were getting wed, then he'd say that we should get hitched too.'

'But what happened?'

'Basically, he laughed. He laughed at me, Vera and then he told me to get lost.'

'And . . .?'

'And nothing. And thank goodness I haven't seen him since.'

'Lily, I'm so sorry,' Vera said, her forehead wrinkling. 'Do you think he'll change his mind?'

'It doesn't matter if he does. It's too late now, anyway,' Lily said forlornly.

'What do you mean? You didn't do anything, did you?' Vera looked horrified; everyone had heard the stories of girls who had got themselves in the family way out of wedlock and the subsequent mutterings about babies that had to be 'got rid of'. Vera had no idea what that meant but didn't like the sound of it one little bit.

Lily sat up straight now and she smiled though the tears were still rolling down her cheeks. 'No,' she said in what was almost a whisper, 'fortunately, I didn't have to do anything. It must have been the shock or something, but I suddenly had a very heavy bleed, and now my monthlies are back to normal.'

Vera let out the breath she had been holding.

'Honest, Vera, I almost went to church to say thanks I felt so grateful. I swear I won't ever do anything like that again. I didn't even enjoy it when we finally did it; it was a big disappointment. Painful and over in a flash.' She found a handkerchief in her pocket and blew her nose, hard. 'All I can say is, be warned. It's not all it's cracked up to be and it's certainly not worth the worry if you're not married. Whatever Bob says, don't let him persuade you. It was horrible while it lasted and then being pregnant, even for a short time, wasn't much fun either. I can tell you I never want to go through that again.' And she shook her head. 'Never!'

'I'm really sorry, no, I'm really glad, well, you know what I mean. Are you sure you're all right now?' Vera sounded anxious.

'I'm fine, but no thanks to . . . him,' Lily said. 'I'm too ashamed to tell anyone and you must promise never to tell a living soul, but I can't believe that Johnny turned out to be such a rotter. And I could never tell my mother that she was right.'

Chapter 11

Elsie Tanner stood between Vera and Lily and all three were gazing solemnly at the wall in front of them, Elsie puffing on a cork tipped cigarette from her freshly opened packet. 'I see they've added another poster since we were here last, Vera,' she said, pointing to one that had been pasted on to the end and curled round the edge of the brickwork. It showed a young girl in trousers and wellington boots and she was holding what Elsie said was called a pitchfork. Vera giggled when Lily said it was used for tossing hay or lifting cut grass.

'That's funny,' Vera said. 'It looks like a very fierce fork to me, more like something that you would use to kill someone.'

'Then that's definitely for me,' Lily said. 'I could use

it to kill Johnny.' She laughed but Vera shuddered, her face suddenly serious.

'Don't make such jokes, Lily, or they might come true,' Vera said.

'We've seen the adverts for the WAAF and the WRENS before, remember, Vera?' Elsie intervened. Vera nodded, for the pictures of the girls in uniform had made an impression on her then, when Elsie had suggested that she might like to consider signing up for the services as a way to leave home.

'But I think this new one looks much nicer.' Vera pointed to the poster headed Join the Land Army. 'The girls certainly look a lot happier working in the countryside than those in the unforms who stand there having to salute.' She wriggled her body. 'Besides, their uniform looks itchy,' she said and Elsie laughed.

'I must admit the Land Army does sound healthy,' Lily said. 'Do come and see what it says here: "Join up for a healthy and happy job." Right at this minute I reckon that would suit us both down to the ground, don't you think?'

Vera nodded and looked thoughtful.

'All I know is I want to get out of here as much as you do,' Lily said. 'I can't face people after the way Johnny treated me and I can't imagine what will be said once the rumours start flying. I think I could do with a bit of something healthy and happy in my life right now, couldn't you?'

Vera looked abstracted as she continued to gaze at the posters. 'That girl with the fork certainly looks much happier than I am,' she said miserably.

'Seriously, Elsie, don't you think Vera and me could do a job like that?'

Elsie shrugged. 'No reason why not.'

'Well, I think it's perfect,' Lily said. 'It would be a chance to live in the country, to grow all our own vegetables and look after a few animals. It's like a dream. The perfect chance to get away from the clacking tongues of Weatherfield and to get out of my mother's hair, not to mention my father.'

Vera giggled. 'Wouldn't my mother be sorry that she didn't let Bob and me get married right away when we had the chance?'

Elsie chuckled. 'I can just picture them all in the Rovers,' she said, 'Ena and Martha explaining to Annie Walker as they wait for their milk stout, that you've left Coronation Street to live on a farm!' And she hooted with laughter. Vera, however, wasn't quite so sure that it would actually be fun trying to sell the idea to her mother.

'I think I might be better off going without saying anything beforehand,' Vera said, her voice quavering slightly, and Elsie slipped her arm around Vera's shoulders. 'I think I'd be best leaving her a note.'

'The more I think about it, the more I want to do it,' Lily said, and she pointed to the picture of the girl with the pitchfork. 'How about you, Vera?'

Vera nodded but not quite so enthusiastically.

'Why don't you find out more about it, Lily,' Elsie said. 'There's an address to contact so you can check it out.'

Vera looked down at the uneven paving stones and shuffled her feet. 'I suppose if Bob can have another job, then why can't I? Growing vegetables sounds like a lot more fun than working in a factory.'

Lily nodded. 'It says there that the Land Army is helping to feed the nation,' she said, her face creasing into a big broad smile. 'Now that sounds all right, doesn't it?'

'And I like what she's wearing,' Vera said. 'It's much nicer than the other uniforms. Do you think you get it for free?'

'Who knows?' Elsie answered first. 'My Arnold gets all his navy stuff free. Not that I get to see him in it all that often, thankfully.'

'It would be fun to wear trousers like that,' Vera said. 'I get fed up with skirts sometimes but my mam would never let me wear trousers.'

'I hope you're not saying you'd join up just because of the uniform?' Lily said with a giggle.

'No, of course not,' Vera said. Then she giggled too, 'But I'd like to see everyone's faces if we turned up dressed like that one day in Coronation Street.'

'I can understand why you don't want to tell your mother what you might be planning,' Elsie said. 'She'd be bound to find some way to stop you, if she knew beforehand; she's proving to be good at that. But are you sure you really want to leave her a note?'

Vera had accepted Elsie's offer of a cup of tea as she knew Ena was still out at the Rovers and now she looked embarrassed. 'I was hoping you would help me to write it, to put it into the right words so she can't argue back. She'll try and stop me whatever I do,' she said, not looking at Elsie who was busy heating some water, 'though you must cross your heart and promise not to tell.'

'Of course I shan't tell,' Elsie said. 'But it has to be in your hand, or she'd smell a rat right away.'

'That's all right,' Vera said eagerly, 'I'll write it, so long as you help me with the words.'

Elsie laughed. 'I think we might need something stronger than tea, right now,' she said. 'How would you fancy a little tipple? I've a nice bottle of sherry I've not long since opened.' And she got out two shot glasses and filled them with the pale-looking liquid. 'Let's drink to a bright, clear future working on the land.' Elsie touched her glass to Vera's and took a sip of the drink.

Vera raised her glass, 'Maybe this will help to put a bomb behind Bob to stand up to my mother. He needs to hurry up and save enough money so's we can get married and I can get out of her house.'

'I think it's a wonderful idea, I must say, and it will

be a good move for Lily too.' Elsie finished what was in her glass and poured another one. 'You know, I've been saying for a while that it was time you got out from that Mission. I only wish I could be there to see Ena's face when she finds out what you've done.'

'Oh no, you can't do that.' Vera looked horrified. 'She can't find out until long after we've gone,' she said.

'Oh, Vera love, you are precious,' Elsie said, and she leaned over the table to top up Vera's glass. 'But you don't have to worry about me. I promise not to tell a living soul until you are safely gone and away.' She raised her glass and chinked it against Vera's. 'Meanwhile, let's drink a toast to the Land Girls of Coronation Street.'

Vera was disappointed by Bob's first reaction when she told him what she had decided to do. If anything, he sounded irritated and she felt she had to justify her position. 'As we can't get married right away, I thought I'd at least be doing something useful,' she said. 'And it would mean I can get away from my mother.'

'I understand that,' Bob said. 'I'll also be glad not to have her breathing down my neck.'

'And now you've got your fire watching it's not as though we see much of each other. This way I'd have my own special work.'

'I suppose it's only a pity that you'll be living away from home,' he said, though he didn't actually look sad.

'But think of it, by the time I get back you should have saved up enough for us to get wed and then we'll be together all the time.' She smiled and felt hurt when he didn't immediately smile back.

'I'm sure we can make it work if that's what you want to do.' Bob's face suddenly brightened. 'It really does sound like a good idea.'

'Will you miss me?' Vera prompted.

'Of course I will, but we can write.'

Vera curled her lip. 'I'm not much of a writer, I'm afraid,' she said, 'though I will try.'

'Never mind. It won't be for ever,' Bob said, and Vera was suddenly anxious that he looked almost too eager that she should go.

Part Two

The Land Girls

Chapter 12

July 1943

Vera had never been on a train before and she was glad Lily was with her when the screeching whistle blasted in her ears and the carriage suddenly shuddered into life. She gasped and stood up unsteadily, fearing that their bags might fall onto their heads from the overhead racks where they had managed to store them. 'What was that?' she gulped.

'Do sit down, Vera,' Lily said. 'It only means the train's ready to go. It'll probably shift again in a minute.' She might have been younger but she was certainly the more experienced traveller.

Vera remained standing. She pressed her face to the

window, though with the smoke and steam swirling about the platform it was not easy to see what was happening outside. 'Are you sure everything's all right? Why is it shaking like that?' she asked fearfully.

Lily shrugged. 'I suppose it's when the engine connects with all the carriages it has to pull to sort of make sure they're all coupled together correctly. I don't know for certain, I've only been on a train to Glossop before, not on a long-distance one like this.'

'Like cranking the engine of a car, do you mean?' Vera said and she tried to smile. She was still not reassured that the luggage hadn't been dislodged, but she sat down, albeit nervously.

'Isn't this the most exciting thing ever?' Lily said, not willing to respond directly to Vera's jitters, though she reached across and squeezed Vera's hand.

'I'm glad our mams didn't come to see us off,' Vera said, 'though mine certainly tried hard enough.'

Lily laughed. 'We all know how disastrous that would have been.'

'She'd have wanted to stay on the train,' Vera agreed.

Vera had been hoping her mother wouldn't find out that they had signed up to be land girls until long after she'd left Weatherfield, but she had reckoned without Ena periodically snooping in her cupboards and drawers. It had been a frightening moment when her mother raised her hand to flash the envelope she'd found in Vera's face – and for a brief moment Vera thought Ena was going to strike her. Vera couldn't deny that the envelope had 'Mrs Sharples' written on the front, so that Ena had every right to open it, and her face had been like thunder when she'd read the contents, written in very strong terms why her mother shouldn't stop her going. It was a good job that the handwriting was Vera's, which Ena recognized instantly, but she didn't try to hold back her fury at the thought of what Vera and Lily had been plotting behind her back.

'And why, might I ask, do you want to go running off to join this Land Army?' Ena said, her voice almost a snarl. 'You're far safer at home with me.'

'Oh, but . . .' Vera began but Ena hadn't finished. 'And what about Bob?' she said. 'You'll be leaving him behind. Does he know about this?'

Vera was on the verge of tears. Why did her mother have to find the letter before they'd even had a chance to get away? She shrugged her shoulders. 'I hardly ever get to see him, these days,' she said miserably. 'Anyways, he said he'll write and it will give him time to save up for a ring.'

'I don't understand you wanting to go away when you've got a perfectly good job here,' Ena started again. 'But that won't matter so long as you've not done anything daft like handing in your notice.'

Now tears did begin to dribble down Vera's cheeks as she confessed that was exactly what she had done. 'I hate working in the factory and you know it!' Vera suddenly stamped her foot and Ena stared at her in surprise. 'Why wouldn't I want to go away? With Bob standing on rooftops looking for fires every spare minute and you hovering over me all the time. If I grow vegetables I'll be doing something *really* useful towards the war effort, won't I? And I'll be a lot safer down in the countryside.'

'How am I expected to manage here on my own?' Vera thought she detected a note of pleading in her mother's voice as she said this. In fact, looking at her, she wondered if her mother's eyes didn't look a bit watery all of a sudden.

'Eh, Mam, you're not taking on, are you?' Vera asked.

'Don't be so bloody daft!' Ena's mouth had set in a thin line again, and there was a flash of anger in her eyes now, not tears, so Vera thought it must have been her imagination. 'There's daughters out there who wouldn't dream of abandoning their mothers like you are, though!'

'But you've said yourself many a time that it's selfish for people not to do their bit and didn't Mr Churchill, the Prime Minister, ask everyone to do that?'

At these words, the ones Elsie had told her to say, Ena tutted and harrumphed and rolled her eyes heavenwards, muttering crossly to herself for the rest of the day, but she gave Vera no further argument.

Vera couldn't wait to tell Elsie how much her advice had helped, because after that conversation her mother had agreed to let her go and the next time she saw Elsie passing by, pushing little Dennis along in his pram while toddler Linda tottered alongside, she stopped her in the street to thank her.

'I'm delighted to have been of service,' Elsie said with a laugh. 'Do you know, I bet that underneath your mam's really dead proud of you, even if she doesn't say so. And remember, if she ever comes at you again, you can tell her that being a land girl is as good as being a soldier any day of the week, only not half so dangerous. Oh, but here she comes,' and before Vera could say anything Elsie had called across Coronation Street to where Ena was carrying a large bag of shopping.

'Oh, she's a good girl is your Vera, don't you agree?' Elsie called out. 'Glad you've finally had sense enough to see that. It's great news that you've let her go and join the Land Army. It'll do her the world of good. I bet you they'll both do all right there, her and Lily.'

Ena stopped and put her heavy bag down on the pavement as she turned to glare at Elsie. 'I don't need your approval, thank you very much, and how come you're knowing so much of our family business, Mrs Nosey Parker? Have you not got enough of your own?' Ena all but exploded.

'I believe in helping out neighbours whenever possible, that's all,' Elsie said, 'which you might be able to see for yourself if you'd only take the time to look.'

Ena snatched up her shopping bag and marched off

but the look on her face was so fierce Vera was afraid that she might have changed her mind.

'Don't worry about it, she'll soon come around,' Elsie assured Vera. 'She's more upset that I know something about what goes on at the Mission than the fact of you signing up. And if there's any more to it than that, then I promise you she'll really have me to deal with.'

When Vera got home Ena turned on her again, much as Vera had expected, screaming, 'How dare you tell that woman about our private business! She knows more than I do about what goes on in this house.' But to Vera's relief there was a knock at the front door before Ena got too far into her stride and Vera opened the door to their neighbour, Albert Tatlock, who often dropped in for a quick cup of tea while he was doing his ARP rounds. For once, she was glad that he had something to say because Ena usually listened to him.

'I think it's just the thing your Vera should be doing right now,' Albert said. 'You've got to let her go sometime, Ena, and going off down south to help the country seems like a good thing to be doing.'

'She'll be going with Lily Longhurst,' Ena said hesitantly, 'you know, Martha's lass.'

'Well, there you are then, she won't be alone, and I'm sure there'll be plenty of folk around supervising them.'

After that, Ena had acted as if the Land Army had been all her idea.

*   *   *

Vera looked over to Lily gratefully as she felt the touch of her hand and she thought once again how glad she was that they were travelling together. There was something comforting about Lily's quiet air of confidence that somehow gave her confidence too. Although she had to admit that her friend had changed following her brief pregnancy scare and no longer looked quite so sure of herself. She had felt so ashamed by the way Johnny had treated her that she, too, had become desperate to leave Weatherfield. She knew there were bound to be rumours and she wanted to get as far away as possible, not only from her angry parents but from all the local gossips.

The top section of the window had been locked permanently open and Vera sensed an acrid taste at the back of her throat and the smell of bad eggs. She got up again to have another look. A never-ending plume of dark grey smoke seemed to be belching out of the engine's chimney. It was blowing back towards the passenger carriages as they slowly rounded the curve of the platform and the train began to pull out of London Road Station. Despite the pungent odour, Vera stood there for several minutes getting used to the rhythm of the metal on metal, wheels on tracks, and she began to breathe more easily.

'I can't believe we made it and we're really here, on our way to London,' she said as she finally sat down again.

'Kent,' Lily corrected. 'Holden Manor where we're

going is in Kent. We're only stopping in London long enough to change trains.' She smiled at Vera.

'I thought my mam was going to have a fit when she realized that I'd not only signed up but had handed in my notice at Earnshaw's without asking her first,' Vera said.

'Well, you are over twenty-one so you didn't really have to ask her permission,' Lily said. Then she grinned. 'And of course I didn't tell them at the recruiting office that I wasn't quite seventeen and a half yet.'

Vera giggled. 'But it didn't seem to matter once we had the papers about all that medical stuff and we'd got the certificate things we needed.'

'No, that's true,' Lily agreed. 'But when my mam said she was washing her hands of it and was leaving it to my dad to sort out, I knew it would be all right. He hates official-sounding forms and doctors; he never wants anything to do with owt like that.'

'Did you not think he might try to stop you then?' Vera said.

'Well, they'd found out that I was going out with Johnny Bradwell and I think they both felt so relieved that I wasn't courting him any more that they were glad for me to leave town before the gossip about me going out with one of the Bradwells really got going, and they weren't that mithered about where I was going. Besides, they've got too many things of their own to fight about,' Lily said and Vera laughed.

'In the end I think my mam was glad to see me go so's I'd stop nagging about the engagement, though it was her fault for making us wait. She's probably hoping I'll forget about Bob.'

'Well, I'd like to think we convinced all of them that they're doing their duty by letting us go,' Lily said. 'That and all the other patriotic guff they tried to sell us at the recruitment centre.'

Vera frowned. 'Oh, but I think we really *are* doing something useful. We're going to help feed the nation and that's very important work.' Then she giggled. 'Mam almost changed her mind, you know, even when she'd said yes,' Vera said.

'No! How come? You didn't tell me that.'

'It was when she found out that Elsie Tanner knew all about it and she was hopping mad that I'd told Elsie what was going on.'

'What made her change back again?'

'Mr Tatlock put his two penn'orth in. He said he thought it were absolutely the right thing for me to be doing, as he'd said from the beginning, and after that she couldn't say anything.'

Vera laughed and glanced once more in the direction of the window. 'I'm getting proper excited now, aren't you? I can't wait to see what Kent's like. It's going to be so good, I'm sure.' She sighed. 'Bob said he'll write but I wonder if he will.'

'Don't worry.' Lily smiled reassuringly at her. 'Hey!

Will you look at that?' She was suddenly distracted. 'Not only fields but cows too.'

Vera followed her gaze. 'I often wonder, don't they get cold always standing still like that for hours?' she said.

'I don't suppose they feel the cold,' Lily said, 'they do have nice warm coats.' She giggled then she clapped her hands. 'I can hardly believe that we're on our way.'

Vera didn't know how far they'd gone when she fell asleep but when she opened her eyes she knew she had missed most of the journey for the train seemed to be pulling into a station and people from other compartments were heaving their suitcases down the corridor and making their way towards the doors. Lily stood on the seat and handed down the bags to Vera who was glad she'd decided to wear a large part of the new uniform she'd been given when they finally signed all the forms, for it meant there was less to carry. Her suitcase was only small and, as they prepared to get off, she proudly took out her regulation mackintosh and slipped it on. She left it unbuttoned so that it folded back showing off her corduroy breeches and green knitted pullover. She had to cover up the green armlet with the red royal crown on it that she was so proud of but she hoped that when her coat swung open at least the Land Army badge could still be seen on her chest. She was also wearing her heavy brown shoes and the fawn, knee-length stockings, having decided to pack her rubber gumboots which would not have been easy to travel in.

She thought she had better squash the dreadful brown felt hat down onto her newly bobbed hair, though – that was one piece of the uniform she didn't like.

'There, I'm ready. Will I do?' Vera asked and she turned to check on Lily as the train came to a juddering halt. 'I presume this is it,' she said, peering out once more, 'though why does it say Easton? I thought we were going to London.'

'This is London,' Lily said patiently, 'and it says Euston, not Easton, can't you read? Come on, then, we'd best get going, we've not got long to find out how to get to Victoria Station where the Kent train goes from.'

People were scurrying in all directions and everyone seemed to be in a hurry so that Vera had trouble keeping up with Lily. But she was glad to have someone to follow, and made sure she kept her friend in sight. She worried that if she lost Lily she would never find her way around the station on her own. The concourse smelled much the same as the one they'd left behind in Manchester and the atmosphere was murky and grimy so that it was difficult to tell whether it was day or night outside; with the steel girders and the high arched roof it looked similar to the Manchester station too. They found a bus that took them to Victoria and the Kent train, when they found it, was much smaller and more crowded with servicemen and a few service-women than the train from Manchester had been. Vera felt proud to be in uniform and wanted everyone to see it, hoping they would instantly know that she was a land girl in the same way as she was able to recognize sailors and airmen as well as the regular soldiers in their khaki uniforms.

'How far is it once we're on the train?' Vera asked.

Lily shrugged. 'I've no idea,' she said. 'But it doesn't really matter; someone should be there to meet us at the other end. All we have to do is to remember to get off at Holden, so no falling asleep this time.'

Dusk was beginning to gather by the time they left the small train even though the station clock showed it was only seven o'clock. They had been on the go for most of the day and when they stepped outside and crossed the bridge, Vera felt as if they had been travelling for days. She dragged her suitcase up the metal stairs, thinking that one thing was very different – the scents. Here was almost a sweetness to the evening air.

'It reminds me of a day when we went for a picnic in Heaton Park back home, once. I remember it because my dad said what I was smelling was the grass that had just been cut,' Lily said.

'Maybe it's that; we do seem to be in the middle of a lot of fields,' Vera said as they dragged their cases down the steps on the other side of the bridge. There were several other people who had got out at the same station and Vera noticed them as she peered over the handrail. She also saw the guard running along the platform they had just left, slamming the doors to the individual carriages behind him as he went. He stopped at the farthest end of the train away from the engine and turned back to wave his green flag at the engine driver. Then he blew one long blast of his whistle. Almost immediately the steaming engine began to pull the train out of the station and gradually picked up speed.

'Miss Sharples!' (pause) 'Miss Longhurst!' (pause) 'Miss Grainger!' Vera heard a male voice shouting out the names like he was reading from a school register.

'Miss Longhurst and Miss Sharples are over here,' Lily shouted in reply.

'And I'm here too, I'm Miss Grainger,' a young girl's voice with a strange accent responded and then the male voice called back, 'That sounds like it's all three of yer at once, thank the Lord. Come and get yerselves shifted over 'ere and then we'll be off.' He was standing by the back of an open horse-drawn wagon covered with straw, with a banner across the back saying it was from the Holden Land Army Training Centre. He held the wagon steady while the three girls clambered awkwardly aboard.

'I'm Jenny, by the way,' the other girl addressed Lily and Vera as they settled back against the boarded sides of the wagon. 'Jenny Grainger from Bow, a bit like in the old song.' She sang a short phrase about someone called Burlington Bertie but it was something neither Lily nor Vera recognized. 'And you are?' She extended her hand.

'I'm Lily Longhurst and this here is Vera Sharples. We're both from Weatherfield,' Lily said. They were trying to adjust into more comfortable positions on the wooden slats but they had to stop so that they could keep their balance as the horse jerked the carriage forward and began pulling it up an incline and out of the station lot.

'Where's that? Weatherfield, was it you said?' Jenny asked. 'From the sound of you I'd say it's a long way north of here.' She giggled.

'Aye, I reckon it is,' Lily said. 'Nearest big city is Manchester.'

'Not like me then, *bawn and bred wivin the sand o' Bow Bells*,' Jenny said and she laughed as she exaggerated her cockney accent.

Chapter 13

'You're late!' They were greeted at the front door by an older woman who came out from behind a sort of reception desk and ushered them into the stone flagged hall. She was carrying a file with a large bulldog clip holding several sheets of paper in place and she was leafing through the written pages without really looking at any one of the new girls. 'I'm Mrs Sykes,' she said brusquely, still searching through her papers rather than looking at the girls.

There were several suitcases and duffel bags piled on the floor near the desk.

'Mr Megson will get your bags down from the wagon shortly and he'll leave them in the hall here for you to collect later. You can take them upstairs to your room after you've eaten. Meanwhile, you're just barely in time for supper so I suggest you get yourselves into the dining room before everything disappears; though what's there is probably cold by now but that's what happens when you don't arrive on time. Bear that in mind, young ladies, as you are to be with us for the next four weeks.'

She still didn't look at them but wagged a finger in their direction as she shooed them through the first open door that led off the hallway. The food smells were not unappetizing and Lily suddenly realized how hungry she was. It was a long time since she had eaten the thin paste sandwich her mother had grudgingly packed for her.

Lily hardly had time to take in her surroundings as she entered what had grandly been referred to as the dining room. There were six rustic wood tables, most with six occupants who were noisily eating and chatting at the same time. She, Vera and Jenny were directed to where made-up plates of food were being passed through a serving hatch at the far end of the room and Lily was given a plate on a small tray that was piled high with chunks of bread spread with a generous amount of what she assumed was margarine. The bread was a grey colour, although it looked as if it had been freshly baked, and when she broke off a piece and hastily stuffed it into her mouth when she hoped no one was watching, she found that it tasted delicious;

it was not like any bread she had ever had at home and there were large quantities of it.

They didn't always have bread at home in Weatherfield, of course, since the war, and never anything chunky and freshly baked like this. She was also pleasantly surprised at the warm golden colour of the spread and she was assured that it was, in fact, butter. It was certainly very different from the dull lardy texture of the margarine ration they usually had at home. There was also a generous-sized portion of cheese on the plate beside the bread and something that looked like a large pickled onion. Then she was given a bowl to hold while the server ladled some kind of orange-coloured broth into it that had probably once been hot. There was an apple on the tray beside the plate and a full glass of milk. Lily had never seen such a feast, certainly not since the war had begun.

'It's like being in a hotel,' she whispered to Vera.

Vera's eyes opened wide. 'Is this what people get to eat when they go away on their holidays?' she asked. 'Mam and I only ever went to Blackpool for the day, we never did stop over.'

'You two may sit here.' Mrs Sykes had been following them without the girls realizing and Lily jumped, spilling some of her precious soup. The older woman pointed to two empty places on a table laid for six and all but pushed Lily and Jenny down onto the bench. She pointed Vera to the empty place setting on the opposite side of the table. They all obediently sat down. The others on the table had finished their meal and stood up to clear away their trays as the three newcomers sat down.

'We'll see you girls later; we're off to unpack,' one of the girls called over her shoulder as they moved away. 'Don't worry, I'm sure we'll get to meet you all soon – we're going to be together in this hellhole for a while yet,' and she laughed derisively as she moved away.

'What did she mean by hellhole?' Vera said. 'It seems all right to me.'

Jenny nodded. 'I know, I've not eaten so much in years,' and she laughed.

'Me neither,' Lily agreed. 'It beats home cooking in our house any day of the week.'

'If it's always as good as this, I'll be well pleased,' Vera said.

When they'd finished eating they were about to follow everyone's example and take their trays and dishes to pile them on a trolley with other dirty dishes. 'Don't worry, you'll get a turn on the cleaning-up roster,' one of the girls whispered with a giggle as Mrs Sykes who seemed to be in charge came over to their table. She flicked through the sheets held in place by the bulldog clip once more.

'Which one of you is Vera Sharples?' she asked.

'I am.' Vera put her hand up. Lily and Jenny also

identified themselves and Mrs Sykes put a tick by their names when she found them on one of her sheets of paper.

'Then we are all present and correct,' she said, in clipped tones with a satisfied smile. Vera thought she sounded like she might be reading the BBC news on the wireless. 'Your bags are in the hall,' Mrs Sykes went on. 'You may take them upstairs and unpack. Your dormitory is up the stairs and first door on the right off the landing. Lights out will be in half an hour so I'll bid you goodnight.'

Vera stared at her, thinking she might as well have been speaking a foreign language for all she understood what the woman had said, then she followed Lily without a word.

The dormitory, as Mrs Sykes had called it, turned out to be a large room with two sets of beds, that were layered in pairs, one on top of the other, each of them so narrow there looked to be barely room to turn over. Vera, used to sharing a large double bed with her mother, looked at them in horror, wondering how she would ever be able to sleep. Someone was already sitting on one of the bottom bunks while the remaining beds were unoccupied.

'Whichever one of you is called Vera is in the bunk above me,' the girl called out.

'That's me,' Vera said, not sure whether she should put her hand up.

'Then here, catch! You'll be needing this, no doubt,' the girl on the lower bunk said and she threw a small but solid looking pillow in Vera's direction. Vera's hands were still holding her bags and she watched with dismay as the cushion landed with a thump on the stone tiled floor when she failed to catch it. It felt leaden when she bent to pick it up.

'Ta,' she said, 'I'm sure I will, but how do I . . .?' She looked around until her eyes lighted on the step-ladder that was hanging over the side of the upper cot. 'Oh!' she said, but no one was taking any notice. Lily and Jenny were eyeing the other beds and the ladder attached to the upper bunk there with equal apprehension.

'I'm Margaret Wiley,' the girl from the lower bunk said, in the kind of clipped tones that made Vera want to stand to attention and salute. 'What's your name?'

Vera looked at her. 'Vera Sharples,' she responded automatically.

'OK, Vera,' Margaret said, 'I've left you the bottom shelf in that cupboard if you want to unpack your things. That's all we get, half a cupboard each.'

'A-and what about the lav?' Vera ventured to ask. 'Where's that? I haven't seen one yet.'

Margaret suddenly giggled. 'Next door,' she said and she jerked her thumb in the general direction. 'Turn right out the door.'

'And the bathroom?'

'You'll be lucky!' Margaret raised her eyebrows.

'How do you mean?' Vera was puzzled.

'You don't honestly expect there to be a bath, do you?' Margaret sneered.

'Well, no.' Vera had taken it for granted there would at least be a tin bath and didn't know what to say. 'I hadn't really thought . . .' She felt foolish for asking. 'Where is it that we can wash?'

'Same place,' Margaret said. 'Next door,' but she gave no further explanation.

Vera heard Jenny apologize to Lily that she seemed to have been assigned the bottom bunk and she watched as Lily boldly climbed up the ladders to check out her bed and Margaret introduced herself to Jenny.

'Margaret, that's nice, then I shall call you Megs,' Jenny said in what Vera now realized was quite a broad cockney accent.

Margaret snapped back immediately, 'No, you certainly will not. My name is Margaret like the young Princess, only without the Rose, and I will answer to no other name than that. Although you may call me Wiley if you prefer.'

Vera didn't want to look at Margaret, she sounded so indignant, so she climbed up to her bed and was trying to straighten out the blanket when the room was suddenly plunged into darkness.

'Damn and blast it!' Jenny's cockney-sounding voice

piped up and Vera had to stifle a giggle. 'When the old biddy said lights out she really meant it, didn't she? Anyone got a candle?'

'Why would we happen to have a candle? Do you think we live in the dark ages or something?' Margaret said, her clipped tones already easy to recognize.

'Because we might as well be plunged into sudden darkness like this at any time,' Jenny retorted, 'or maybe that doesn't happen in whatever high-and-mighty part of the country you come from.'

Vera felt too afraid to move in case she fell off the bed until suddenly there was a tiny pinpoint of light flashing from the other top bunk.

'I forgot, I've got a torch,' Lily said, 'but I don't know how long it'll last if they turn out the lights so early every night.'

'Ouch!' A sudden cry went up. 'Can you shine it in this direction?' It was Jenny again, but this time she sounded to be in pain. 'I've just stubbed my bloody toe on the ladder. How are we supposed to find our way around this place if they won't let us have any light?'

'I give up,' Lily said. 'I'm about ready for bed anyway and as I'm already up here I reckon I may as well stay put and call it a night.' She yawned. 'I'm tired enough to sleep all night and all day after all that travelling. How about you, Vera, are you all right?' she called.

'Yes, thanks, I'm fine,' Vera responded, hoping her voice wouldn't betray how scared she really felt. She was already lying flat in her cot, not daring to move for fear of dropping over the side. She desperately wanted to go to the lav but couldn't risk trying to find it in the dark. She felt tears of frustration and weariness trickle down her face as she lay as still as she could. But all she could think about was, 'What have I done?' It was as though the enormity of her actions was striking her for the first time. She was such a long way from home. If she could have hopped on a train and gone home now she would. Inside she was crying, even calling for her mother, though she knew she couldn't voice any of those words out loud.

'It'll be all right in the morning when we can see things again.' Jenny's hearty voice sounded surprisingly bright in the dark, but Vera didn't bother to reply. Then she heard Lily say, 'I think I'm going to get up early and explore. Things always look better in the morning. You can come with me, Vera, if you like. Goodnight, everyone, I look forward to getting to meet you all properly in the morning.'

There were a few grunting noises in response but then the room fell silent almost immediately until Vera plucked up the courage to shout back, 'Goodnight!' into the darkness. She had said her prayers silently and now she closed her eyes though she doubted she would ever be able to fall asleep.

The next thing she knew a high-pitched alarm bell was piercing through the house. Every item of free-standing furniture, including the bunks, seemed to be vibrating noisily on the linoleum and all the girls shot out of bed and made for the door.

'Where's the shelter? They forgot to tell us where the shelter is!' Jenny cried in a panic-stricken voice.

'Never mind that, we must get out straight away so follow me.' It was Margaret's coldly authoritative tones and with a commanding gesture, as if she was wielding a sabre in battle, she led the way out of the door. She was closely followed by Lily who was surprised to see groups of girls emerging from several of the other first-floor doors. There were more people in the house than she'd realized. The blackout curtains were still closed tight and the lights were on all over the house, even if they were only dim. She was met by Mrs Sykes coming up the stairs.

'Girls, girls,' she said in a calming voice. 'There's no need for panic. It's not an air-raid alarm. It's the morning alarm call for waking everybody up.'

'Why? What time is it?' Lily asked. 'We've only just gone to bed.'

'It's four thirty in the morning,' Mrs Sykes said with a smug sort of smile. The girls all blinked in astonishment. 'Whenever we have a new intake of girls we always like to give them the opportunity to get up a little earlier than usual on their first morning. They're not used to our countryside ways, but the animals don't know that. They still expect to be watered and fed at their usual time.' She gave a little laugh. 'It'll help you all to adjust to your new routines to have an early start. It also will give you time to have a proper breakfast. Set you up properly for the day.'

Vera had landed heavily on her ankle when she had jumped down from the second rung of the ladder and she hobbled painfully out to join the others on the already crowded landing. She yawned and rubbed her eyes against the light, thankful that the dreadful noise of the bell had stopped.

'In case you were wondering, we will be having an air-raid drill later,' Mrs Sykes announced. 'To show you where the shelters are and all that.'

'Air-raid drill?' Vera said to no one in particular. 'I thought we'd come to the country to get away from all them bombs.' She sounded puzzled.

'Yeah, me too,' Jenny agreed.

'Don't be so naive, whoever told you that?' Margaret Wiley said with some contempt. 'Most planes have to fly over Kent first, after they've crossed the Channel, before they fly anywhere else and don't forget we are pretty close to the Chatham dockyards. And even if they don't drop their bombs on this part of the country on their way in, they will most certainly drop any leftovers on the way back.'

'And in between they head for one of the big cities to drop the bulk of their cargo?' Jenny queried.

'Exactly,' Margaret said. 'I doubt there's anywhere

down south, or in the whole country you can call safe right now.'

Mrs Sykes held her hands up for silence. 'Now that you know what the morning reveille alarm sounds like, why don't you take advantage of the extra hour that gives you this morning and get yourselves washed and dressed in time for an early breakfast? There's plenty of water in the ewers and in July you don't have to worry about the water being frozen.' She smiled as if she had said something funny. 'And of course, there is the loo outside for those willing to brave the mud – we have had rather a lot of unseasonal cold and rainy weather, recently.'

The groups gradually dispersed with disgruntled murmurings of, 'Four o'clock in the morning? I've never been up this early in my life!' 'No, but I've sometimes been going to bed at this hour,' someone said and everyone laughed. 'Is this what we've got to look forward to?' 'How come nobody warned us?' others were saying as they wandered back to their own rooms, debating whether they dared to go back to bed.

Now that she had been awakened, Vera realized just how desperately she needed to go to the bathroom and she hurried to the room next door that Margaret had previously pointed out. She opened the door and was shocked to find a row of chamber pots tucked neatly under a low-hanging shelf. On another shelf halfway up the wall was a line of large china bowls, each containing a large matching china jug, that had been filled with brackish-looking water. There were no sinks, no means of heating any water, no flushing toilets and certainly no baths, even tin ones. She wondered what this 'loo' thing was that Mrs Sykes said was outside in the garden. Did she mean the midden? Maybe she'd go exploring with Lily later, but first things first. Even though they disgusted her, she had to make use of the facilities.

In the dining room, breakfast was laid out on small trays like the night before and consisted of more bread, some of which was rather staler than it had been the previous night but it was still covered with lashings of what Margaret pronounced to be 'definitely real butter'. There was more milk and more cheese, which neither Vera nor Lily were used to eating at that hour of the morning, and some weak-looking liquid in a glass that the servers referred to as tea. This time all four of the girls from the dormitory were guided by Mrs Sykes to sit together on the same table, and she indicated that from now on these were to be the group's set places at mealtimes. Lily gathered her tray, added a glass of cold water and came to sit next to Vera.

'Eat up,' Lily whispered. 'I bet we won't get anything else until dinnertime.'

'Do you think so?' Vera whispered back. 'But I can't eat any more. I'm not that hungry and I certainly can't eat any cheese right now.'

'No, I know what you mean, 'Lily said, 'I feel a bit that way myself, but I bet we'll be glad of it come dinnertime.'

'I tell you what,' Vera said, 'why don't I put it in my pocket for later?'

Chapter 14

As soon as breakfast was over Mrs Sykes announced that all the newcomers were to make their way to the meeting room and the sleepy-eyed girls, still yawning and stretching, shuffled across the hall to the large room she had indicated. There, she promised, the arrangements for the four weeks they were to spend at the centre would be explained.

Mrs Sykes with her now-familiar bulldog clipboard climbed the steps to the raised dais at one end of the room and stood ready to address the group like a headmistress at a school assembly.

Jenny was standing between Lily and Vera. 'Gosh,' she said, 'I'd no idea there were so many of us last night. They must have all gone to bed by the time we arrived.'

'How many do you think are here now, then?' Lily said, trying to gauge numbers as she looked around the room.

Jenny shrugged. 'About forty, I reckon,' she said, but Mrs Sykes had raised her hands once more to order silence.

'This talk is essentially for the newcomers,' she began. 'The rest of you please check the cork board for your new assignments for the week and then you may leave, though quietly please.' She paused while more than half of the girls clustered round a bulletin board at the back of the room and then filed out, chatting noisily.

'The rosters will be pinned up on that noticeboard each morning.' Mrs Sykes raised her voice to block out the chatter, though not entirely successfully. 'Please make sure you all read it in good time to get to wherever it is that you are working that day as this will keep changing.'

The newcomers turned as she pointed to the board. 'You will all be expected to cover a range of different tasks during the month you spend with us doing your training and we will do our best to make sure you each get an opportunity to take a turn at most things. That way you will be equipped to carry out any task that might be assigned to you when you move up to the big house.'

She paused for a moment to glance at her notes and there was much muttering among the girls. She cleared her throat and began again.

'The big house, for those of you who don't know, is called Holden Manor, and it is half a mile up the road. It's where Lady Edgefield of "a hundred different species of dahlias" fame lives and you will be billeted there when you leave here. She will be in charge of you once you make the move.'

'Fancy that! We'll be living in a stately home,' Lily whispered to Vera. 'I'm dying to see it.' She chuckled. 'I can't wait to write home and tell Mam and Dad about that.'

'But for now,' Mrs Sykes said, 'you'll be living here and all you need to know is what tasks you will be undertaking each day and where you need to go. At the end of the day supper will be served in the dining room as it was last night. Please check to see if you are on one of the cleaning-up rosters. If you have any queries you may leave a note for me at the reception desk, and any emergencies should be reported at the desk immediately.'

For some reason Lily giggled and poked her elbow into Vera's ribs, but Mrs Sykes didn't seem to notice. 'There is a bellpull by the side of the desk,' she said. 'Please ring it once – but only once, in emergency – and someone will attend to you instantly.' She paused. 'And I do mean emergencies only.' Finally, Mrs Sykes put down her clipboard. 'Now,' she said, 'unless there are any burning questions, I will leave you to find out the nature of your first tasks of the week and all those who have been assigned to the dairy should be ready to follow me in five minutes precisely.' She hesitated as a hand shot up. 'Unless there are any burning questions.' She reclipped her loose papers onto the board as Margaret stood up.

'We all thought this morning's alarm call was because of an air raid,' she said without a trace of nervousness, 'and none of us seemed to know what to do. You mentioned earlier that there would be an air raid drill later but in the meantime, please can you direct us to the nearest shelters where we would be expected to go should there be an actual air raid?'

'Ah, yes, I was coming to that.' Mrs Sykes' face coloured slightly. 'And as I said before, there will be a full drill later because unfortunately, as you know, we are not air-raid free here in Kent. I'm afraid we're too close to the Chatham docks for comfort sometimes. So we have to be constantly on the alert and should the air-raid siren sound you must run for the nearest shelter. The main ones are shown on the map on the pinboard.' She pointed once more to the board at the back of the room. 'Please study the map carefully and make sure you familiarize yourselves with their locations. Memorize them. And you will be shown those that are closest to your place of work whenever you start a new job. As a general guideline there are some Morrison shelters in some of the outbuildings such as the dairy and the cowsheds, and there are several underground Anderson shelters dotted about in the more open areas of the grounds. If, for any reason, you are caught while in the house here, then make your way calmly but quickly down to the basement using the cellar stairs. They're the stone steps that lead off from the hallway. You can't miss them. But a word of warning; it is very dark down there, so make sure you pick up one of the torches that are kept permanently on the table by the entrance to the basement. And don't forget to replace them once the all-clear has sounded.' She didn't actually say, 'dismiss!' but Vera felt as if she was on one of the parade grounds she had seen in films and she almost wanted to salute. Instead, she made her way to the bulletin board as they'd been instructed.

'Hey, I'm on gardening duty.' Lily grabbed her arm. 'That should be easy enough. How about you?'

'I'm in the dairy.' Vera didn't know whether to be pleased or disappointed when she saw her name on the list, for the thought of working with Mrs Sykes frightened her. But at least it meant she'd be working indoors.

'See you later then, have fun,' Lily said and Vera felt a sudden lump in her throat as she watched her friend disappear.

'I'm in the dairy too.' Jenny bounded up and took Vera's arm. 'I think it's all very exciting. Let's go to find the old dragon, shall we? No doubt she'll be waiting by the desk.'

Instead of taking them directly to the dairy parlour,

171

Mrs Sykes led the two young trainees to the cowshed and told them this was where they were to report each morning of their first week. 'I will be seeing you later in the dairy parlour,' she said, 'but first you will be in the capable hands of Bert here, who will show you how to milk the cows, a task that has to be undertaken twice a day, no matter what.'

'That's right.' A middle-aged man with a slightly balding head came into the shed at that moment, dressed in a short-sleeved T-shirt and knee-length breeches. 'Now, the missus is right there,' Bert said, his hand gently patting one of the cows who were lining up quietly in the stalls. 'Cows don't want to know that you're feeling poorly or you overslept, so make sure you're here on the dot each day, in the morning and again at teatime, cos they'll be waiting for you and so will I.' He tried to look stern but there was a twinkle in his eye. 'The only way cows can tell the time,' he said, 'is by the amount of pressure they feel on their udders.' He bent down and pressed hard against the first cow's obviously full udder. 'That's how they know what time it is, when the pressure builds and they know it's time to get shot of all that milk.' He guffawed and slapped his leg as he said this, as if he had cracked a joke. 'Come with me and I'll show you how we put them out of their misery.'

Vera's image of a cowshed was of milkmaids sitting on cute three-legged stools, pulling on the fleshy udders like they were church bells. But as Bert sat, legs splayed on a tiny stool, he soon put her right. 'First off, you don't pull,' he said as if he could read her mind, 'not unless you want to the poor thing to have udders stretching to the floor. What you do is to close off the top like this and then you squeeze,' he stated, demonstrating the movement so that shots of milk squirted into the pail. 'Once it starts to flow you keep going until you get up a nice steady rhythm.' He worked the udder for a few minutes while the two girls watched, fascinated, as the cow let down her milk, full flow, and he made it look easy as he seemed to draw out a few inches into the bucket in no time at all. 'It should take you no longer than half an hour for each cow,' he said when there were several inches of milk in the pail.

Bert then stood and watched while Jenny tried her hand. Unfortunately, Vera could see immediately that it was not as easy as Bert had made it look, for no matter what Jenny did the cow kept kicking out at the bucket and refused to give up her milk. Bert shook his head and pushed Jenny aside for a moment.

'She's got to trust you,' he said, and he began gently coaxing the cow, guiding Jenny's hands along the teats under his. When he was satisfied that the cow was no longer objecting and there was finally some evidence in the pail, he turned to Vera. 'Here, you have a go with this one,' he said, settling her onto a stool, and he demonstrated the milking action once more. To

Vera's surprise, the cow let down her milk almost immediately and she quickly picked up a rhythm. Bert stood back, nodding approvingly as the milk began to flow.

To her amazement, Vera found she was enjoying it as the milk gradually began to fill the pail and she was able to get into her own rhythm as Bert had suggested. When she finished her first cow, Vera sat back with some satisfaction. Her hands were sore and her arms were stiff from holding their position and she rubbed her back which was aching from being hunched into an awkward position for so long. She massaged her sore fingers back to life, pleased with her work, but wishing she'd brought some Fuller's Earth cream with her to soften her skin.

It wasn't until then that Bert pointed out that there were fifteen more cows in the herd and that they, too, needed milking twice each day.

Chapter 15

'I think this is the last one.' Jenny jumped up and came over to where Vera was finishing milking a much smaller-looking cow, no doubt the daughter of one of the more elderly beasts. 'I can't believe how many we've done, considering it's our first morning.'

'Have we really only been working for a morning?' Vera asked. 'It feels like we've been at it the whole day!'

Jenny smiled and Vera was pleased that they were together, for Jenny was proving to be fun to be with. She couldn't always understand her cockney accent, particularly when she talked about things using funny kinds of rhymes, but at least she was a jolly soul.

'I'd never have believed that milking a cow would

be such back-breaking work,' Vera said. 'And to think, we've got to do it all over again this afternoon . . .'

'And tomorrow, and then again the day after that!' Jenny added.

'I know,' Vera agreed, her smile dropping, 'It's funny, at first I didn't really like the cows – if anything, I felt a bit afraid of them – but I'm getting to like them more now, with their big soft eyes and the way they just stand there looking at you. Though do I feel as if I'll never be able to move my arms again in any other way than this.' She took up the milking position and they both spluttered with laughter.

At that moment the door opened and Bert came back. 'If you've got time for a joke, girls, then you're obviously not working hard enough,' he said, and though his tone was jolly Vera felt she had better take him at his word.

'We've finished all the milking,' she said.

'For now,' Bert added.

'Yes, of course, I meant for now.' Vera's face flushed.

'Then you can grab some milk to drink from one of them jugs, if you like,' he said, not unkindly. 'We put them out fresh each day for you to help yourselves. And now would be a good time to eat your sandwiches.'

'Sandwiches?' both girls said together.

'Didn't you fetch them with you from the kitchen?' Bert asked.

'No one told us there were any sandwiches,' Jenny

said and when she closed her eyes for a moment, Vera was worried that she was going to cry.

'Oh well, I might have spoken out of turn. There might not have been enough for everyone; there's often not on the first day,' Bert said.

'Never mind, Jenny,' Vera said, 'I saved summat from breakfast. You can share it with me if you like, though I'm afraid it's only cheese.'

Jenny's face lit up. 'That doesn't matter – I could eat a horse right now.'

Vera put her hand in the pocket of her dungarees and felt something warm and sticky. She swivelled about trying to see what it was and realized that, against the warmth of her skin, the creamy cheese she'd taken from the breakfast tray had melted into a soggy mess and had stuck together the two sides of her pocket.

'I'm really sorry,' Vera said and to her relief Jenny was laughing.

'Never mind,' Jenny said, 'I'll live. I'm only sorry for you, having to carry that sticky goo with you all day. But we'll both know not to make the same mistake tomorrow.'

'Better have an extra glass of milk before you go on to the dairy,' Bert said, 'but be quick about it. Mrs Sykes doesn't like to be kept waiting.'

Mrs Sykes was standing by the door of the dairy parlour with her inevitable clipboard in hand and as the two girls approached she looked at the dainty fob watch that was pinned to the reverse of her white overalls. She kept her eye on the clock as if she was counting down the seconds and when they arrived she pointed to a pile of white overalls and head coverings which were folded neatly on a shelf by the door. With no further preamble she began her instruction.

'Today I'm going to show you how to make butter and one of our basic cream cheeses,' she said, 'and when you've finished with that it will be time for you to go back to the byres for evening milking.'

Vera stared at her. Lily had been right, not only was there not to be a break for dinnertime, but having missed the sandwiches there was going to be nothing to eat either. She wasn't sure she could stomach any more milk even if it had been offered.

Vera's back was breaking, her hands were still sore from the milking and she could hardly lift her arms by the time she had finished churning several pounds of butter. Continually winding the handle on the barrel-shaped churn was bad enough, but by the time she had creamed off the buttermilk to be stored elsewhere, then repeatedly washed the butter ball until the water ran clear, she hardly had any strength left to knead the pure lump of butter that remained into a usable slab.

Fortunately, Jenny had already completed her own tasks satisfactorily and Mrs Sykes didn't object when, towards the end of the day, she offered to help Vera take all her newly formed products into the cool stone room where they were to be stored. Vera was glad of the help, for when the time came to hang up the bags of cheesecloth in order to separate the whey from the newly formed cheese curds, she was no longer working as efficiently as she had at the beginning and the pungent smell of the soured cream was beginning to overwhelm her and to make her feel sick to her stomach.

It was almost seven o'clock when the two of them finally finished for the day and dragged their weary bodies up the long driveway to the hostel, both complaining about having a sore back and aching arms and legs. They were hungry, too, but most of all they wanted to crawl into bed and go to sleep. And then on the path Vera was delighted to see Lily. It was the first time since breakfast and she perked up, a smile suddenly crossing her face.

'It's so good to see you again, Lily,' Vera said. 'Are you all right?' and she moved forward eagerly to embrace her friend. But she stopped before she got too close.

'Phew!' Vera held her nose. 'Will you get a whiff of that!'

'What have you been doing all day?' Margaret came up the path to join them and she too took a step back.

'Sorry about the pong,' Lily said with a laugh. 'I've sort of got used to it. I don't even smell it any more.'

'Where were you? I thought you were supposed to be on gardening duty?' Vera said.

'I was, but they changed their minds so I ended up in the stables for a large part of the morning, cleaning up after the horses. Believe me, they don't call it mucking out for nothing. I've never been so knee deep in muck in all my life.'

'It certainly smells like you've brought most of the muck with you,' Jenny said.

'I can see I'll be popular for the rest of the evening,' Lily said and she chuckled. 'It reminds me of when I was a kid and my dad made me go with him to follow the coal cart and collect the muck from the horses so that he could grow some roses in a pot in the back-yard.' She shuddered. 'No one would speak to me for days at school. I thought I'd never get the smell out of my nose and yet here I am now and I can't even smell it.'

'Were you at it all day?' Margaret asked.

'No, I did lots of hoeing, first thing, trying to keep the weeds at bay from rows and rows of beets and turnips. Then I was breaking my back trying to get some wretched potatoes out of the ground and most of them didn't want to come. That was not only dead painful but deadly boring too. And look at my poor hands.' She held her once neatly manicured hands out, palms up, to show the red sores and blisters then she flipped them over to reveal the broken and cracked nails.

'Then I was feeding and watering the chickens before I went on a hunt for eggs. Now that bit *was* fun. I found over thirty eggs, would you believe, all in different places. You'd be amazed at all the hidden places where I found them. After that I spent the rest of the day washing dishes and cleaning up the kitchen and helping to prepare the supper for this evening.'

'What! Smelling like that?' Jenny said.

'No one complained,' Lily said with a shrug. 'There was too much work to be done, and not enough hands to do it.'

'I hope we're getting more than bread and cheese to eat tonight,' Vera said.

'And if I drink any more milk you'll be able to milk me,' Jenny grumbled. 'Seriously, though, were you cutting up more bread?' She sniggered.

'No, there's no bread tonight,' Lily said. 'It's some kind of stew, I think, with lots of vegetables in it, though it seemed to me to be mostly potatoes. All I know is I've been peeling pounds and pounds of spuds, turnips, swedes and carrots – oh yes, and then pickling onions which isn't easy when you start off with blistered hands.'

'Well, I'll eat anything put in front of me because right now I'm starving.'

'Me too,' Jenny said, and Vera nodded as well.

'Did any of you know there were sandwiches that we could have taken with us?' Lily asked. 'One of the girls who'd already been here a week, told me about them. I was going to tell you, Vera, but you and Jenny had already left.'

'I heard about them but by the time I got there they were all gone,' Margaret said, 'though I believe they were hardly worth fighting for.'

'There was fish paste or fish paste from what I could see,' Lily said scornfully. 'No different from home. So I'm starving now too. Though I did manage to munch on the odd carrot when no one was looking.'

'We had a couple of pints of milk for dinner,' Jenny said and she looked at Vera and they both burst out laughing.

'What's so funny?' Lily said. 'Where were you?'

'Jenny and me were together in the dairy,' Vera said, 'and as far as Bert was concerned we could have drunk milk all day long.'

'Was it easy work? How did you get on?' Lily wanted to know.

'I wouldn't exactly call it easy,' Jenny said. 'I don't think either of us can move our arms.' She demonstrated to prove that she couldn't lift them above waist level.

'And my back is killing me from that stupid milking stool,' Vera added, 'but apart from that it was OK.

Maybe I'll sleep better tonight. I won't be so worried about falling out of bed cos I won't be able to move!'

'Well, I'm sorry you're all so tired and have had to work so hard today because I've had a fun time and feel fresh as a daisy,' Margaret said with a grin.

They all stopped and turned in her direction.

'Why? What have you been doing?' Jenny wanted to know.

'I've been driving a tractor,' Margaret said with some satisfaction, as though it was something she did every day. 'But best of all I've been learning how to tinker with a tractor engine; I've always wanted to know how to do that.'

'How is that fun?' Lily said with some disdain as she looked once more at her poor, blistered hands.

'Oh, but it is, I can assure you. Of course, I'm used to the driving bit,' Margaret boasted. 'When I was at home, sometimes my father let me drive a military truck, he taught me as soon as I was old enough; said he would even buy me a car after the war when hopefully petrol will no longer be rationed,' Margaret said loftily. 'It really is great fun.'

'I dunno that I'd want to be breaking my nails learning about engines, even if I ever learned to drive,' Lily said. She was trying to inspect her hands once more but it was getting too dark to see them clearly.

'It seems to me there's not many jobs round here that *won't* hurt your hands,' Vera said.

'I can't say mine hurt, though I have been working as hard as anybody,' Margaret protested.

'I don't know about hard work, from the sounds of it you really did have fun.' Lily had difficulty keeping the scorn from her voice.

'I think we're all extremely tired, and very hungry, and it's getting quite cool,' Jenny intervened, 'so shall we hurry up and get back right now? Let's make sure that we're not late for supper again.'

The inside of the hostel felt warm compared with the surprising chill of the late July evening that had settled outside and the girls trooped in and headed straight for the dining room. As Vera passed the reception desk she noticed a slate that she hadn't seen before propped up near the bellpull at the far end of the countertop. Several names had been scratched onto it with a charcoal stick, and hers was at the bottom. A young girl she hadn't seen before was standing behind the desk, looking as if she was a shop assistant on duty. She stepped forward as Vera scrutinized the board.

'It means there's a letter for you if your name's on there,' she said to Vera.

'A letter for me? Vera Sharples?' She was surprised, but the girl handed her a brown envelope. At home brown envelopes meant bills to be paid and she inspected it with a frown.

'You're lucky. Who's that from?' Lily asked coming up behind her.

'Dunno,' Vera said. 'It's not my mam, I know that. But right now I'm too hungry to be mithered.'

Vera waited until she was sitting on the top bunk with only a few minutes to spare until lights out before she retrieved the brown envelope and her torch and slid her finger under the gummed flap. Inside was a single sheet that looked as if it had been torn out of a child's exercise book. It had been written with a fountain pen that had deposited blobs of excess ink after every few words and a spider seemed to have jumped into the miniature pools before crawling drunkenly over the page.

Dear Vera, she managed to read,

Your mother told me that you had gone away for a little while and that I should write to you. I hope you are having a good time and not working too hard. Everything is exactly the same in Weatherfield and I am still working with my dad. What work are you doing? I went to see a film called Casablanca *with Humfry Boggert. Have you seen it? At the end everyone was crying though I am not sure why. Is there a cinema near where you live?*

Take care.
ERIC BOWMAN

She had just read the signature which was written in childish capital letters when the lights clicked off and she shuddered as she slid down under the flimsy blanket. She didn't know what to make of it and was unable to stop shivering. She had left home to get away from her mother, but somehow Ena was still managing to interfere in her life. Vera felt a flash of shame as she realized she hadn't yet written to Bob since she'd arrived though she'd said she would do so as soon as she got to Kent – but when had she had time? Still, she'd thought of him often while she'd been working, and she thought of him now. Then she thought of Eric. There was no comparison, so why did her mother persist in trying to push the rag-and-bone boy onto her?

She pictured going to the cinema with Bob and she was overcome by a wave of homesickness. She genuinely missed him and she hoped he missed her. It made her sad to think that he might be going to the cinema on his own and she felt angry at the thought of her mother still trying to take over her life. If it hadn't been for Ena's meddling, Vera would probably have been married to Bob by now. She couldn't stop a sob escaping. She tried to cover it with a cough. but now that she had seen Eric's so-called signature on the bottom of the page, she realized that her mother would not leave her alone until she had got her own way, and she couldn't stop the flow of tears that spilled down her cheeks or the low sob that escaped her. Vera vowed to write to Bob the following morning before she started work and tell him that she missed him.

She heard Lily's voice call out, 'Everything all right, Vera?'

'Uh huh,' was all she could reply.

Chapter 16

Vera tore Eric's letter into small pieces for she had no intention of replying and hated the very idea of anyone ever seeing it. Even if she had wanted to she would have found it difficult to make the time to write back. Every minute of every day was filled with tasks connected with the cows, for feeding and watering them had now been added to her list of things she had to do several times a day; and if it wasn't related to the cows directly, then there were things to be done in the dairy parlour.

She would come in at the end of the day, joints aching, eyes stinging from tiredness and so generally exhausted that she didn't have the energy for additional tasks, even something as simple as sitting down to write a letter, as Lily frequently complained.

'This is inhuman,' Lily wailed when it finally began to sink in that these were to be their working hours and conditions.

'Oh, don't be such a wimp!' Margaret snapped. 'I don't know what you expected.' She was the only one in their dormitory who was up each day before the alarm, while the other three dragged their feet and found it difficult to get going.

After that first early morning call they were granted an extra half an hour before the alarm woke them up, but it still felt as though it was the middle of the night. Vera complained that she never had sufficient time to relax properly and Lily too was constantly tired, with barely enough energy to get through the day.

As August came in, bringing even more unseasonal weather, the hostel became extremely damp and cold. Vera couldn't stop shivering once she was awake and she dressed as quickly as possible, ready to go down for a hastily snatched breakfast. But before long she began to function automatically as she grew used to the new routine. She was surprised at how much she enjoyed working with the animals and for their sake, despite her aching body, she always tried to be there on time.

Poor Lily on the other hand was not always able to drag herself out of bed in good time each morning and she was constantly hungry. She worked slowly as the blisters on her hands from the hoeing took time to heal, and she was frequently being punished by Mrs

Sykes with additional tasks or reduced rations every time she was late reporting for work or coming back for the evening meal.

Lily always seemed to be tackling some new task, whereas for Vera there was something comfortingly familiar about the repetitiveness of her work and, once she had completed the cycle of that first day for a week, she was able to repeat the tasks without having to think too hard about what she was doing. Vera was locked into a tight schedule that was dictated by the animals' nature and needs and yet there was a freedom about her daily routine that she had never felt at the factory, working with her mother, and she went about her business with an air of quiet confidence. She was sure she would never get used to the sheer drudgery of it all, the permanent ache in her limbs and the constant tiredness. But she took a pride in her work and she found she was surprisingly good with the animals. She wished that Bob and her mother could see her milking and churning as though she had been doing it all her life.

Towards the end of the first week Vera was told that Friday was to be her last day in the cowsheds and on Friday morning she was upset to find that she was later than usual leaving the hostel. Jenny had already left and Vera knew she'd have to walk quickly if she wanted to catch up with her and be at the byre in time for the start of milking. But as she stepped outside and began to walk down the path, she was enveloped in an unusually heavy fog that the earlier risers had dismissed as merely low-hanging cloud. Whatever they called it, Vera soon found to her cost that it was the kind of fog that made it difficult to see more than a few yards in any direction and she could only hope when she set off that she was heading for the cowsheds.

Vera hadn't gone far when she was overtaken by a sudden sense of unease and she realized that she couldn't be sure she was still heading the right way. She shouted Jenny's name in the hope that her friend might not be far away, but she was greeted by an eerie silence. It was as if her words were left hanging in the air and she was aware of being completely disorientated. She was in no doubt now that she had lost her bearings and, in the all-enveloping gloom, she didn't know where she was.

It was purely by accident, as she admitted later, that she came across the cowsheds. She was breathless from running fruitlessly back and forth and she hurried inside with a sigh of relief, anxious to begin milking before anyone noticed that she was late. But although the shed she went into had looked the same on the outside, it didn't look the same on the inside and it took her some time to find a milking stool. For some reason the cows didn't look the same either. There were fewer of them, for a start, and they didn't seem to be standing in the same order as they usually did. The stalls seemed to have higher sides than she remembered and each beast was individually tied up with a thick rope that led to a chain of sturdy metal links, firmly attached to the wall. Her hand was shaking slightly as she sat down on the stool beside the first animal and went to feel for the reassuring fullness of the udders. She had barely touched the beast when, without warning, it lashed out with a strong backward kick that landed painfully on her stomach. Vera's scream as she was knocked off the stool and the clatter of the pail as it fell onto the hardened mud floor brought the dairyman running.

'What the bloody hell do you think you're doing?' Bert shouted the moment he set foot inside. 'Get away from there or you'll get us all killed!' And he picked up a pitchfork that was leaning against the whitewashed wall. It looked exactly like the one Vera remembered the young girl carrying in the advertising posters, only this one looked menacing as Bert took a firm stance and aimed it at the bucking animal.

Vera gasped as if she had suddenly woken up to her surroundings and realized they were definitely different, although she still couldn't say where she was.

'Oh, my goodness, I think I've come to the wrong place!' she cried. 'I got lost in the fog this morning and . . . This isn't the regular cowshed for milking, is it?' She couldn't help the tears that were falling because she really was in great pain and it was difficult to speak as she nursed her bruised stomach.

'You daft bugger, of course it's not!' They were harsh words but Bert's breathing seemed to be calming down. 'I'll say you're in the wrong place. You're lucky he didn't kill you.'

'Where am I? I've never made a mistake like that before,' Vera sobbed. 'I only put my hand up to test the udder was full—'

'You did *what*?' Bert shouted.

She repeated what she had said and he shook his head in disbelief. He was still holding on to the pitch-fork, in readiness, keeping his eye on the animal, but thankfully it had stopped kicking. It snorted heavily and tossed its head as if trying to slip the leash.

Bert flashed a disdainful look in Vera's direction. 'Hasn't anybody ever told you the difference between a cow and a bloody bull?' he asked with heavy sarcasm. 'These bulls are waiting to be taken out into the fields to service the cows, you're blooming lucky he didn't try to service *you*.'

Vera gasped, her hand flew to her mouth and the tears flowed faster when she realized the enormity of her mistake. Bert put out his hand to help her get up off the floor but she was still bent double as she tried to stand up. When she did eventually manage to pull upright she didn't lift her head. She had never been so humiliated.

'You'd better get out of here before you do any more damage,' Bert said without sympathy, then he said something she didn't understand about her cock and bull story being a load of bullshit and if she wanted to see a real stud in action it was a pity she was a few years too late. She presumed whatever he said was meant to be a joke, for he roared with laughter as he said it. But she didn't ask him to repeat it; in fact, she resolved never to mention the incident again and she prayed that he wouldn't, for fear that everyone in the hostel would laugh at her as the story spread.

She spent the rest of the day in the dairy nursing her painful stomach but trying not to let it show. She desperately wanted to keep up the output of milk and said nothing, for no one had any time for a complainer. But when she finally found some privacy to inspect the damage she was not surprised to find that, from the waist down, her normally pale skin was all shades of black and blue. Vera thought of home as she rubbed her hand gently over her painful stomach in the kind of comforting gesture she'd often wished her mother would make. She smiled ruefully. In reality she knew better than to ever expect any real sympathy from Ena. She would have tossed her head and called Vera stupid for making such a mistake in the first place.

The fog had lifted during the day although there were heavy clouds as Vera made her way back to the hostel and she paused to watch the stream of nightly bombers that filled the sky. No sirens had been sounded but no doubt they would shortly be heard in different parts of London; wherever the planes were heading to drop their deadly loads. Vera shuddered and clutched at her stomach, grateful she didn't have to run for a shelter. At least she would get a chance to have a rest for a few hours tomorrow. All the girls in her group had been told they would be getting a half a day off over the weekend and she was on the list for a break in the morning.

'Not that there's much for us to do,' Jenny had grumbled when the notice went up, 'we might as well be working.'

'Not at all,' Margaret sounded perky. 'I intend to read and write letters.'

Vera wondered if she might write to Bob or to her mother.

'I want to stay in bed and to sleep until the last possible minute,' Lily said. 'At least give my poor hands a chance to recover.' And she patted her flaming palms together as if to cool them down.

'Is half a day off all we're ever going to get?' Jenny asked. 'I think that's pretty tough for the hours of work we put in.'

'Don't worry.' Margaret assured her, 'I'm told on good authority that we'll get a whole day off when we get up to the manor house and it will be good because there'll be far more to do and people to do it with. I hear they have parties and dances going on up there all the time.'

'Wow! Really? You mean with real men?' Jenny asked, and Margaret nodded. 'Oh yes, it will all be quite different when we go there.' And to Vera's astonishment, she winked.

The dinner that marked the end of their first week of work at the training centre contained actual portions of meat and all the girls ate heartily. They had all worked so hard every day but the bread and milk, even though it was readily available, never seemed to fill them. So, when a spotted dick dessert appeared, drowned in a creamy-looking custard, the girls all fell on it and for once no one complained that they were still hungry.

Chapter 17

Over the next few weeks the girls had to complete their training and they rotated round all the different tasks that needed to be done on the farm. Vera had the opportunity to learn how to do most of the work that would be expected of her when they moved on to the big house. But if she thought life might get easier when they moved, she found she was very much mistaken. She had no sooner mastered one skill than she was moving on to learn the next, pushing herself to new limits of exhaustion.

'I don't know about you, but I ache in places I didn't know I had,' she said to Lily one evening when the two of them were dragging their weary bodies in from the fields. They had both been on gardening duty;

harvesting rows and rows of vegetables and it had been back-breaking work.

'The only thing that amazes me is that I'm getting used to some of the hard work,' Lily said. 'Even my hands are getting hardened. After a bit, some of it doesn't seem so bad. Though don't tell my mother I said that.'

'Me too!' Vera nodded in agreement and they both laughed.

'Maybe it won't be as bad when we get up to the big house,' Vera said, trying to straighten her back.

'I dunno, from the sounds of it the gardens are twice the size of what they are here.'

'Well, maybe they'll have twice as many people working on them,' Vera said.

'At least we'll get some proper time off when we get there and from the sounds of it there'll be more people to share it with,' Lily said.

They walked in silence for a few moments then Lily said, 'I don't think I'll ever get used to getting up so early every day. I can't wait to have a full day off when I can stay in bed all day if I want to.'

'At least we get some decent grub here most of the time,' Vera said, 'even if there's not always enough of it.'

'Don't complain – I've found bits of meat floating in the stew sometimes,' Lily said. 'And I've never even heard of half the vegetables they have here, except for spuds, of course, and we all know about them,' she said with a laugh.

'It beats my mam's cooking,' Vera said, 'though I know that's not saying much. I only hope it will be as good up there.'

By the time they were ready to move up to Holden Manor, Vera's bruises were reduced to yellows and pinks and the terrible mistake she had made in the cowshed was beginning to fade from her mind. She had mixed feelings about making the move now that she had settled into the centre, but from what she had been able to see of the house from a distance, a part of her felt very excited. There were stories about the kind of accommodation the manor offered, which ranged from sleeping in tents in the extensive grounds to each person having their own bedroom with access to a bath. Vera didn't know what to believe.

On the final Friday night at the centre, Mrs Sykes announced in the dining room that the trainees who were leaving would be going on Saturday. 'That way you will have plenty of time to settle into your new surroundings up at the House, and will be ready to start work fresh, first thing on Monday morning.'

'What, at four o'clock?' Jenny whispered, reminding them of their first morning in the Centre. 'We'd probably sleep through the alarm this time.'

'At least we won't think it's an air raid warning,' Lily

whispered back and Mrs Sykes glared at her. 'You will have your beds stripped and your bags packed straight after breakfast – and that includes you, Lily,' she said pointedly.

'What time will the wagon be picking us up?' Margaret asked.

Mrs Sykes frowned. 'It won't,' she said sternly. 'You will make your own way. It's only half a mile down the road.'

'What about our—' Jenny began, but Mrs Sykes cut in, 'I should think carrying your suitcases will feel like nothing to you strong girls by now and you will be given instructions about where to go once you get to the main gate.'

Chapter 18

Long-distance views of the manor were deceiving, for what they hadn't been told was that the house was nearly a mile from the main gate and though they set off at a smart pace along the gravel driveway it wasn't long before they had to slow down.

'I don't know about you lot, but my suitcase is getting heavier by the minute,' Jenny grumbled.

'That's bound to happen now that it's begun to rain,' Margaret called over her shoulder and they agreed to stop to put on their uniform mackintoshes.

'At least I can stop my hair curling,' Jenny giggled and she pulled her regulation hat as far down over her face as possible.

The house was set well back from the road which was why they had never seen its full splendour, and when it first came into view as they'd turned the corner into the private drive Lily caught her breath.

'No wonder they call it the big house,' she said to Vera who was walking beside her. 'It looked big enough from the top fields at the Centre, but the closer we get, the more magnificent it looks.'

From that distance it did indeed look beautiful, even in the rain, and they stopped for a moment to admire the original white stone façade that glinted as if it was new.

'It looks like Tara in *Gone with the Wind*,' Lily said.

'Whoever would have imagined for one second that we would end up living in anything quite so grand?' Vera said, gazing at it in awe.

'Don't get carried away, we're hardly going to be living in the house itself, now are we?' Margaret pointed out. 'And there seems to be lots of signs up there saying, "Keep Out" and "Danger No Admittance".'

'I don't care,' Vera said. 'Would anyone back home believe us if we told them we were even camping in the fields that belonged to a house this size?'

The sheep grazing on the oversized front lawn added a picture-postcard touch to the general view, for it was as though a rich green carpet had been stretched from the steps that led up to the house down to the thickly entangled hedges that seemed to have taken the place of boundary railings.

It wasn't until they got closer that Lily could see that the whole building was badly in need of redecoration and that most of the outbuildings, in a separate block to the side of the main building, were in need of some repair. At the top of the driveway was an arch and Margaret assured them, as if she lived there, that it led through to the stables and to large outhouses where the coaches would be kept. Vera wasn't sure that she believed her, but she had no alternative but to follow her through the archway to the back of the main house and into the courtyard where several pathways led away from the house to what looked like a largely wooded area.

A middle-aged man with a well-weathered face was standing at the top of the concrete steps at the back of the house and he came slowly down to greet them as the girls arrived. Margaret looked as if she was about to salute him but then changed her mind and offered a firm handshake instead. He was wearing muddied work clothes and oversized boots that were loosely laced and he rubbed his hand on the leg of his dungarees before shaking her hand. Then he quickly scooped his woollen hat from his head and introduced himself as Alf Clarke the head gardener.

'But it's not me you'll be needing just yet,' he said, 'as I know they're waiting for you in the house,' and he pointed to a huge oak door at the top of the steps. 'Mind how you go, there's a couple of them as needs fixing,' he said, indicating the broken slabs of concrete. Margaret stepped over them carefully and lifting the wrought-iron latch pushed open the door. Warm baking smells greeted them as the girls crowded into what they were surprised to find was a large, modern-looking kitchen.

'Wow!' Vera couldn't help exclaiming. 'This is bigger than our whole flat at the Mission!' She was looking at the well-scrubbed table that stood in the middle of the room. There were benches on each of the long sides that could seat at least twelve people and a hefty chair with curved arms stood at either end.

'Look at all these modern gadgets and things,' Lily said, keeping her voice low, 'see the size of that range.'

'And what's that?' Vera's eyes alighted on a large white cupboard-type object that looked not unlike the refrigerator that stood next to it. 'It says, B-E-N-D-I-X,' she spelled out, 'but I don't know what that is.'

She heard someone clearing her throat, followed by what sounded like a chuckle. 'It's a machine for washing clothes and bed linen and the like,' the voice said. 'It runs off electricity, which is why it's in here.'

'Oh gosh, sorry. I didn't mean to be rude,' Vera said, seeing the woman for the first time.

'Not at all,' the woman said. 'You'll soon get used

to what everything is and you'll be using things yourself before long.'

Vera looked up properly at the woman who appeared to be at least middle-aged and older than Mrs Sykes, though her face was softer and frequently creased into a smile. An extraordinary number of keys jangled freely on a chain round her waist, warning of her approach.

'Welcome, young ladies,' she said and her eyes joined in the smile that was already on her lips. 'I'm Mrs Temple, the housekeeper, and no doubt you will be seeing a lot of me. For now, I'll show you your living quarters where you can drop your bags.'

They went out the way they had come in, being careful to mind the broken step, and this time they crossed the courtyard and she showed them the stable block on the other side. Behind this was an old barn that looked as if it had been newly painted.

'The other land girls are in a separate part of the house but this is where you'll be staying while you're with us,' Mrs Temple said. 'It's been done up specially.' She hesitated, but none of the girls had anything to say, they were taking it all in. 'Right then, I'll leave you to settle. And if you decide to have a look around be aware that there are other people sharing the manor grounds with us right now, so please be mindful of the signs. Supper will be served in the kitchen, but unless you have a specific reason to be there, the rest of the house is off limits. Tonight we'll be eating at five o'clock because her ladyship wants to have a word with you all, though on normal working nights you'll eat between seven and eight o'clock, depending on when you finish your work. Anything else you need to ask, you can usually find me somewhere close to the kitchen.' And with her keys jangling, she disappeared and left them alone.

As they went inside the barn, they were struck by how clean it was and how it smelled of fresh hay and new paint. The large downstairs space was filled with overstuffed couches and several well-worn armchairs that were spread about the well-swept floor. In one corner there was a large cupboard against the wall where it seemed they were expected to store their belongings. An additional floor had been added under the high, arched beams of the vaulted ceiling and it was quickly apparent that that was to be their sleeping quarters. The new floor stretched from one end of the main barn to the other and could be accessed by either one of the ladders that was propped up at each end. Margaret was eager to climb up to inspect their new home and she scooted up the ladders before anyone could stop her, making appreciative noises about their new accommodation.

'Hey, girls, you must come up and look at this,' she called down before she had even stepped off the ladder.

Vera was happy to let the others go first and when she tentatively climbed up to join them she was so anxious she had to pause for breath on the top rung. She looked about her and was pleased to see four well-stuffed palliasses spread across the floor with a good deal of space in between. Each had a neat pile of bedding on top, consisting of a sheet and a pillowcase, a blanket, a small hand towel and a feathery pillow. Vera saw Margaret touch each of the mattresses with her foot then stand back as if she expected something to happen.

'No obvious sign of any livestock in there,' Margaret said, 'and it doesn't look like they're filled with fleas either.' She gave a sigh of relief.

Vera was shocked but she'd hardly had time to take it all in when she heard Jenny shouting from below, 'Look what I've found!' and she was pressured to go back down again quickly to where Jenny was standing beside a hotplate with a small kettle.

'They surely don't expect us to cook on this?' Jenny said.

Margaret laughed. 'No. What this tells me is that we've got electricity in here, thank goodness, so there must be a light switch somewhere. I hardly think we could cook anything on one little ring, but we might be able to make a cup of coffee if anyone's got any essence?' She looked around the group, eyebrows raised, but silence greeted her question.

'Didn't Mrs Temple say supper would be in the kitchen?' Lily said. 'I don't think we could be expected to eat in here.'

No one noticed that Jenny had slipped outside and now she came back in with a triumphant look on her face.

'Guess what else I've found?' she said teasingly and when nobody answered she announced, 'A privy, a loo or whatever you want to call it, but – wait for it – it's got a proper flush and there are two sinks, a big one and a little one, both with taps and running water.'

'Hot water? And a bath?' Lily wanted to know.

Margaret snorted. 'Come on, don't be ridiculous.'

'Actually, there is a tin bath hanging on the back of the door,' Jenny said, 'if you fancy carting hot water over from the kitchen.'

'Then it's not exactly the height of luxury, is it?' Lily sounded disappointed.

'It depends which way you look at it,' the ever-optimistic Jenny said. 'It's a whole lot more than we got at the training centre and it does seem as if we've got it all to ourselves.'

After they'd unpacked their bags, Lily and Vera took a stroll around the grounds so that they could become familiar with their new surroundings. The first thing that struck Lily as she and Vera wandered about was how many men there were about the place, just as Margaret had forecast. She had seen them at a distance as soon as they had entered the boundaries of the estate and she had assumed they were farmworkers or people working on the estate, but now she could see that they were mostly wearing British airmen's uniforms although some seemed to be wearing soldiers' uniforms that she didn't recognize.

'We're not used to seeing so many men together in one place – I wonder where they've all come from?' Lily said. As they watched, a small group of young airmen marched smartly by while someone with stripes on the sleeves of his jacket barked orders that were almost impossible to interpret.

'There were hardly any men at the training centre, none that we could talk to at any rate,' Lily whispered as they went by.

'What makes you think we'll be able to talk to any of them here?' Vera said.

'I'm sure we could find a way,' Lily responded and sniggered.

'I've not seen so many servicemen in one place since I went to that dance at Burtonwood,' Vera said, and suddenly she felt guilty, thinking that she hadn't written any letters to Bob as she had promised. They were halfway down the drive when Vera stopped to look back at the house. How could she ever begin to tell anyone in Weatherfield about all this in a letter? She didn't think she had the words. Besides, there were so many things she had to tell about now that she wouldn't know where to start.

As she and Lily returned to the kitchen, Vera realized she'd be glad of an early supper because they hadn't eaten since breakfast. The other girls appeared and, as they began to jostle together to claim a seat at the scrubbed pine table, Vera noticed that three more people had joined them. Mrs Temple was keen to introduce them before they all sat down and so she held up her hand for silence.

'Girls! Gentlemen!' she said with a nod and a smile. 'I'm sure you would like to know who is sharing your table tonight. Some new faces for all of you, as you haven't yet met, so please allow me to introduce you to each other.' She sounded rather formal, though she gave a little laugh. 'Of course it's easy to recognize our Land Girls, in their smart new uniforms,' and she insisted that each of them gave their name and where they were from. 'And now, girls, this is Mr Grayling, our butler here at Holden Manor,' Mrs Temple went on, nodding towards the white-haired gentleman who had carefully positioned himself at the head of the table. Then she turned to a young boy and an even younger-looking girl. 'And these two special people are what remains of our staff. They are bravely soldiering on in order to look after our dear Lady Edgefield and the family, despite all the privations and difficulties involved in trying to run a house like this when there's a war going on.'

It was easy to see that the butler was too old to serve in the army, Vera thought, but it was not clear why Jones, who Mrs Temple referred to as 'the last remaining footman' had managed to escape conscription. Tucker, the girl, seemed to be the only maid left at the house from what had once been a whole hierarchy of maids. It seemed she had been the youngest and she was now, no doubt, doing the work of several others. According to Mrs Temple, when she wasn't working she was to be found tucked away in her own little room in the eaves of the main house, or at home with her family in the village on her days off. It was not difficult to see why she was happy looking after Lady Edgefield rather than working in some boring job down at the docks.

'What does a footman do?' Vera, bemused by Jones' title, whispered to Lily as they all sat down and began to pass the bowls of soup piled high with vegetables to the end of the table. To her embarrassment, it was Margaret who responded in far too loud a whisper that could be heard all about the table.

'In a house of this size there's usually more than one footman,' Margaret said casually, 'but with all the other servants gone I imagine he'll be a sort of general dogsbody.'

Everyone suddenly became interested in their soup

and Vera felt sorry for the poor boy as she saw his face and ears begin to redden from his neck up.

Fortunately, Mrs Temple stepped in before sitting down opposite Grayling. 'The only other member of the family you may come across from time to time,' she said heartily, 'is the Marquis of Holden, Lady Edgefield's son. He is in the army, of course, and posted several miles away from here, but he drops into the manor whenever he can get leave.'

They were woken the next morning by someone ringing a handbell downstairs in the barn, followed by the sound of a door slamming shut.

'It's six o'clock! Rise and shine everyone!' Margaret's strident voice was the first to pierce the chilled air.

'She's missed her calling, that one. She should have been a sergeant major,' Jenny grumbled.

Vera rolled over on her mattress, infinitely wider and more comfortable than her bunk bed had been. 'Do I really have to get up?' she said. 'I thought we were having the day off.' She yawned and stretched.

'We are.' Margaret's head popped up over the top rung of the ladder. 'But there's a message from Lady Edgefield with apologies for not appearing last night but she says that she'll be waiting to meet us all in the drawing room at the big house at eight o'clock this morning instead.'

'I suppose we'd better get up then, though I could get used to lying in bed,' Lily said.

'What's so special about a drawing room?' Vera asked. 'Do you think there'll be lots of drawings on the walls? Or is it a place to sit and draw?'

Lily laughed. 'We're about to find out,' she said, as she pulled on her dungarees and pullover.

Chapter 19

Vera was disappointed that the drawing room was no different from any of the other rooms she managed to peek into as they made their way deeper into the house. As far as Vera could see, there was a sprinkling of satin-covered chairs with ropes across the arms that she would have been afraid to sit on even if they were free, and family portraits covered most of the walls. The only difference in this room was the grand piano that stood in one corner, its closed lid full of family photographs. Lily leaned across to inspect some of them.

'Hmm, he looks nice,' she said, running her finger over the image of a particularly handsome young soldier, 'I wonder who he is?' But before she could share the picture with Vera, the lady of the house appeared. It was not a very comfortable-looking room and they were not invited to sit down even though Lady Edgefield smiled at them warmly.

Kathleen, Lady Edgefield looked to Vera exactly as she had imagined a 'lady' should look, and when the two black labradors trotting behind her settled quietly at her feet in front of the hearth, Vera thought she looked as if she was actually posing for a portrait. She had on a plaid skirt that was pulled flat across her stomach and held in place at the front by a large fancy safety pin and the heavy woollen material fanned into chunky pleats at the back. It was Margaret who said that Lady Edgefield was actually Scottish and that the weave of her kilt was probably in her original family tartan, a whisper that passed among the group.

Lady Edgefield wore a pale green twinset that picked out one of the background colours in her kilt, the shade the sea was sometimes painted on funny postcards. At her neck she wore a single row of pearls, just like Vera had seen Queen Elizabeth wear when she was photographed with the King, and she wore a single pearl drop in each ear. The only thing that looked at odds with her elegant style was the stout-looking shoes she wore which were heavily laced and made her look as though she was set for a day's hiking in the mountains. She had a very pretty face with a smooth complexion, and her thick fair hair was drawn back off her forehead and finished neatly in a French pleat behind; a style Vera envied though it was never possible to achieve with her wispy locks, even before she'd had them bobbed.

Like the housekeeper, Lady Edgefield smiled a lot as she welcomed the girls. Vera wanted to smile back and tell her ladyship how glad she was to be there, but she had a feeling the others would laugh at her and she held her tongue.

'I would like to welcome you all to Holden Manor,' Lady Edgefield began. 'As you may have noticed, you are not the only guests we have staying with us right now, so we would ask you to stick to the rules meticulously and follow the signs about where you may and may not go. A reminder of these rules will be pinned up in the kitchen as well.' She held up a piece of paper the size of a small poster. 'Please make sure you read them and obey them; it's vitally important for the smooth running of both the farm and the house. We do have some other Land Army girls with us who have been working here for some time and you will no doubt be working with them on the farm.' She stopped and smiled. 'But you are special for they don't live on the estate; they are boarded out at a hostel in Redridge, the next village, so you probably won't see much of them, I'm afraid. You are the first land girls we have been able to accommodate in our own grounds.' She paused. 'If you have any queries about anything at all, please address them to Mrs Temple who will do her best to help you. She and Mr Grayling, our butler, are in charge of the day-to-day running of the house.'

She paused again to beam at the group and make eye contact with each of them, then she bent to tickle the ears of one of the dogs.

'You'll be getting your instructions from Ken Abbott at breakfast about where you are to go each day; he is in charge of the farm. Alf Clarke is the head gardener for those of you lucky enough to be working in the gardens.' She smiled. 'Always my favourite place when the roses are in full bloom and, of course, the glorious dahlias we are known for, but sadly you won't be seeing any of them this year because all the gardens have been turned over to growing fruit and vegetables.' She took a moment to look at the group again and sighed.

'Now I know you were all expecting to have the rest of the day off, but I hope you won't mind if you get straight down to it today. There is a lot to be done. You will no doubt be working hard, in quite a different way from me deadheading my roses.' She paused and smiled. 'But then you knew that before you came. In fact, that's exactly what you've come for and I'm sure you will find it all worthwhile.' She beamed once more at everyone in the group. At the same time the dog she had been tickling lifted its head and gazed in the direction of the girls before stretching out, head on paws, by the hearth.

'On behalf of everyone here at Holden Manor I would like to say thank you for all the work you have done so far and for the work you are about to do. You have answered the call, recognizing that your country needs you as much as it needs the boys and the men, and I'm sure everyone is proud of your attitude and grateful for your contribution. You truly are an asset and you will be helping to feed the nation and keep the country going. I don't know if you realize it, but as the sea blockades are tightening, so your work becomes more and more essential. I see you as being the equivalent of the gallant sailors on our Royal Navy ships who are battling it out right now in the Atlantic. Thank you.'

Vera couldn't help beaming at the lady of the manor and was gratified when her ladyship beamed back.

'I hope you will have a happy stay here,' Lady Edgefield concluded and with that she withdrew, the dogs suddenly stirring and trotting off dutifully behind her.

The girls began to move away and Vera had a sudden urge to stroke the dogs' heads. But before she could reach them they had disappeared from view.

The girls assembled in the kitchen, waiting for Ken Abbott to allocate their duties, but before he appeared they heard the jangle of keys and Mrs Temple announced that she had something further to say.

'Her ladyship has asked me to remind you about the places that are out of bounds. It's all there.' And she pointed to one of the cupboard doors where a large hand-drawn map had been pinned next to the poster listing the house rules. 'The other thing is to make clear about the "other guests" her ladyship referred to. Firstly, there's a whole squadron of airmen in the west wing of the house.' She pointed to the map. 'I don't know if any of you have come across them yet?'

Jenny rubbed her hands together and her face lit up. 'Ooh, that should be interesting,' she said.

'No, it won't,' Margaret said, pointing to the poster on the door. 'It says here it's completely out of bounds. Strictly no fraternizing.'

'What does that mean?' Vera whispered to Lily.

'It means steer clear of them,' Lily whispered back, though she couldn't suppress a giggle.

'Then there's the bit of the house that used to be called the Summer Wing.' Mrs Temple was speaking again and she pointed to the opposite side of the map. 'Before the war, the Edgefields were well-known for their generous weekend parties and that was where their real guests used to stay.'

Vera frowned. 'So what kind of guests does it have now if they're not real?'

Jenny giggled. 'I'd say not very welcome ones as it didn't look very inviting when I saw it yesterday. It was covered in barbed wire and looked more like a prison.' She got up from the table and went to peer through the kitchen window at the building in question on the other side of the courtyard.

'That's because it is a prison, of sorts,' Mrs Temple said. 'It's where the Italian POWs live.'

There was a collective gasp.

'You mean there are actually prisoners of war living there?' Jenny said.

Mrs Temple nodded.

'But they're within touching distance!' Jenny sounded incredulous.

'That's the point. Hence the rule, Absolutely No Trespassing!' Mrs Temple said firmly.

'But if they're prisoners . . .?' Vera started to say. She looked very uncertain.

'You don't have to worry,' Mrs Temple hastily assured her. 'They are definitely not the dangerous kind of prisoners and it's extremely unlikely that any of them will ever try to escape. It's a lot safer for them to be here than on the battlefield, and they know which side their bread is buttered. But that's why the rule is for us to keep well away from the entire Summer Wing which is where they're living. Regard it as out of bounds, as is the rest of the big house.

'Anyway, it's all here so you can come and look for yourself,' Mrs Temple said, pointing to the poster. 'The only time you might get special permission to enter the house will be if you want to use the library. Or, of course, if there is a social event, although there hasn't been any of those for a while.'

'I can't see that I'll have much time to read many books while I'm here,' Lily sniggered.

'Oh, you never know when you might want to have an excuse to visit the house,' Jenny said. She had a mischievous tone to her voice and Lily peered at her.

'In that case,' Mrs Temple said brusquely, 'you'd have to go and ask Lady Edgefield yourself.'

'What about the work roster?' Vera suddenly asked. 'When's this Mr Abbott coming to talk to us?'

At that moment a gust of wind blew through the kitchen as the courtyard door opened and a man came in, grabbing the cap from his head as he did so and releasing long, straggling locks of hair. He was in his thirties, Lily estimated, his chin thick with a sharp gingery stubble though the abundance of hair on his head was dull blond. His woollen jacket seemed too flimsy to protect him from the elements though his ruddy cheeks looked warm enough, but from the thick mud that coated his green wellington boots it seemed as if he had spent the morning so far tilling the fields behind a horse-drawn plough.

He introduced himself as Ken Abbott, the farm manager, and he was carrying what looked like a roster for the day's work. Tasks seemed to have been allocated in much the same random way as they had been at the training centre and he pinned the list on the cupboard door so that the girls could check off their names. There was no doubt Holden Manor was a busy working farm and that there was much to be done in order to keep it running smoothly and efficiently; from the jobs listed it seemed as if all of the girls would be involved in hard work for long hours of the day.

Vera was pleased at first to see she was on what was called Maintenance Detail, until Margaret explained that it probably involved mostly cleaning and mucking-out duties, but then she discovered that it also included feeding and watering most of the animals as well, a task she looked forward to because it was one she knew she would really enjoy.

The list of individual instructions Mr Abbott had given her directed Vera to begin with the small animals that were kept on the far side of the fenced-off Summer Wing in what was labelled on the map as the old tennis courts. She passed through what had once been the prized rose gardens and the famous dahlia beds which had now been turned over to huge patches of vegetables. As she skirted around the barbed-wire fencing that enclosed the buildings she had been warned were out of bounds, she felt her heart suddenly begin to pound, even though she told herself she was being silly. Hadn't they been assured that no one would jump out at them? The men inside the compound were soldiers who had been unfortunate enough to be caught by the enemy. How dangerous could such prisoners of war really be? And, scared as she was, she was also curious and she wondered if she dared sneak a peek as she slipped behind the prison that was in the heart of the manor's extensive grounds.

But all she saw when she plucked up the courage to glance in that direction was a row of arched windows with leaded panes that threw a great deal of light into a large room. There were a number of men milling about inside, but she could see no faces or any other details.

Vera had no idea if they were handcuffed or restrained in any way and she wondered if they were ever let out on their own. She pressed closer to the windows, her breath coming faster, but then a loud noise behind made her jump away and she almost fell into the tangled shrubs that shrouded the barbed wire. Somehow she managed to hang on to the pails of feed she had brought with her and, with them clanging, she ran the final few yards to her intended destination – the tennis court.

The wired netting that still surrounded the old court was held together by a padlocked gate. She could see that inside the chickens were strutting and squawking as they vainly pecked at the old cracked surface, furiously searching for grain among the clumps of broken tarmac. As she pushed her key in the lock, she had a sudden sense that someone was watching her and she glanced over her shoulder, but she could see no one. She slipped the lock back onto the bar as she entered, remembering the 'never leave gates open,' first rule of farming that had been instilled into them at the training centre.

As she entered the courts, she noticed that the

markings on the crumbling tarmac had long gone, together with the net that must have once stretched across the centre of the playing area. She managed to fill her empty bucket with water from the standpipe in the corner and tipped most of the contents into a nearby trough for the hens. Then she cautiously began to scatter the seed and grain that she had brought with her, as she had seen others do back on the farm. But as she did so, she still had the feeling that she was not alone and, like a game of 'What time is it, Mr Wolf?', she kept looking over her shoulder trying to catch the culprit creeping up on her unawares. However, she could still see no one as she made her way to the hutches at the far end of the court that she'd been told housed the rabbits. She topped up their little water troughs and replaced the old leaves and root tops with new crunchy vegetables and went hurriedly in search of the morning's clutch of fresh eggs.

As she carefully reset the padlock in place, she realized her legs were trembling and she took a few moments to look about her to calm down. There was still no one to be seen and she took a few deep breaths then ran all the way back to the kitchen, praying that she wouldn't drop any of her precious charges.

She deposited the eggs in the ceramic container on the marble countertop and replaced the rooster-shaped lid that looked as though it was trying to hatch the contents. Almost immediately a man came pounding into the kitchen behind her. He seemed to have been running, even though he dragged one of his legs stiffly. As the door shut behind him, she could hear that he was breathing hard.

'I'm looking for someone called Vera,' he said gruffly and, as he pulled off his cap, Vera recognized Ken Abbott the farm manager.

'That's me . . .' she said hesitantly.

His bushy eyebrows, even more gingery than the roots of his beard, drew together as his eyes clouded and his face took on a thunderous look. 'Then what the hell are you doing in here when you should be down at the stables?' he said.

Vera looked at him blankly. He strode over to where the roster had been pinned onto the cupboard door and ripping it down he thrust it at her. 'What's this then? Can't you read? Not much point in having a timetable if you can't stick to it.' He raised his voice several notches and Vera wanted to crawl away into a corner and hide her face. 'Them horses should have been mucked out ages ago. And what about the byres, have you cleaned them yet?'

'No . . . I didn't know . . . I've been feeding . . .'

'Never mind that now.' He was actually shouting as Vera was trying to find her name on the roster to prove him wrong. But she could now see that she hadn't realized that Vera Sharples actually appeared in more than one place.

'You needn't waste my time with useless excuses, you'd best get over there now and get on with it,' he snapped, his voice still sounding angry. 'I can tell you them horses is not happy and I'm in need of one of them for the thresher.'

'I'm sorry, I didn't realize I had to—'

'Get that horse harnessed and fit for use, girl. The threshers need it *now* not tomorrow or the next day.' He shook his head and then rammed his hat down over his abundant hair. 'I don't know,' he shook his head, 'wandering about like tomorrow will do.' And he held the door open so that Vera had no choice but to head directly across to the stables, aware that Mr Abbott was following her.

Everything took much longer than she had imagined, because Holden Manor farm was very much bigger than the farm at the training centre; by the time Vera had mucked out the stables and cleaned the byres, it was time for her to check on the chickens and the other small animals again, and she retraced her steps to the old tennis court as quickly as she could. She was concentrating so hard on avoiding the barbed wire that she didn't notice the two Collie dogs that had followed her from the stables until they actually came nuzzling about her legs. She jumped in fright, then stood still for a moment, wondering if it would be all right to touch them. But they looked at her soulfully and let out a high-pitched whine so that she felt she had to bend down to stroke them and utter soothing words. They seemed to like this and only wanted to lick her hand as she crouched down to their level. She didn't know who they belonged to and she was afraid of being too friendly towards them; however, as their behaviour didn't seem to be threatening, neither did she want to shoo them away. It was pleasant to be able to talk to creatures who couldn't shout or answer back, if only for a short while.

Vera had always wanted a dog when she had been a little girl but there was no chance that her mother would ever entertain the idea. 'Filthy beasts!' Ena always curled her lip as she said it. 'They need house training; they're worse than babies.' Besides which they were an added household expense that she felt the Sharples' family didn't need.

Vera had once been followed home by a brown and white bundle with long, silky ears that she longed to keep but her mother had made her take it down to the animal shelter in the centre of Weatherfield in case someone claimed it and Vera had always imagined some lucky little girl being able to adopt it. They had had a cat for a while at the Mission, after Ena was convinced they had mice, but she had made sure it had no babies and when it had died of what she had been at pains to tell Vera were natural causes, it had never been replaced. But Vera was on her own now and it felt good being able to chat to the dogs as she carried out her duties.

Suddenly Vera became aware of an extremely high-pitched whistle and she couldn't fail to notice how the dogs' ears pricked up almost immediately. Both dogs crouched low as if preparing to pounce and, with a sudden spring forwards, they shot off in the direction of the fields that were home to the Holden Manor sheep. She was imagining the dogs rounding up the sheep and hadn't realized she had come close to the POW wing once more, so she was shocked when a young soldier in a uniform she didn't recognize stepped out in front of her and she jumped back with a loud gasp. He put his finger to his lips.

'Please, no scream. I not hurt you. I am good man, I no mean to frighten you.'

Vera stood stock-still, trying not to show her fear.

'I see you before,' he said. 'You look inside window.' He pointed to where she had indeed crept up to the windows earlier.

Vera looked up at his dark brown eyes and nodded, though she waited until her breathing calmed down before she spoke. 'I promise I won't scream,' she said, 'though I must admit you did scare me.'

It was almost like being in a film. She'd thought for a moment that she was going to be kidnapped but then she argued in her head that the POWs were not really like dangerous criminals. They were mostly ordinary men like their own British soldiers, with families, who had got caught up in a war and were now thousands of miles from their homes. He won't hurt me, Vera had kept repeating in her head. And it was true. From the way that he spoke in hesitant, heavily accented but understandable English, he did indeed seem nothing like she imagined a regular prisoner would be.

'My name is Pietro Esposito,' he said, holding out his hand. Then he reeled off a long number and fingered two metal tags that were on a thin chain round his neck.

Vera took his hand and shook it tentatively. 'Vera Sharples,' she said.

'I grow grapes, they make wine. I good farmer with fields in Tuscany in Italy.' He drew the outline of a map of what she guessed was Italy in the palm of his hand and pointed halfway up to where Tuscany was.

'I long way from home right now,' he said, and Vera noticed his dark brown eyes looked a bit glassy when he said this. 'I much miss my family.'

He took one of the empty buckets from Vera's hand and, as she began scattering the grain, he filled it with water from the standpipe. When he began to pour it into the troughs, Vera was able to look at him properly.

He was not particularly good-looking; in fact, he looked very ordinary except for his eyes that were very big and very brown and also kind. His hair was thick and wavy and the only frightening feature on his dark face was his eyebrows. There was something about the way they met in the middle, drawing a thick straight line across his forehead, that did make him look a bit scary. Or was it the fact that he looked as though he could do with a shave, like Humphrey Bogart in one of his gangster films?

As he handed back the empty pail she noticed that he wasn't wearing handcuffs and remarked on it.

'We Italians, we left free to . . .' He searched for the word.

'Wander?' Vera supplied.

'Si, si. To wander, free. When not work. Us Italians, we never wanted to go to war, so authorities know we not run away, but we are locked up at night. And nowhere to run to anyway.' He smiled and looked ruefully down at his scarred, calloused hands. 'Italy is a long way.' He sighed. 'And I not have to work. Officer,' he said and he stood to attention as he indicated the insignia on his shoulders. 'But I like to help. At home, every day I am working in vineyards. So where you go now? I go with you. I help you.'

She indicated the stables.

'And no guards?' Vera asked, looking over his shoulder as they walked away from the chickens. There was a solitary British soldier standing watching a team of men who were working in the fields stacking huge bales of hay and she wondered how many prisoners he could see at any one time.

'Yes, but stay in open, they can see you, nobody care,' Pietro said. 'Yesterday I walk into village. I meet people. They speak to me. "How do you do?"' he said in his best English accent and he pretended to lift a hat from his head and bow as if he were being introduced. 'They know but they are very nice.'

'So, you *could* just run away?' Vera said softly, and she was surprised when Pietro laughed.

'I suppose so,' he said, 'but no one runs away. Take me, where would I go? Here bed, work, food.' He paused as he rubbed his hand across his flat stomach. 'Some food. But not enough.' He put his hand inside his trouser pocket and pulled out into the palm of his hand several pennies and halfpennies, a couple of shilling pieces, and some sixpences and threepenny bits. Out of the other pocket he proudly produced a single half-crown which he held up to show her.

'And I earn money.' He gave a deep-throated laugh. 'Enough I buy cigarettes.' He showed her a small green packet of five Woodbines, one of which was already half-smoked. 'I no escape. But if I try escape, I no go far or I need new clothes. See this, you see from long way away,' and he pointed to two large and obvious red circles that had been sewn onto his jacket and trousers. 'You see, you know, instantly.' He pointed to some imaginary figure in the distance. 'That man prisoner of war.'

Vera didn't want to admit that she hadn't known

about the red circles when she had first seen the POWs in the grounds, but he was obviously very much aware.

'Do you mind being a prisoner?' Vera asked as they made their way to the stables. 'How long have you been here?'

Pietro shrugged. 'I not count. Two years, I think. Three, four years I not see my home. I was in Italian army in Africa. We surrender. I volunteer to be co-operator, so they bring me here. Is cold here, but OK.' He held his thumb and forefinger together. Then he turned his face skywards and spread out his arms. 'I miss sun,' he said, 'and family, but glad no more fighting. I no like politics. Only hard work.' He smiled. 'Like you.' They had reached the stables where he stopped to pat the horses and say a few gentle words to them in Italian.

'I like the garden. But also like the animals.'

Vera nodded in agreement. 'Just be glad you don't have to muck out the horses and the cowsheds every day,' she said and she held her nose between her finger and thumb.

'Perhaps we meet tomorrow. Same place. Like today.' Pietro spoke as he began to walk away. 'Though maybe I help men lift hay.' He gestured to indicate what they had seen the other POWs doing.

'It's been nice to talk to you, Pietro,' Vera said sincerely.

'And you Miss Vera. They make you work too hard. You call for Pietro. I help.'

Vera giggled. 'Wouldn't that be nice?'

And there was something she could do in return for him. She could bring him some extra food, even if it was only bread. She must be able to find something she could share with him.

Chapter 20

Lily thought she had landed a reasonably easy job when she saw she had been assigned to the threshing team and she didn't envy Vera having to work so hard cleaning out the animal quarters and being responsible for their feeds when what she'd really wanted to do was to work in the dairy. Threshing was not one of the tasks Lily had handled during the month of her training but she was confident that she could do it. How difficult could it be when it was the machine that did most of the heavy work? Unfortunately she found out the hard way that the tasks that had to be undertaken by the team who worked with the threshing machine were considered to be among the least desirable on the farm.

She had been pleased and proud at first when she found out she was going to be doing the most important job for the threshers until she realized that as one of the newest recruits she had been given the dirtiest and most uncomfortable job on the team. She was responsible for cleaning out the chaff from under the thresher, making sure that it couldn't clog up the machine, but nobody warned her that the remnants of the corn husks and the broken and mangled bits of straw that she had to handle produced a choking dust which got into everything. Not only did it cling to her clothes and fill out her hair, but it made her cough as she breathed it into her lungs through her nose and her mouth and she couldn't stop it penetrating her ears and making her eyes sting.

She had wanted so much to do well on her first day, but instead she was painfully aware of the constant chiding she received from the senior farmworker who was responsible for driving the machine. She'd done her best but it had never seemed quite good enough for the team leader and now, as she trudged back to the house that she had almost begun to think of as home, she was feeling despondent about her lack of achievement and her entire body was aching from keeping a constant watch on the machine. She had worked as hard as she could for she knew how dangerous it would be if, for one moment, she lost concentration; it could even prove fatal; but now she had such a headache she worried that she wouldn't be able to continue to work at that level. She thought the team had pulled well together today, for they had managed to thresh several of the fields, but the driver had never seemed satisfied that Lily was working hard enough and she was worried that she might be reported and thrown out of the group.

Now she was trying to forget about the harshness of the day and the gloomy prospects for the rest of the week; she was even trying not to think about what she must look like and what the corn dust had done to her face and hair. She was grateful that the gathering dusk was helping to make her invisible as she walked slowly back from the fields. Her eyes felt scratchy, her whole body was aching and all she was dreaming about was the luxury of soaking in hot water the way she occasionally had been allowed to do at home when she filled the tin bath in front of the fire; but she knew that was not something she was likely to be able to indulge in here, no matter how many pans of water she might try to carry across the courtyard.

Her eyes had almost begun to close, trapping the image, but that was when she saw him, the boy from the photograph, and her eyes flicked open immediately. She stared in his direction for a few moments, not sure if he had seen her. Then she straightened her back and ran her fingers through her dust-filled hair, fervently wishing she could do something more positive to improve her appearance quickly so that she could make a good impression.

He was tall and even better-looking than in the photograph on the grand piano, though she had no difficulty recognizing him even in his uniform. He had a large canvas bag and, as he seemed to be striding towards the house, she wished she could think of some positive way to attract his attention. He took a shortcut across the grass and seemed to disappear for a moment behind the trees, then suddenly he popped up in front of her and put down his kitbag so that it stopped her on the path.

'Blimey, you look in a bad way, if you don't mind my saying,' he said, eyeing her up and down. 'Been rolling about in the hay or the barley or something?'

Lily came to an abrupt halt. She could feel the blush rising from her neck and she had to look away. 'I've been working on the threshing machine,' she said simply, not sure why he should be interested. She thought he sounded like an actor in a film, like David Niven or Trevor Howard.

'Good for you, though it looks more like the machine's been threshing you.' He burst out laughing. 'I presume you're one of the new land girls so I suppose you've got no choice. You have to work wherever you're sent?'

Lily nodded.

'Where have you come from?' he asked.

'Manchester,' she said quickly, not wanting to give

him the opportunity to scoff that he'd never heard of Weatherfield.

'Are you staying in the old barn?' He seemed genuinely interested. 'The mater's very proud of that, you know. First time she's been able to accommodate the girls actually on the farm. What's your name?'

'Lily Longhurst,' she said, discovering that her voice was not strong due to all the corn dust and she wasn't sure what the word mater meant.

'Better get yourself cleaned up then, Lily. Cos right now you look like anything but a lily. You've so much fine dust on you I bet even your best friends would think you were a ghost.' And he roared with laughter again.

She looked away, feeling very self-conscious, but then was overtaken by a sudden impishness. 'Am I allowed to ask your name now that you know mine?'

'Of course, why not, though I'm surprised you don't know,' he said, 'when my mother insists on having my photograph stuck up all over the house. Captain Edgefield, at your service, ma'am.' He saluted, then he laughed as he took a mock bow. 'Or Duncan to my friends. And right now I'm off to get cleaned up at the house.'

'Do you not live in the barracks in the grounds here, then?' Lily asked, feeling confused.

'No, I'm army, not air force. I'm stationed a few miles up the coast and I'm home on leave for a few days.' With a smile, he hauled his bag up once more.

Lily smiled more hesitantly now, no longer sure whether she should be continuing this conversation. But she didn't have to for the captain took charge. 'Well, Lily,' he said. 'I look forward to bumping into you again soon. Though once we've both had a chance to get rid of all the dust we may no longer recognize each other. Either that or my mother will have thought up some new house rules in the meantime to prevent us from communicating.' He laughed.

Oh, I'll definitely know you, Lily thought and she flashed a quick look in his direction from under half-closed eyelids. Duncan chuckled and saluted again, then, with a grin, he marched across the grass and disappeared through the carriage arch. Lily followed him, her slow pace suddenly picking up as she hugged her secret to herself. Lady Edgefield had warned them about not fraternizing with the airmen from the barracks in the grounds – but she hadn't said anything about not speaking to a soldier, especially her own son.

Chapter 21

Lily was excited after her encounter with Captain Duncan, as she now thought of him. It was all she could think about as she went into the barn and tried to clean herself up as best she could with cold water and very little soap. She was anxious to share her news with Vera before she forgot any of the details, but all the girls were coming back from work now, desperate to use the bathroom, and she had to clean up as quickly as possible so that they could all be in time for their evening meal. And as the girls and the servants of the house assembled around the large wooden table in the kitchen, bowing their heads while Grayling gave thanks for the food they were about to eat, she realized that any kind of private conversation would be impossible. Not only were there eight of them seated in close proximity so that they were party to each other's conversations, whether they wanted to or not, but she could see that even Margaret and the normally bubbly Jenny were finding it difficult to get a word in as the maid Tucker was holding forth at great length. Lily would have to save her story until bedtime, when she could perhaps have a private word with Vera.

Tucker seemed anxious that everyone at the table should know how well in she was with the Edgefield family. According to her she was far closer than any junior servant was normally allowed to be. And while Mrs Temple dished out large helpings of potatoes, dotted with a fine crust of burnt cheese and decorated with thin slivers of home grown-tomato, Tucker boasted about her knowledge of the aristocratic family she served. She claimed to know all the relevant aspects of their history that had led to their status today and implied that she understood completely what was and wasn't socially acceptable behaviour among people at that level of society.

Tucker paused for breath only briefly, but when she then launched into a lecture about the cutlery and glass-ware usage and the etiquette of fine dining, Margaret could no longer stifle her giggles and Lily was grateful when Grayling finally interrupted the flow. She was developing a headache and she stopped listening after the butler explained that the rules Tucker had been referring to were only relevant to the more formal meals that were served in the family dining room and did not apply to the eating of the simple cheese and potato pie they were currently enjoying, for which a simple fork and a tumbler for water sufficed.

'Have you worked here long?' Jenny eventually asked Tucker, even though all the girls were beginning to yawn.

'Long enough to have my own room, in the main part of the house,' Tucker said proudly, omitting to mention that it was an attic room hidden away under the eaves. 'I've seen most of the hired help going off to fight, even the young Marquis.'

'The young Marquis?' Lily said, suddenly alert.

'Yes, you know, the young master,' Tucker said.

Lily didn't know what to say. Had she really been chatting so casually to a real-life Marquis? Not that she knew what a Marquis actually was, but it sounded so grand, almost royal, and of course he was grand, grand enough to live in a house like Holden Manor. Should she have curtsied or something, rather than talking to him as if he was one of the Weatherfield lads? She didn't know what she would do if she met him again, now that she knew.

'Of course, he's not here much any more,' Tucker was saying. 'He's in the army now, but you must have seen his pictures, they're all over the drawing room. I like to tease him that he's the good-looking one,' she said, lowering her voice, though she had the good grace to blush when everyone at the table turned to stare at her.

'Lady Edgefield preferred that he didn't wait for war to be declared,' the butler put in as Tucker looked away quickly. 'She made sure he signed up to the regular army and naturally, because of the family's history and his own educational background, he was assessed for a commission. Bright young man. Her ladyship is naturally very proud of him making captain so young.'

'That's what I wanted to do.' Jones, the young footman suddenly spoke up. 'Sign up for the local regiment. But they wouldn't let me on account of the rheumatic fever I'd had as a kid.'

'And how long is the – the Marquis . . . on leave for right now?' Lily thought she would break the awkward silence and take the opportunity to ask.

Tucker turned to Lily with a patronising smile. 'He's not on leave,' she said.

Lily looked at her in surprise.

'He couldn't be or I'd have been told to make up his room,' Tucker said.

'Then how come I spoke to him on my way in?' Lily couldn't resist saying.

'You couldn't possibly . . .' Tucker began, pouting, her lank hair falling over her eyes.

Lily shrugged. 'He told me himself he was on leave.'

Tucker's blush flared once more but this time she made no attempt to answer.

'Perhaps they'll remember to tell you when he gets shipped overseas,' Lily said and without even glancing at Tucker she took her empty plate over to the sink where she washed it carefully in the bowl of cold soapy water.

Vera was keen to share with her friend the story of her extraordinary day and could hardly wait for bedtime so that she could whisper her story to Lily in private.

'Tell me more about the Marquis,' Vera said, giggling, as she and Lily pulled their mattresses closer.

Lily put her finger to her lips. 'We'd better talk really quietly, so as not to disturb the others, but there's nothing more to tell, really, except that he said he hoped he might bump into me again.' Then she giggled too. 'Though I honestly can't imagine why he said that. I looked such a mess after all that threshing.'

'And is he really as good-looking as he seems in the photographs?' Vera wanted to know as she bunched the blanket under her chin.

'Better, I'd say,' Lily whispered. 'He looks a bit like Cary Grant, you know the film star, only his hair is shorter.'

Their beds were almost touching now so that they might not be overheard. 'But enough about me, what about you?' Lily said. 'How did your day go?'

Vera smiled, forgetting that the barn was now in darkness, and launched into her story about meeting the prisoner of war.

All four of the girls complained that after a hard day's work their food rations were not enough and that they were always hungry. Nevertheless, Vera slipped into the habit of wrapping up a portion of her food at each meal and putting it on one side to take to Pietro. They met every day, usually after supper, even if only for a few minutes. But sometimes they sat together in a warm corner of the barn and chatted. Vera found Pietro was easy to talk to and she was soon telling him about Bob, sighing as she told him about their long engagement, and the difficulties she had had with her mother.

'Your mother, she love you very much,' he said.

'I'm sure she does,' Vera said, 'but sometimes she has a funny way of showing it. She still thinks I'm a little girl and treats me like I haven't grown up. The other main problem is she doesn't like Bob very much,' and she told him how Ena was always trying to push Eric the rag-and-bone man on to her.

'But you love him? This Bob.'

'Yes, of course I do,' Vera said quickly, suddenly thinking she owed him a letter.

'Then only that is important. He very handsome?'

Vera laughed. 'He looks like Alan Ladd, the film star.'

Pietro looked at her blankly, then he opened his hands,

palms up. 'I love my Sophia,' he said, 'she very beautiful. I want to go home now,' Pietro whispered, 'to see my Sophia.' Vera could see his eyes were shining with tears. 'Perhaps we marry when I go home. You also?'

'Yes.' Vera nodded enthusiastically. 'First we'll have an engagement party, then the wedding.' And she found that the more she talked about it with Pietro, the more she began to believe once more that it really would happen.

Chapter 22

The girls fell into a routine that was harsh and unrelenting, whether it was the back-breaking work of making dibber holes for planting celery, transplanting cabbages, or getting callouses on their hands from lifting out maincrop potatoes and beets. Vera began to tackle even the most boring repetitive jobs automatically, trying not to think about what she was doing or how long she had to do it for. When it came to the apple-carting season in late October and early November, each day they prayed that it wouldn't rain, for they learned very quickly that it was no fun wading in oversized gumboots through the mud carrying sodden cartons of wet apples. There was no question that they felt much heavier than dry ones and Vera was often glad of Pietro's help on some of the cold wet mornings as he didn't seem to mind getting wet. But the girls had to get togged up specially, in rain hats and macs and remember to tie up their sleeves with string at the wrists to prevent the icy water from trickling up their arms. If they got too wet they would have to spend the whole night drying their clothes and they would often still feel damp the next morning.

Vera's rewards came mostly when she was working with animals and her feelings for them deepened as her skills in handling them improved. At first she had been afraid of the larger animals and had been put off by the strong smells, not only of the stables, the byres and the pigsties, but also by the smells of the animals them-selves. Thanks to Pietro, she learned how to approach them gently but firmly, and the more time she spent with them, the more her confidence grew.

'See how much he love you,' Pietro said one day as one of the temperamental shire horses came to nuzzle her hand when she slipped into the stall to groom him. 'He look for apple or carrot. He know you kind person. Not like some people,' and he pointed to several of the mean-looking whips that were pinned up on the wall.

Vera was thinking about this at the dinner table one night as she felt one of the dogs brush by her leg then stop to lick her hand as she leaned down to pet it. She felt a flash of pride and smiled, trying to picture her mother's reaction if she suggested they should have a dog at the Mission. Suddenly Mrs Temple stood up and tapped a spoon against one of the teacups, calling for silence. Everyone stopped eating their vegetable stew and looked up in surprise because she rarely interrupted their meal.

'I'm sorry to interrupt,' Mrs Temple said, 'but I do have an important and not unpleasant announcement to make.' She beamed at them until she had everyone's attention. 'As you will have noticed, since you have been here it hasn't been possible to have any social get-togethers like those we used to have in the past. In fact, you've had very little to do during your time off except occasionally go into the village. Well, whether you realize it or, not we used to have regular social evenings once a week and the main attraction was that they were held here at Holden Manor. One of the reasons why they became such a popular tradition was that it gave some of the village folk an opportunity to come to visit us, which they always seemed to enjoy.'

Vera could see Mrs Temple was looking at Tucker as she said this and the young maidservant was nodding enthusiastically.

'Every Saturday night,' Tucker said, 'regular as clockwork, we had a do in the barn where you lot are now sleeping. I must say we've missed them, haven't we?' she said looking directly at Jones.

'Yeah, they were good fun,' he agreed. 'It's a pity we've not had any recently. I reckon it's ever since them Eyeties have come. Once the prisoners were here, folk were probably too scared to come.'

Mrs Temple ignored his outburst. 'Obviously the barn is no longer available to us for that purpose,' she went on and she nodded towards the girls with a smile. 'To make up for that, her ladyship has suggested that we hold a special social next Saturday in the main house, and she insists that we invite as many local people as possible.'

'Woo hoo! That sounds like fun,' Margaret whooped. 'So who would you invite?'

'I've already approached a couple of the local community centres in Holden who always liked to come and then there are several church groups who've also enjoyed our hospitality in the past. We always ask the men from the onsite barracks and there are plenty of those this year. Then there are the other land girls, the ones who have been here much longer than yourselves and who board out. Oh yes, and this time we are going to include the Italian POWs, I don't think anyone will mind and I think they will enjoy it.'

'But that's taking a huge risk, isn't it?' Jones said. 'After all, wasn't it their fault the dos got cancelled in the first place? Because no one trusted them?'

'I don't think so, Jones,' Mrs Temple said icily. 'I don't know where you got that idea from.'

'I'd have thought they'd have been on their best behaviour,' Jenny said. 'They aren't our enemies any more, they're our allies. Didn't Italy declare war on Germany in October? I'm sure they aren't going to ravish us all in our beds!' Her tone was joking but there was an awkward pause. 'They'd be the first suspects, wouldn't they? And they haven't so far, anyway,' she said.

'Of course, and no one's suggesting anything of the kind, Jenny,' Mrs Temple said. 'We've never had reason to believe they are anything but perfectly nice people.'

'Once you get past their unfortunate politics,' Margaret said under her breath. 'But I suppose it just sounds funny, that's all, to say you're inviting prisoners.'

'I think you'll find that most people around here refer to them as POWs rather than use the actual word prisoners, for that very reason,' Mrs Temple said a little primly.

'After all, it wasn't their fault they got caught up in the war.' Vera spoke up with some spirit, but quickly sat back when no one else commented.

'And what will we all be doing at this social?' Jenny broke the moment of tension that followed. 'Will there be any music?'

'Well,' Mrs Temple began, 'her ladyship is offering the use of the drawing room this time, so there is the piano on offer, and one of the local community groups have already said that they'll be able to provide a small swing band from among their members, as they have done in the past, and possibly with a singer this time. If we can roll back the rugs, I think you'll find the wooden floor underneath is perfect for dancing.' She beamed round the group once more and there was much head nodding, with no one offering any opposition now.

'And the Marquis has some gramophone records he will lend us for the evening, when the band members need to take a break,' Mrs Temple said. 'The only condition is that someone should take responsibility for looking after them and for playing them at the appropriate time. So long as that happens, then we shouldn't be short of music.'

'Will there be any refreshments?' Jenny asked.

'There is plenty of homemade lemonade that has been sitting in the ice box waiting for such an occasion and Mr Clarke should be able to supply enough bruised fruit for me and Mr Grayling to make up a tasty punch bowl – without alcohol, of course.' She paused and looked up and down the table. 'So, as it's now official I take it you approve and would all like to come?' There was a sudden buzz in the air and a general aura of excitement as everyone began talking at once. Vera giggled and looked over to Lily with a knowing smile. At least they would both have something interesting to tell their mothers when they next wrote home.

Chapter 23

The talk among the girls for the rest of the week was solely about what they called the Big Party, although Mrs Temple insisted on referring to it as The Social. They talked about who they might be able to dance with and what kind of music they preferred and Tucker seemed to take every opportunity to visit the drawing room as if she was responsible single-handedly for all the arrangements.

'I think she likes to show off her knowledge of the family and her familiarity with the house,' Margaret said one day when Tucker had been particularly obnoxious. 'She will keep talking about the "young master" as if he belonged to her. The latest is that he's promised to help her roll back the carpet to make sure the room's fit for dancing.'

'And is he going to grace us with his presence?' Lily asked, not wanting to admit that her blood was racing at the very thought of Duncan appearing at the party.

'According to Tucker he is,' Jenny said.

'What on earth does one wear to a "social"?' Lily asked. She dispiritedly pulled out a dress that had been stuffed at the bottom of her suitcase since she had first packed for the trip to Kent and she shook her head. They had hardly had much social life since they had arrived at Holden Manor so her leisure clothes hadn't mattered before; but she had forgotten about the dress and now unfortunately it was badly crumpled. It was in a pale blue fabric that looked like crepe de Chine and which creased as badly as the natural silk, even though it was only an imitation.

'I'll iron it for you, if you like,' Jenny offered. 'I think there's an iron on the range in the kitchen if there are any hot coals to put in it.'

Lily stood up and held the dress against her. 'Do you think it's retrievable?'

Jenny shrugged. 'I'll do my best.'

Vera had brought a lemon-coloured pleated skirt and a white organza blouse that she liked to wear with it; to her amazement it didn't look too bad as far as being creased was concerned. Her mother had insisted she put it in her bag at the last minute.

'In case there's any need for you to dress up for best. You never know, you might even go to church one day,' Ena had said. Vera had taken no notice of that but it was one of Bob's favourites and it made her feel good whenever he told her how nice she looked in it. It would remind her of him if she wore it tonight and it would give her confidence.

Lily helped herself to a glass of punch for courage, although she knew there was no alcohol in it, and she kept her eyes fixed on the drawing-room door, trying not to look too obvious as she eagerly awaited the arrival of the young marquis. She hadn't seen Duncan since she had first met him in the grounds and the idea that he could have such a fancy title to his name still made her laugh. He sounded like one of the exotic Sheiks or Counts who were usually the dashing heroes in the cheap novels she loved to read from Boots Book-Lovers' Library. The crowd was trickling in and the band had already begun to play.

Lily had already turned down offers from several of the airmen from the barracks who had asked her to dance, but her patience was rewarded when Duncan finally arrived. She couldn't help feeling a little flustered when he came over to talk to her almost immediately, but she did her best to keep her composure.

He was dressed in plus fours with a fine 'v' necked wool pullover that showed off the long pointed collar of the casual shirt he wore underneath. He looked as if he was going to play a round of golf rather than attend a dance but the outfit did mark him out as different. Lily was immediately aware of Tucker glaring at her as Duncan continued to engage her in conversation but she tried not to take any notice. She actually found it funny when Tucker tried to find every excuse to interrupt. The young maidservant kept offering them drinks on a silver tray and, when the band paused, insisted on asking his advice about how to operate the large mahogany radiogram, even though the corporal in charge of the records seemed to be having no difficulties in making the gramophone work.

When the live music started up again for the next set of swing numbers and couples stepped once more onto the floor, swaying and jigging, Lily was delighted that Duncan asked her to dance. She loved it as they shuffled across the floor together at some speed and with much merriment while the band swung their way through a completely new set of numbers, but by the time the musicians paused for refreshments again she was so exhausted that she was not sorry when Duncan dropped his arms and asked if he could get her a drink. Despite the chill of the evening, she was now very hot and she welcomed the break and the sharpness of the homemade cordial that revived her.

'Well, I'm sure this is all a great deal of fun,' Duncan said with a grin, as he patted his brow with a large white square of handkerchief, 'and I thank you for that.' Then he tilted his head and lowered his voice as he suddenly leaned towards her. 'But I think there is a whole lot more fun to be had elsewhere.'

Aware that he was now staring at her meaningfully, Lily suddenly felt coy, for she was not sure whether she had fully understood his meaning. But when he leaned in even more closely and whispered, 'Why don't you come to my room? We can make our own music and I've got a bottle of bubbly we can pop,' she clearly understood what he meant, though she wasn't sure how to reply.

'Ten minutes?' he said.

'Oh, but I don't know . . .' she began.

'You go up the main staircase and follow the landing to the left,' was his immediate response. 'It's the third door on the right at the end of the corridor, next to the nursery,' he said, as if she should know where the nursery was. Not wanting to appear ignorant, she didn't ask for more specific details though her heart was pumping wildly as she imagined herself trying to find her way about the large house. But she couldn't speak and she felt the blood rise from her exposed neck right up to her cheeks and beyond as she considered what they might get up to when she found him. For a moment she had a flashing image of Johnny, and knew she could never let that happen again, but she was confident that she had grown up and matured since then and this time she knew what she had to say.

The village band had paused for a few minutes when Duncan left and Lily stood alone. People were chatting in small groups and it gave her time to control her breathing and to think very carefully concerning what she was about to do as she slowly surveyed the room. Margaret and Jenny seemed to have become attached to two of the British airmen who had stripes on their sleeves and she was not surprised to see Vera no longer standing on her own, but deep in conversation with Pietro. Lily allowed a respectable length of time to elapse before she followed Duncan out of the room and she made no attempt to acknowledge any of her friends as she left.

She took what she assumed was the main staircase, but when she counted the rooms off the landing she realized she had clearly made a mistake and she wasn't sure what she should do. She knocked gingerly on the only door on the right-hand side of the corridor and, when no one came to answer it or called for her to enter, she cautiously turned the handle and peeped inside. It turned out to be a large bathroom with a freestanding bath on clawed feet and she hastily shut the door again and went back down the stairs.

She was relieved when she finally found what she now recognized as the main staircase. It swept majestic-ally round both sides of a central flight of stairs and when she stepped onto the landing and veered to the left as Duncan had instructed, she was able to count up ahead to where she could see the third door on the right. However, as she did so, she saw someone entering the corridor from the other end and come walking towards her. Hoping she hadn't yet been seen, Lily took a step back into the shadows until she was almost entirely hidden by an enormous velvet drape that covered the wall and casement window from floor to ceiling. She stood perfectly still and held her breath, counting off the moments she thought it would take for the figure to pass her hiding place, but when she heard no sounds and felt no movement, she ventured to peer out from behind the curtain. She was just in time to see Tucker, carrying a glass of what could have been whisky on a small silver tray, stop outside the third door on the right and give a timid knock. She heard nothing more, though she assumed someone must have responded for Tucker grasped the handle boldly and disappeared from view.

Lily stared aghast, as the door shut firmly behind the maidservant and she hardly dared to breathe as she waited for Tucker to reappear. But Tucker didn't, and although Lily waited for some time it became obvious that neither she nor Duncan would be making a further appearance. It wasn't until the giant, free-standing clock in the reception area below struck ten that Lily realized how long she had been waiting and she was tense and stiff from having been frozen in one position. Feeling foolish, yet hardly able to believe what she had witnessed, she cautiously slid out from her hiding place. She made sure there was no one else about before she went slowly downstairs and made her way back to the drawing room.

There was slow music now issuing from the gramophone where the corporal and another soldier seemed to be in charge of the records, and only half a dozen couples were wrapped in each other's arms on the dance floor, swaying slowly to the gentle rhythms. Everyone else, including Vera and Pietro, seemed to have disappeared. Lily smiled up at the two airmen and pretended to look at some of the titles of Duncan's large collection while she tried to decide what to do. She was hardly able to see the words on the labels through the mist that was clouding her vision, but in her mind's eye she could see the determined look on Tucker's face and she wondered if she had had a narrow escape.

Lily spoke to no one as she wandered slowly across the courtyard and back to the barn where she scaled the ladder and threw herself down on her mattress. 'What's wrong with me?' she was crying in her head. 'Why do I always manage to pick the wrong boys? Boys who seem interested in me at first but who, when it comes to it, always manage to let me down?' Fortunately, she had not been seen by Tucker and she was thankful that none of her friends had been there to see her humiliation either, though she couldn't be sure if anyone else was in the barn now so she knew she had to cry as quietly as possible.

Vera hadn't known what to expect from something that was called 'a social' and she was pleasantly surprised to find it involved much scope for dancing and drinking delicious fruit punch. She had danced with several of the airmen from the barracks before the POWs put in an appearance but as soon as they arrived, she naturally gravitated towards Pietro. His eyes widened when he saw her and for a moment he held her at arm's length.

'You look very pretty,' he said.

Vera smiled shyly. That was what Bob always used to say when she wore this outfit.

'Bob very lucky man.'

They danced several times and Vera couldn't help wondering what it might have felt like to be dancing once again with Bob, until eventually she felt so overwhelmed by feelings of homesickness that she had to pull away and suggested they have a break.

They took their drinks to a quiet corner of the room, away from the band. There they sat at one of the small tables that had been carefully covered by a special cloth and talked without being drowned out by the music. Jones was wandering about the room with a large glass jug, offering to refresh people's drinks, but it soon became clear that his offer of service was not extended to the POWs. Pietro made no comment but got up and collected their empty glasses. 'I go. I get more to drink,' he said, pointing to where the punch bowl stood on the table next to what was left of the snacks.

'He not nice person,' he said, indicating Jones. 'I not understand but he no like Italian people.' And he quickly came back with two full glasses. Vera found she couldn't stop her body swaying in time to the music and her foot was gently tapping on the wooden floor. You want more dance?' Pietro asked.

Vera shook her head. 'No thanks. Maybe later,' she said.

'OK. Then now you see picture.' He put his glass down on the table. 'See, I bring special to show you,' he said, and he delved into one of the front pockets of his uniform shirt. 'This my fiancée,' Pietro said proudly as he laid it on the table. Vera picked up the picture of a girl with thickly braided dark hair and a broad smile and studied it.

'She beautiful, no?' Pietro said. 'She really like film star also.'

Vera stared down at the dark-haired young girl in the photograph and was struck by her bright shining eyes. Even in the cracked, much-handled picture her beauty shone out.

'She's lovely,' Vera agreed with a smile. No wonder

he couldn't wait to get home to her, she thought, but would such a lovely young girl still be waiting?

'You have picture of Bob?'

Vera shook her head. It hadn't occurred to her to ask Bob for a picture when she saw him every day, and her mother hadn't allowed them to have their picture taken together when they first talked of getting engaged.

Pietro laughed. 'Never mind.' He leaned over and peered into her glass. 'You finish drink?' he enquired. 'You want more?'

Vera took a final gulp and emptied her glass. 'No, thanks,' she said, 'I've had enough.'

'Then come, we go for walk now. We see big moon. Very bright. Very beautiful.'

Vera hesitated and shivered involuntarily.

'Too cold to walk?' Pietro said.

'Not at all,' Vera said. 'I have my shawl,' and she drew the large woollen scarf from the chair where she had thrown it and put it across her shoulders and around her arms as she spoke. Pietro put his hand under her elbow to steer her from the room and as he led the way out of the house, Vera was suddenly aware of his closeness.

'We see moon then we find shelter,' Pietro said. 'I know place.'

And he led her away from the manor to a glade in a small stand of trees, above which the moon rose in silvery splendour. Vera was struck by the warmth of him as he stood behind her and wrapped both his arms around her. She had to admit it was very comforting and also romantic standing under the full moon like that.

'It's very beautiful, just like in the films,' she said out loud, and her first thought was that she was sorry that Bob wasn't with her. But if she was honest, Bob was never one to be overly romantic although she was sure that even he would have been moved by this magnificent moon. She had really missed him recently, hated that he hadn't written to her for ages, even though she had sent him one recently as she had vowed to do, and she thought about what he might be doing right now at home. Was he missing her, she wondered? Pietro was convinced his Sophia was waiting for him. Would Bob actually be waiting for her?

'Tonight is night for love,' Pietro suddenly said and Vera felt a moment of alarm as she was shaken out of her reverie. 'Is good, yes?' he said. 'But too cold. We need warm. I show you. Why not enjoy?'

He pulled her closer to him, embracing her with the bulk of his body as they walked towards the gardens where they had been working so hard during the day. Then she remembered the little hut-like structure where they had sought shelter one afternoon when the rain had been particularly heavy. They stepped inside where it was quiet and surprisingly warm and suddenly Vera felt Pietro's lips descend on hers. Then she gave herself up to his kiss.

A moment later Vera pulled away and looked into Pietro's kind eyes. His kiss was nice – but all she could think about was Bob and how she would feel if she knew he was kissing a lass down at the Rovers. She also hadn't felt that warm, funny feeling in her stomach that she got when Bob kissed her.

'I'm sorry, Pietro,' she said, pulling back. 'I don't think I can give you my love tonight.'

Pietro looked into her eyes and sighed. Then he dug into his pocket and pulled out the picture of his Italian girlfriend, Sophia. 'The eyes of those we love still see us even though they are not here, yes?'

Vera nodded.

'Long time it has been since I hear from Sophia.' He gazed at the pretty Tuscan girl in the picture. 'I write to her at home, but no reply. Maybe she is gone or married to another. Maybe she not survive?'

'I'm sure she's all right, Pietro,' Vera tried to reassure him. 'It must be very hard for her to know where you are.'

'You think so?' he asked her earnestly.

'I'm very sure. And at least there are umpteen thousand miles and a war between you and her – I'm not sure what Bob's excuse is for not writing to me when he's only in Weatherfield! Even Eric the Bogeyman put pen to paper.'

'Ah yes, the boy with the dripping-tap nose you tell me about.' Pietro nodded.

'That's the one.' Vera shook her head despondently.

Pietro tutted gently. 'No one can really know what is in a man's heart.' And he lifted Vera's chin gently with his fingers. 'What is that phrase you English say, about keeping the pecker up? Your Bob loves you, I feel it. You are kind and lovely woman.'

Vera smiled and reached towards him to give him a friendly kiss on the cheek. 'Thank you, Pietro.' She looked at her watch. 'Lord, we must be getting back.'

It was late as they made their way back to the barn from their shelter in the little hut and, as they passed the Summer Wing, they noticed to their horror that the POW dormitory had already been locked up.

'Don't they count how many men they should have?' Vera asked, surprised.

Pietro shrugged. 'No, now we are allies. Also is easy to see everyone.'

'It can't be that easy if they didn't notice you were missing!' Vera said.

'They not expect . . .'

'But someone must have noticed you weren't there?' Vera was appalled.

'Maybe not.' He shrugged again.

'Well, you can't spend the night outside, it's far too cold and you can hardly go back into the house,' Vera said, 'so all you can do is to come back to the barn with me.'

'I see you back home. Yes,' Pietro said.

'No, I can do better than that,' Vera insisted. 'There's a store of hay kept in one corner of the barn downstairs – we all sleep above – so you can kip down there; it's very dark and it will be warm if you tuck yourself deep in the hay. No one will see you so no one need know. You can go back to your quarters first thing in the morning and hopefully no one will notice you've been missing all night.'

When they made it back to the barn, she showed Pietro where she meant and he burrowed into the sweet-smelling hay and fell asleep instantly. For a moment, watching him, Vera felt so sorry for this kind man, so far away from all his loved ones. She made her way back up to her own sleeping area and, as she picked her way amongst her sleeping pals, Lily whispered to her, 'Where have you been, it's the early hours?'

'I'll tell you in the morning,' she whispered back.

Vera was a light sleeper and at the first flicker of dawn she crept down and woke Pietro.

'You must go back to your billet now,' she urged him as he rubbed the sleep from his eyes. 'They'll have unlocked the gate for the early shift of POWs helping the cow men.'

Pietro popped his cap back on and made to leave. 'Goodbye, Vera, we have good adventure last night. And remember – Bob, he will be your husband one day and you make him very happy.'

Vera smiled and waved him off, his words making her feel warm inside. Maybe letters weren't that important – she knew how hard she found writing them – and maybe, as she was thinking of him, Bob was thinking of her and making plans back home on Coronation Street?

Chapter 24

It was later than usual when the four land girls went across to the main house for their breakfast the next day. Their wake-up call had been delayed as a special concession after the previous night's festivities, but they were all surprised to find the kitchen in an uproar. Mrs Temple and Tucker were fussing over the porridge that was still bubbling on the cooking range, trying to spoon it into individual bowls before it stuck to the pan, while the footman, Jones, was sitting at the table with an angry scowl on his face. Vera was astonished to see Pietro standing by the door with his hands tied together with a piece of washing line. He was looking bewildered while Jones pointed his finger accusingly at him shouting, 'It was him! It was him!'

It looked as if Mr Grayling was trying to smooth things over, but it was plain he wasn't doing a very good job.

'If you will all calm down,' Mr Grayling was saying in his normal, level tones and he raised and lowered his hands in a soothing gesture. 'Now that everyone is here we can go over it from the beginning.' He turned to Tucker, but it was Jones who jumped up and squared up to Pietro, poking him in the chest with his finger as he shouted, once again, 'It was him! I'm telling you, it was him!'

'Jones, will you please give Tucker a chance to explain the situation to the girls. You can't make wild accusations like that, not without proof,' Grayling said.

'They're not wild. I *have* proof,' Jones insisted. 'I saw him, what do you expect of a prisoner of war,' Jones sneered, 'and an Italian one at that?' Jones seemed determined to go ahead with his story. 'When I was on my way to start my shift, I saw him out by the POW huts, creeping back from somewhere.'

'Maybe, maybe not, but for now shut up, and let Tucker speak,' Grayling snapped.

Tucker turned away from the range, leaving Mrs Temple to dish out the last of the porridge, and faced the girls who had gathered round the table.

'What's happened is,' Tucker began, fixing her gaze on Margaret, 'I came down early this morning to put the final touches to her ladyship's breakfast tray as I always do, only to find that her favourite silver cruet set had gone missing. It's only tiny but she loves that set and I always put it out with her breakfast. It was there last night when I set things out on the tray, but this morning it was gone. Poof!' She snapped her fingers as if she were a magician capable of making something disappear in a puff of smoke. 'And when I went to the cupboard where I always keep them to see if they were there, I found that one of the silver sugar sifters, the most expensive one, I reckon, the old family heirloom that her ladyship is forever telling me about, had gone an' all.'

'And *he* took them!' Jones began shouting again the moment Tucker paused, pointing once more at Pietro.

'I mentioned it to Jones,' Tucker continued, ignoring the outburst, 'as he was the only other person here at the time, and he immediately said he knew who must have taken them.'

'I've had my suspicions about him for a long time,' Jones snarled, glaring at Pietro. 'He's always hanging around the kitchen. I found these in his knapsack!' Jones brandished the silver cruet set in his hands.

'What time did you put everything out on the tray?' Margaret asked Tucker in an effort to defuse the awkward moment.

'It must have been about midnight,' Tucker said, 'just before I went to bed. But I didn't notice them missing till this morning.'

'And did you lock the kitchen when you went to bed?' Margaret asked.

'Depends what you mean by locked,' Tucker said. 'It's not possible to get into the kitchen from the outside once I've locked the door, but someone could have entered from inside the house.'

'I saw him,' Jones suddenly announced and that brought an immediate denial from Pietro. 'What do you expect of a prisoner of war,' Jones sneered, 'and a dirty Italian one at that? He's really a criminal at heart and you must report him immediately to the police, Mr Grayling.' Jones seemed determined to plough ahead with his story.

'No, no! You not see. Nothing to see. I leave big house early last night. I not come back . . .' Pietro started to protest, but then he caught Vera's gaze and stopped.

'This morning, after Tucker told me, I went immediately to the POW wing,' Jones said, 'and when I said why I was there *he* looked so guilty that I knew instantly I was right.' He sounded triumphant.

Vera looked at Pietro. She knew why he had looked so guilty and it had nothing to do with the stolen silver. It was not that she and Pietro had done anything wrong, but she began to panic. Pietro refused to make eye contact but he looked so miserable that she knew she would have to say something soon, before someone acted on the false accusation. Vera knew that Pietro couldn't have stolen anything, for at that time he had been a long way away from the house and the kitchen with her. She couldn't let him take the blame for something he didn't do, even if it meant her getting into trouble . . .

Trembling, Vera stood up and cleared her throat then she spoke out as boldly as she dared. 'It couldn't have been him,' she said, 'because he was with me.'

'The whole night?' Jones said scornfully.

Vera was just about to speak when Pietro interrupted her. 'No, not whole night, I just walk her back to barn and say goodnight.'

'There, you see,' said Jones with a nasty sneer on his face. 'I told you it was him; he must have snuck back and taken them after that.'

Vera wrung her hands, desperate to speak as she knew this couldn't be true, but Pietro looked at her and shook his head, indicating for her to be quiet. Vera was on the verge of tears.

'That's it then. Follow me,' Jones said. 'I'm taking you to Lady Edgefield and she will call the police.'

Vera could only look on, appalled, as Pietro was escorted out of the room, knowing that he could face prison if he was found guilty. She was aware of the stares of the other staff and land girls as they absorbed what she had said. Now they all knew she'd been with Pietro.

That night she sat on the side of her palliasse, after a fretful and miserable day at work, wondering what had happened to her Italian friend, and she told Lily about what had happened the previous night and how it couldn't have been Pietro.

'What are you going to do?' Lily asked Vera.

'I don't know,' Vera said sniffing into her spotted handkerchief. 'If I tell the truth they might not believe me and think that I was up to no good with him in the barn.'

'But if you don't say owt, he'll have no alibi.' Lily remembered the word from a detective novel she had once read.

Vera thought about what her mother would say if she found out what she'd been up to and felt a knot in her stomach. 'Me mam will go mad if she knew I'd been cuddling up to an Italian POW after midnight.'

'Happen you're right – but I also reckon your mam would want you to tell the truth,' Lily said with feeling.

Vera thought for a moment then she nodded. 'Yes, Lily, you're right – I can't let an innocent man be sent to jail.' The drama of the moment wasn't lost on them. 'Let's go and see Lady Edgefield now,' Vera said decisively.

Chapter 25

Vera felt her knees trembling and she wished she could sit down as she stood in front of Lady Edgefield in her study, but neither she nor Lily were invited to sit during the gruelling interview. Instead she stood on the other side of the large mahogany desk that filled the study, wishing for the comfort of stroking the long, soft fur of the two dogs that were lying by the hearth.

'Thank you for coming forward, Vera, it can't be easy speaking out like that in front of your colleagues and I'm sure we all appreciate it. And your explanation of events goes some way towards illuminating the mystery, if not actually solving it because it is obvious Pietro is not the culprit,' her ladyship said. 'We've never had any trouble with our Italian POWs, apart from a bit of illicit moonshine production and fraternizing with you land girls and I shall not be taking any criminal action against him. However . . .' she leaned forward and looked severely at Vera over the top of the half-moon glasses that were perched on the end of her nose, 'I must make it clear that I do not approve of your behaviour. You were given clear rules to follow before you began working here and you have quite clearly contravened them.'

It wasn't a word Vera was familiar with but the angry expression on her ladyship's face told her all she needed to know.

'For the remainder of your stay, therefore,' Lady Edgefield continued, 'I forbid you to see any of the POWs and certainly not the gentleman concerned, unless Mr Abbott or Mr Clarke deem it necessary for your work. Even then,' she said sharply, 'I shall give strict instructions to Mr Abbott that, as far as possible, your work schedules should not overlap and that you be heavily supervised.'

Vera looked down at the floor, face fiery with the blush that she could feel settling on her face.

'I think I have been extremely generous with all of our employees,' Lady Edgefield said sternly, 'and in return I expect you to behave yourselves and not to overstep the mark. Under the circumstances I am prepared to draw a line under the incident – but I warn you: one more breach of behaviour like this and you will be reported to your superiors.'

Vera swallowed hard, bracing herself for what she knew she still had to come. 'Naturally I shall be reporting the incident to the POWs' commanding officer and I shall leave him to deal with the matter as he sees fit regarding that particular soldier's fraternization.'

Vera looked at Lily, puzzled for a moment, then she remembered Lily explaining that word when they had first read through the book of rules – and all she could think about was how she was going to get her extra parcels of food to Pietro. They had discussed a safe place to use in an emergency when she had first started bringing him extra rations, but would he remember?

There was a strange mood among the dormitory girls who were working out in the fields the following day and Vera felt it especially sharply as she set about feeding and mucking out the animals without any help from Pietro. After such an eventful previous day, the incident hung over them all and they skulked about as if they each felt they were personally to blame. Then, at supper, Grayling announced that he had some good news to tell them and everyone looked up eagerly.

'I'm delighted to be able to tell you that the sugar sifter that was stolen has been found,' Grayling said, beaming at each of them with a satisfied smile. 'And I can tell you that it is now safely under lock and key in her ladyship's study. Unfortunately, the family will have to think twice about using it again. This is the sort of situation that reminds us how valuable a piece it is and they may decide not to risk it disappearing again.'

At this, they each exchanged glances and looked as if they expected him to produce the sifter as proof of its safe return, but he made no such offer. 'All I can say is that it appeared as mysteriously as it had disappeared,' Grayling went on, 'but her ladyship is extremely grateful and she has asked me to tell you that she is satisfied that as all the stolen items have now been retrieved she considers the incident to be closed.'

'But does she know who stole the items if it wasn't the POW?' Jones seemed anxious to know. 'Isn't she afraid the burglar could strike again?'

'Not really, not if it was just a petty thief,' Grayling said with disdain. 'Whoever it was must have realized he'd made a mistake and that it made rather more sense to return the items than to hang on to them once he knew the value of the sugar sifter. It would have been of no use to him because he'd never have been able to sell it.'

'Why's that,' Jones persisted, 'if it was so valuable?'

'Because unless the culprit was part of a gang or a large organization he – or she – would have a great deal of difficulty trying to sell any of those pieces, the sifter in particular.'

'What makes you say that?' Tucker was interested now.

'You said yourself that the sifter was a family heir-loom,' Grayling said, 'and frankly, once the police issued a description of it, it would have become too easily recognizable to sell and much too easy to spot. That particular piece was so intricately fashioned it would be instantly identified, so the moment it came onto the market the thief would have been found out.'

Vera was thinking of Pietro, glad that his name had been cleared and that as Grayling said now, the whole incident could be put behind them.

She was hoping Pietro would get to hear the story of the return and wondered whether she herself might be able to snatch a few moments to tell him when she snuck out after supper to leave her parcel of extra food in their safe emergency place.

Chapter 26

Duncan, Marquis of Holden, sat back in the deep leather chair in his mother's study and put his feet up on the desk, careful not to let the finishing polish on the fine leather of his riding boots come into contact with any of the papers that were splayed across the desktop. He glanced up at the clock on the wall that signalled ten minutes to midnight. May as well make myself comfortable, he thought, I might be here for some time.

It had been a strange few days since he had been home on leave, first Tucker turning up like that and practically demanding the attention she felt she deserved given their previous history, when he had been expecting to have a bit of spontaneous fun with the land lass, what was her name? Oh yes, Lily. It was funny how Lily had never appeared at all, he thought, so he might well have been left in the lurch if he'd relied on her. A bird in the hand and all that. But imagine the shock she would have had if she had come across him and Tucker while they were otherwise engaged! Still, it was a shame – he had quite fancied trying out a new bit of skirt. But he could see now that Tucker wasn't going to let go of her previously established position without a fight. Never mind, maybe another time.

But now he had got embroiled in the troublesome little problem of a petty theft and it angered him to think that there might be someone at the manor who thought they could help themselves to a trophy from the silverware cabinet with impunity. Well, that wasn't going to happen on his watch, for watch he would. Tonight, whoever they were, they were about to have a rude awakening.

His mother had agreed to their using the study as bait and Grayling had given out the false information concerning the whereabouts of the finest piece of silver that had been taken, and he and Grayling had each volunteered to sit up for half the night in the study in the hope of catching the thief red-handed. Only the real thief would know that, regardless of what Grayling had said, the sifter hadn't actually been returned yet. But if everything went according to plan the robber would be tricked into coming to check what it was that they had under lock and key in the study. They were hoping that the stolen goods would, in fact, be returned tonight.

Of course, Duncan had his own suspicions as to who the culprit might be, but he needed proof before they could present the case to the local police and ask them to investigate further and charge someone. Duncan grinned in the dark. The idea of catching a burglar with the evidence in his hands appealed to his sense of adventure. A jolly jape, he would have called such a plan when he was young and at prep school, though what his mates in the army would call it now was anybody's guess.

Duncan wasn't sure whether it was the click of the door handle or the flash of the torch that woke him up, but he made sure not to move an inch in case it alerted the intruder. He lifted his eyelids a fraction, trying to absorb what little light there was, as he saw what looked like a hooded male figure creeping across the room. The figure stood in front of one of the glass cabinets on the opposite side of the room and carefully lifted the latch. Duncan opened his eyes wider and felt for the short, sturdy stick that he had slipped into his pocket for protection. As he watched, the cabinet door swung open and a hand lifted down the silver-plated sifter that they had used as bait in place of the solid silver one that had been stolen. In one move

Duncan swung his legs off the desk and lashed out with the stick, aiming for the robber's shoulder, and from the cry and the groan that followed it he knew he had connected sweetly. The moaning continued but Duncan took his time switching on the light and pulling back the black hood.

'Well, well, if it isn't Footman Jones,' Duncan said. 'I would say you'd been caught in the act, wouldn't you?' But Jones didn't reply; he was too busy nursing what he was convinced was a broken shoulder.

Chapter 27

Ena Sharples carried her regular favourite, milk stout, back to the table in the snug at the Rovers Return where she and her friends liked to sit at this time, early on a Saturday evening. Ena and Martha Longhurst had made a habit of meeting in the pub to swap news since the girls had gone away and Ena's friend Minnie Caldwell usually joined them. It was normally a quiet time in the Rovers, before a proper Saturday night got going; a time when it felt pleasantly sociable and not too busy and a couple of pints and a gossip could put them in a good mood for the rest of the weekend; but tonight Ena sat down heavily and scowled.

'Have you heard from your Lily, then?' Minnie asked Martha. She was carefully avoiding talking to Ena about

Vera, for the last time she'd asked about her, Ena had all but snapped Minnie's head off.

'Not since she first changed over from the training place to that fancy stately home where they're all living now,' Martha said, not without pride. 'She told me she was working on this amazing machine that did something with the corn they'd been collecting, but I didn't understand it, I'm afraid. Not that she ever told us much, really. Her father keeps threatening to go down to this place to see for himself but I don't even know where it is.'

'Somewhere in the countryside, no doubt, a long way south from here. Somewhere safe at least,' Minnie suggested with a smile.

'Oh no,' Martha said quickly. 'I've since found out it's not as safe as she first said. Seems they get lots of alerts and they even get bombs dropping so they have to run to the shelters. It seems the wretched Jerries will sometimes drop the bombs on them when they're on their way home if they haven't already dropped them. I don't know what to make of it all,' she said shaking her head.

'Whatever you hear from Lily you can't get less than this.' Ena suddenly seemed to stir. She took out a flimsy piece of lined notepaper from a small brown envelope and threw it on the table in disgust. 'This is what my daughter thinks can be called a letter to her mother,' she said angrily, not seeming to care that the paper had landed in a puddle of beer. 'As you can see, I've no idea what she's getting up to down there in this here army thing. The only people she talks about are what she calls POWs and Italian ones at that, so you work it out.'

'I can assure you we don't get no better information from Lily.' Martha tried to placate Ena.

'But Lily isn't expecting her mother to keep an eye out for her fiancé, watching what he's getting up to while she's away, is she?' Ena snapped crossly.

'How do you mean, Ena? What makes you say that? You make it sound like he's been up to something,' Minnie said. 'Like what?'

'Like nothing and everything, I hope,' Ena said mysteriously. 'Nothing that I've heard of, but I'm always hopeful that he'll do something daft that will make Vera change her mind about him, that's all.'

'Ooh!' Minnie's eyes sparkled at the thought of some juicy gossip. 'Do you think there's a chance of that, Ena?' she asked.

But Ena merely sighed. 'How would I know? I only see him occasionally at work so I've no way of knowing what's going on with him – and the last time I saw him he just said Vera hadn't written to him for ages.'

'I bet he's upset,' Minnie said,

'Not as upset as he should be,' Ena said sharply. 'From what I hear lately he's taken to hanging around with that lot that are always messing about on the

Field. Ever since they put up that Anderson shelter there it's been a haven for them young men of an evening, cheaper than going to the pub, isn't it? Not that I've seen them there myself because it's not a place I go to, but other folk have seen him and make it their business to tell me about it.' She shook her head. 'Goodness only knows what they get up to over there.'

'I wonder why she's not written to Bob, then?' Martha frowned.

'I've no idea. Since they moved into what she calls the Big House all I've really heard about – when she does deign to write – is how tired she is because she isn't getting enough sleep, and how hungry she is because she doesn't get enough food. And that doesn't make much sense to me, as there seems to be lots of bread and fresh milk and cheese available there, not to mention all the vegetables they grow. I've told her to count her blessings. She's far better off than she would be up here. I don't know what she thinks *we're* eating.'

'What kind of job is she doing there?' Minnie asked.

Ena shrugged. 'Lots of different things, if she's to be believed, like mucking out horses, milking cows and making cream cheese, but you can never tell with my Vera. She always was fond of making up stories, so I take much of what she says with a pinch of salt. But now she's talking about falling in love with some dogs that seem to be following her about.' She pointed to the beer-soaked piece of paper on the table as if it was of no consequence, then took another sup of her beer. 'I honestly don't know what to make of her sometimes,' she said. 'I wrote and asked her, have you gone all that way to look after someone else's dogs? But she didn't reply.' Ena shook her head.

'It wouldn't surprise me to find that the only person she has written to is Elsie Tanner,' Minnie suddenly said and at that Ena banged her glass down on the table, making them all jump.

'You what?' she shouted, glaring at Minnie and not seeming to care that everyone in the snug was staring at them. 'Are you telling me that as a fact, that you know for sure, Minnie Caldwell, or did you just make that up?'

'Oh no, Ena.' Minnie cowered back into her chair. 'I don't know anything for sure. I was only suggesting that that might be the case. I haven't talked to Mrs Tanner, but she and Vera were certainly very friendly before the girls left.'

Ena made a sarcastic harumphing noise and her face set into even harder lines as she continued to glare at Minnie. 'I wouldn't expect the likes of her to tell me even if she'd had a letter from Vera this morning,' Ena said, her jaw tight. 'I reckon she's too busy with her own affairs right now; too concerned about them GIs that she's so fond of.'

'I think you're wrong about Vera, you know, Ena,' Martha said. 'I honestly don't imagine she would have written to Elsie and not written to you.'

'You can never tell what my daughter might do,' Ena said. 'The way that girl's mind works is not like anyone else's I know. She doesn't seem to think for one minute that I might be sitting at home on my own, night after night, worrying.'

'It's a right shame after all you've done for her,' Minnie agreed.

'Well, I can tell you something for nothing, I'm not relying on that Bob Lomax to straighten her out.'

'How do you mean, Ena?'

'I mean that I still don't think he's the kind of man that she needs by her side. Can you imagine the two of them together, picking their way through life – or more likely *muddling* their way through. It would be nothing but disaster. No, I'm telling you, he's not right for her, isn't Bob Lomax. As far as I'm concerned we've not seen the last of Eric Bowman. He's still keen on her, you know, and, quite frankly, my money's on him.'

'Oh, Ena, you mean you've been stoking the fires?' Martha chuckled, glad to break the tension.

'Where's the harm in helping things along a bit?' Ena suddenly smiled.

'I think I'd have been tempted to do the same,' Martha said, 'if only our Lily's beau hadn't gone by the name of Bradwell.' She almost spat out the word.

'He might only be a rag-and-bone man, but at least Bowman is an honest name round these parts,' Ena said with a glint of triumph in her eyes.

'So how do you intend to tell your Vera what you have in mind regarding Eric? I presume you've not said anything to her yet?' Minnie was all agog.

'That's not the reason she's not written, is it?' Martha checked.

'What do you take me for?' Ena scoffed. 'I've been biding my time, watching Bob Lomax. He's pretty exposed since I persuaded him to take up fire watching and believe you me the minute he puts a foot wrong – which he's bound to, hanging out with that lot on the Field – then I shall be telling Vera about it. That way I'll be able to make her see sense. It'll force her to forget about Bob Lomax and to see Eric Bowman for the good lad that he is.'

'Heard from your Vera, then?' All heads turned as Elsie Tanner came into the snug, port and lemon in hand. She interrupted their conversation but she didn't attempt to sit down. She pointed to the letter that Ena had left floating on the table and took a step towards it as if trying to read what it said upside down. Ena snatched it up, even though it was wet, and folded it back into the torn lining of her handbag.

'What's it to you?' Ena said.

'Only that we'd both have heard from her at the same time, that's all' Elsie said. 'I know she doesn't get much time off, so why would she want to waste what little she does have writing letters? I imagine she must be out having fun, particularly now that they've got all those men on site, even if half of them are Italian POWs. Let's face it, they're much more fun than writing letters home.' Elsie stared at Ena, an innocent look on her face while Ena did her best not to react. 'And of course, they've the big party to organize for the weekend, so I don't imagine she has any spare time.'

Ena somehow contained her fury. 'Of course,' she said. 'She may as well enjoy it all while she can.' Ena barely opened her jaw.

'I thought I might write back to her later this evening. Give her some ideas about what she might wear and tell her all the news from here. Shall I send her your love when I reply?' Elsie said mischievously.

'Thank you very much,' Ena said, her haughty tone her only defence. 'But I'm perfectly capable of telling her myself.'

'I don't doubt that for a minute,' Elsie said and she swept out to the main bar, leaving Ena seething.

Chapter 28

Bob Lomax wandered slowly down to the spare ground known as the Field which he and his friends used as a meeting place. None of them had much money so it was cheaper to buy from the off-licence and meet at the Anderson shelter. As usual, by the time he got there they were already bolstered by bottles of beer as they sat in the shadows of several torches. They had started off as a fairly large group, but their numbers were dwindling as, one by one, they were being called up to the armed forces.

Bob had proudly told them that he intended getting married soon and he was surprised to see how impressed they looked when he said it was his choice and no, there was no baby on the way. This made him brag more than was warranted about Vera and he was proud to see that he'd gone up in their estimation when he'd hinted that they were as good as married anyway, in all but name. Bob hoped he'd sealed his reputation by boasting of the importance of his maintenance work at the factory and of his value to the neighbourhood as an indispensable fire watcher.

Tonight he'd been thinking, as he'd trudged across the cobbles, how much his boasts were justified, for it had been a particularly hard night, not only for the fire watchers but also for the firemen. Although he and his team had spotted several incendiary devices only moments after they had landed and had managed to smother most of them before they flared up into anything serious, there had been one bomb dropped on an end-of-terrace house where there had been more damage than usual. The local brigade and the AFS had had to be called to help fight that fire as it had spread more quickly than they could cope with. It had been almost impossible to contain and had threatened to rip through the entire street of back-to-back houses.

When he'd arrived at the Field, the lads were already discussing the notion of taking a trip to go dancing and Bob was glad to take his mind off the carnage of the fire he had just left behind, in which thankfully only property and not people had been seriously hurt.

'Hey, Bob! Have you heard about the new Palais de

Dance that's opening not far from the American barracks at Burtonwood?' It was Al, their self-appointed leader, who called to him as he grabbed a bottle of beer and sat down heavily on the hardened mud above the shelter. Bob shook his head.

'I think we could have a lot of fun,' Al said and in the semi-dark Bob had seen him wink and felt the friendly gesture of an elbow in his ribs.

'They reckon there's going to be truckloads of girls coming from all over Weatherfield, imagine that,' Al said, closing his eyes for a moment.

Bob's first reaction was to decline the invitation, thinking that he couldn't entertain the idea of going to a dance without Vera. But as the others ribbed him he began to change his mind.

'Just because you're engaged to be married doesn't mean you have to be tied to her aprons strings already,' one of them scoffed, 'especially when she's not even here to object.'

'You know what they say about what mice get up to while the cats are on their holidays,' Al said, chuckling at his own wit.

'Make the most of it, I say,' another voice added and several of the others muttered, 'hear, hear.'

'Never mind his fiancée, from what I hear it's his future mother-in-law he's afraid of,' another said cruelly and several of them sniggered.

'But how would she ever know?' Al said. 'Besides,

you've no way of knowing what Vera gets up to all those hundreds of miles away, have you?'

That did make Bob suddenly sit up and think. In her last letter Vera had mentioned a party coming up. How did he know what would be going on there? He had been thinking about it. Maybe it would do no harm to let Vera worry about what he might be doing for a change.

'So, are you with us or not?' Al asked, grinning. 'We're all waiting to hear whether you're a man or a mouse.'

'Definitely with,' Bob said without hesitation, though he did feel a moment of guilt as he said it. He wasn't normally much for dancing, but he realized that he was already looking forward to a different night out as they began planning how they might be able to use some of the GI soldiers to help them get out of Weatherfield and back again on Saturday night.

Bob didn't want to admit that the taunts about Ena Sharples were not that far off the mark. Vera might have gone away, but her shrew of a mother certainly hadn't and he generally tried to put some distance between himself and Coronation Street so that there was no danger of coming across her accidentally. Whenever he was in that part of Weatherfield he always felt as if she was spying on him, deliberately tailing him, watching him, waiting for him to put a foot wrong. But he decided, as he plodded home along the dark streets, that he had done the right thing. He was not going to let a woman like Ena Sharples damage his hard-won reputation among his mates. He plunged his hands deep into his trousers pockets and he walked the last part of his journey more jauntily, wondering why he had hesitated in the first place.

Bob sat back in the army truck that Al had arranged to pick them up to take them to the Palais, thinking that he now understood how Vera must have felt when she had finally escaped from her mother's watchful eye and had gone to the Burtonwood dance with Elsie Tanner all that time ago. Tonight, however, they were not going to the GI army camp but to the inaugural dance at the brand new dance hall that had been created from some old shops and warehouses. Bob had told no one outside of his immediate group about the dance for fear that Ena Sharples or one of what he called her henchmen might waylay him before he had even arrived there. Somehow, Ena seemed to have eyes and ears everywhere but he was satisfied that on this occasion she had no inkling of what he was up to.

The truck came to a sudden halt and everyone piled out, then Al banged on the wooden tailgate to tell the driver he could move on. Although the new Palais de Danse had been put together recently, it was far from smart-looking. The bricks had been refashioned from old structures and there were bars on the blackened windows. But once through the thick wooden doors, which had also been painted black, Bob was surprised to find the inside had been brightly decorated and was festooned with flowers and bunting for the special occasion. The band were just setting up and a female singer in a glitzy dress was testing out the microphone.

Al led the way across the room to the bar, which was already open for business, and as Bob stepped onto the empty dance floor he was surprised by the bouncy spring to the special wooden flooring. Some girls were already sitting at the tables that lined the walls, pretending not to notice Al and the gang as they went by, heading straight for the bar. Most of the other early arrivals clicked off in their high heels to a door marked Ladies, no doubt to adjust their make-up and put the finishing touches to their hair.

'The money's on you tonight, Bob,' Al said slapping Bob on the back as he ordered them each a beer. 'So don't let me down.'

Bob looked puzzled. 'How do you mean?'

'I've had a bet, between us, that you're the one who'll walk away with one of the lasses tonight. So make sure you don't get too sozzled to help me win my money back.'

Bob laughed as he stood with a pint in his hand, his elbow leaning on the bar as he surveyed their surroundings.

'I'll do my best,' he said and noticed that most of the other lads had taken their drinks and were spread about the room, pretending they weren't looking for potential dance partners. It looked as though it should be easy enough as there were several small groups of likely-looking girls at the tables that were dotted about the room. They all seemed to be dressed up in their finest and were alternately staring and then turning away to giggle behind their hands. Bob, too, looked away at first, not wanting to pay too much attention to any particular gaggle of girls but then, almost without realizing, his eyes kept coming back to the same group of three on the opposite side of the room.

'Who've you got your eye on?' Al said.

'Who says I've got my eye on anyone?'

'Come off it! You might as well have a telescope rammed up against it,' Al said and laughed. 'You know what they say, never kid a kidder, and I know what you're up to because I do the same thing myself, all the time.'

'And what's that?' Bob wanted to know.

'I make sure that they're eyeing me up and down as much as I am them, then I go for a different one altogether.' They both laughed. 'Keep 'em guessing and always on the hop, never let 'em know who you're after, then swoop and strike,' Al said.

'Sounds like a perfectly sensible strategy to me,' Bob said. 'So, which one do you reckon fancies me?'

'I'd say the one in the green dress,' Al suggested. 'She looks as if she's bought herself a drink before she's even started to dance. No doubt, trying to look as if she's Mrs Independent. But don't be fooled. I bet what she's got in that glass is water. If you go over there now, she'll down that lot so fast you'll feel obliged to offer to buy her another one and then she'll stiff you for something expensive.'

'That sounds pretty elaborate,' Bob said. 'Do you really think she would go to all that trouble?' He was thinking of Vera, who he knew was guileless. 'Do you really think girls are capable of plotting such things?'

'They are not only capable of it, but they actually do it frequently,' Al said. 'Look at her now, she's talking to her mates but she's got one eye on you. Wants to know if you're watching her. She'll take out her powder compact in a minute, pretend she's fixing her lipstick when really she'll be swinging the mirror round to watch you behind her.'

'Nah! You're kidding. She doesn't fancy me,' Bob said dismissively.

'But do you fancy her? That's more to the point' Al said.

'We-e-e-ll, not really,' Bob said, wondering if the joke had gone far enough.

'I don't believe you,' Al said. 'So I say get over there now and ask her to keep the first dance for you. Then you can relax and as soon as the band gets going, you're off.' He turned to one of the other lads who was listening to their conversation. 'Hey, Derek! Come and settle an argument.'

'See that small group of girls almost directly under the glitter ball?' Al said when Derek sidled up, pint in hand. Derek nodded. 'Which one would you say is trying to give Bob the eye?'

'The one in the green dress,' Derek said without hesitation.

Bob frowned. 'But how did you know that?' he asked.

'Because she's the only one trying to pretend she's not even looking at you when clearly she is,' Derek said.

When the band struck up, almost immediately everyone started marking the beat in time to the music. Then the singer picked the microphone out of its stand and tap-danced her way from one side to the other of the tiny stage. Al gave Bob a gentle push in the back that made him spill his beer onto the countertop.

'OK, I'm going,' Bob protested. He could hardly say that he was waiting until his knees didn't feel as if they were about to give way. But then he thought of Ena. He needed to show her that she couldn't run his life. And at the thought of Ena Sharples, the young girl he was pursuing suddenly looked very attractive indeed so he set off slowly and carefully, picking his way across to the other side of the room, more determined than ever to enjoy the evening. He had left Al in charge of his beer at the bar and when he reached the table under the glitter ball he immediately made eye contact with the girl in the green dress. His eyes slid sideways, indicating the dance floor, and he twitched his head almost imperceptibly to one side, the way he'd seen others do in places like the Ritz in Manchester when he'd been with Vera.

To his amazement, the girl seemed to read the message without question, for she passed her handbag to her friend to look after and took a step towards where Bob stood on the wooden sprung dance floor. He grabbed hold of her arms, not too elegantly, and guided her into the small space he seemed to have reserved. He began to shift his body back and forth in time to the music without any particular fancy footwork and, incredibly, she followed.

She said her name was Doreen. 'But I'm known to all my friends as Dolly.' She told him she came from the other side of Weatherfield and that she'd come with two of her special friends. Bob told her his name, but neither could say much after that as the music seemed to suddenly grow much louder. It didn't take long for the specially designated dance area to become over-crowded and people were spilling onto the carpet to dance in front of the tables and around the chairs, often pushing them out of the way to accommodate yet more people. Bob had never been to a dance hall that was so crowded and he soon realized that it didn't matter that he didn't really know how to dance, for in no time at all there wasn't room for anyone to move their feet more than a few inches in any one direction, certainly not in any kind of recognizable dance steps.

Bob was about to try the old favourite and ask her if she came there often when he remembered that the Palais had only just opened and he said instead, 'What do you think to this place?'

'It looks very nice.' He read her lips rather than heard her say as she took in the full view of the room. 'And the music's not bad either.'

Bob would have given up at the end of the first set when he returned to his pint at the bar as the musicians paused for their own refreshments, but Al and the boys pushed him back onto the dance floor as soon as the band struck up again and insisted he have another dance with a different girl. Dolly in the green dress had not been much of a dancer, but this girl was so gawky and poorly coordinated that she kept bumping up against him and treading on his toes. He didn't wait for the set to end before he returned her to the table where she had been sitting with her friends.

'Thanks, but I'm feeling tired,' he said as he dumped her unceremoniously and he shivered. He didn't care that he could feel her making faces behind his back as he walked away.

'Narrow escape there, pal,' Al said. 'You should have seen the look on her face.'

Bob ignored him. 'What about you?' he said. 'Why aren't you dancing?'

'I might do later but it's more important that we get you set up first,' Al said. 'You need to be your own man again now that Vera's not around – and most of all we need to get you away from that dragon who's going to be your mother-in-law.'

'Oh don't remind me,' Bob sighed. 'I thought I was supposed to be having fun tonight. Have I not passed the test yet?' he quipped.

'You're doing well,' Al said, 'even better than I thought, if you look over there.'

Bob glanced across the room where he saw that Dolly was staring in his direction.

'I'd say Lady Green Dress has now got green eyes to match, wouldn't you?' Al said. 'She's dead jealous that you chose someone else to dance with and didn't ask her again and now she's angling for another go at it. That was a smart move, Bob, I must say.'

'Maybe I'll ask her for the next set then,' Bob said, delighted that he was finally feeling able to relax and enjoy it.

Al laughed. 'So long as you don't look too keen,' he said. 'And don't be surprised if she turns her back on you at first. Remember, she'll be doing her own bit of playing hard to get.'

Bob felt Al's hand prod him in the back again and he was propelled once more in Dolly's direction.

By the time the tempo of the evening began to slow down and the band were only playing slow numbers, the crowd had begun to thin and Bob was glad the evening was coming to an end. He was tired out, not used to so much excitement or so much of that kind of exercise. If he were truthful, he really was finding it a struggle to think of things to say to Dolly and he could barely hear her over the music. He'd got so used to being with Vera that he'd forgotten what it felt like to be with someone else and he had to admit he found it flattering the way she clung on to his arm. So much so that, when it came time to say goodbye he was reluctant to let her go without making some move to see her again.

'Got a telephone?' he heard himself ask, although a part of him was wishing that she didn't.

She shook her head. 'But our next door neighbour's got one,' she added quickly. 'She could always come and fetch me if you rang on Friday night about seven.'

Bob was surprised that she seemed to have it all down pat and felt he couldn't refuse. 'Then why don't you give me her number,' he felt compelled to say, 'and I can give you a call. Would you like to step out with me one night?'

Dolly raised her eyebrows and looked at him

enticingly as she wrote the number on a scrap of paper she tore from a tiny notebook in her handbag.

'Aye, happen I will. I'll look forward to that, Bob,' she said with a giggle and, as she grabbed hold of his arm, he wondered if he had done the right thing. When she showed no sign of letting go he removed her hand firmly.

'I've got to go now – that's my ride home.' He indicated the truck that had pulled up close to the front door, where the young soldier who had brought them was revving the engine. 'If I don't go now it'll take me till Friday to get home.' Bob gave a little laugh and headed straight for the truck.

'Wait! I thought I might . . .' Dolly called after him but before she could gain any ground on them, Al was hoisting Bob into the truck and they were being driven away.

Chapter 29

Bob didn't think that anyone had seen Dolly giving him her phone number but he was wrong; and the ribbing started almost as soon as they began their journey back.

'Thanks for winning my bet for me. How soon can you phone her?' Al asked. 'Though you'll probably be home before she will so you'll have to hold your fire a bit.'

'On the other hand you've got to take advantage of Vera being away or else you're not doing your duty by us,' Derek quipped. 'I wish I'd met someone who gave me the come-on like she did to you, I'd have been all over her in a shot.'

'Where's the harm?' Al said. 'You don't know what

Vera's getting up to, do you? Let her worry about you for a change. I'm all for that.' He grinned. 'Otherwise it would be like a wasted trip for you if you hadn't picked someone up, and I'm sure you wouldn't have wanted that. You've got your reputation to think of.'

But instead of laughing as Al had intended, Bob responded defensively. 'What if Vera finds out?' he said.

'How can she? No one knows you in Burtonwood, do they?' Al said. 'And none of us are going to tell.'

'That's true,' Bob said and he moved inside the truck away from the tailgate where he could avoid everyone's gaze.

At first Bob tried his best to forget about Dolly. He conveniently forgot where he had put the phone number she had given him and he immersed himself in work during the day and filled his evenings as usual with his conscientious fire watching. But he couldn't actually stop thinking about her; and when he came across the piece of paper with her neighbour's telephone number on it, he decided to take the plunge and ring. He had nothing to lose and the possibility of everything to gain.

There was a telephone box on the corner of the street where he lived with his parents. It was well-used and often vandalized by the street's youngsters when they were bored and had nothing else to do, so that several of the window panes in the door and on the side were cracked or smashed completely, but tonight the phone itself seemed to be in working order and he went armed with enough coins to make more than one call if necessary. There was a dank, musty smell as he pulled open the door but before he got cold feet he dialled the number. It rang several times and he was about to hang up when a voice said a gruff, 'Hello,' and he pressed button A to connect. When he explained who he was a young-sounding woman cut into his planned speech and told him to ring back at eight o'clock when Dolly would be available to speak. When he returned an hour later, Dolly answered the phone and they slipped into an easy conversation. At least it was easy listening from his point of view, for once he had pressed Button A it was like throwing an 'on' switch. Dolly began talking and there was nothing that could stop her.

Bob lost track of how long they had been talking until a young lad banged on one of the window panes of the phone box that was still intact and mouthed angry-looking words. He kept pointing to his wrist and shouting at Bob to finish his conversation, until Bob thought he had better heed his words.

'I've got to go, Dolly, other people need the phone,' Bob cut across her, 'so how about we arrange to meet up? We could go to one of the cinemas in town?' he suggested, anxious now to bring the conversation to a close.

Bob was no longer sure he wanted to see her at all

but he needed to do something that would get the rest of the gang off his back. Besides, he kept thinking of the promise there had been in the provocative look she had given him before they had parted on the night of the dance. A tantalizing look that had made him dream of what might be on offer in the dark anonymity of the cinema; a town cinema as far away as possible from Weatherfield so that there could be no danger of being seen by someone he knew.

They met outside the Paramount cinema on Oxford Street and Bob thought he would impress Dolly by suggesting they sit in the more expensive seats. He was cautious about offering to buy any sweets or drinks to take with them, but before he could say anything she had made her way to the kiosk in the foyer. She picked out a box of Black Magic chocolates which she claimed were her favourites and a carton of Kia-Ora orange juice and then she stood aside, waiting for him to pay once more. Bob had hoped he might guide her into the back row but she said she wanted to be nearer to where the organist was playing and she led the way to the front row of the dearer seats.

Bob sat with his coat in his lap and, as soon as the lights dimmed for the Pathé Newsreel before the second feature began, he slid his hand under it and reached for her leg. Without saying anything she shook him off and returned his hand back to his lap. After a few minutes, without turning his face in her direction, he put his hand onto her thigh once more, making a valiant attempt to slide it upwards. When she once again removed it and placed it firmly back in his lap he began to regret the extra money he had paid for the seats and he had to accept that he had misread her signs.

When the lights came up at the end of the second feature, she once more gave him a sexy smile and tried to peer at him from under half-hooded lids. But he was no longer fooled, for he had come to the conclusion that she was nothing more than a silly little tease. He felt so cross he didn't suggest buying ice creams in the interval, but she did, and he was fuming as he joined the queue to the usherette's tray.

Bob sat for a few moments after the film had ended, trying to read the cast list while the credits were still rolling before the lights went up. But Dolly began to talk the moment the words The End appeared on the screen and despite his ignoring her she didn't shut up. By the time the auditorium was fully lit, most of the audience had already left.

'I hope you enjoyed that,' Bob muttered as he got up to leave, though he knew the sarcasm in his voice would be lost on her.

'I did, thank you,' Dolly said, beaming at him. She glanced up at the clock on the back wall. 'And I've still got lots of time till my next bus.'

Resigned to the fact that he would be forced to wait with her, Bob suggested that they went for a drink and he guided her into a pub at the back of the town hall, thankful that the noise level of conversation drowned out much of Dolly's inane chatter.

He ordered a small beer for himself and she asked for a port and lemon with the kind of confidence that made him assume she was used to drinking. It all seemed to go all right until she asked him to get her another one after sinking her first drink rather quickly. As if that wasn't enough of a cheek, he thought to himself, it only took a few sips of the second port and lemon to prove him wrong about his theory that she was used to the effects of alcohol. The drink seemed to go straight to her head, for she suddenly began to laugh loudly at everything he said, while she talked in a high-pitched, shrill voice several decibels higher than necessary. It was not the kind of behaviour he was used to, except in someone who was very drunk, and it made him appreciate Vera, who rarely drank much when they went to the Rovers Return.

Dolly was already slurring her words and her behaviour was fast becoming embarrassing. Bob was glad that he was a long way from home but she didn't seem to be in any hurry to end the evening. He looked up at the large clock on the wall.

'I think it must be time for me to walk you to your bus,' he said hopefully.

'Not yet, I've not finished my drink,' she said and he was sorry he'd mentioned it for she suddenly began to gulp it down far too quickly, her behaviour worsening with each mouthful. He wished he could walk out and leave her there.

'OK,' she said with an enormous hiccup, when the glass was empty, 'if we go now we'll have enough time to get some fish and chips at Carole's.' She tried to stand up but she had to quickly sit down again. 'Oops!' she said. 'Try again.'

Bob's eyes opened wide; he was anxious to be gone, but there was obviously no point in trying to rush her.

Dolly giggled. 'Don't look at me like that,' she said. 'I always have fish and chips from Carole's whenever I'm in St Peter's Square.'

Bob continued to stare.

'You must know Carole's?' she said. 'They do the best cod in town, not to mention the mushy peas.'

The whining tone that had crept into her voice was really irritating him and he didn't want to think about how much money he had already spent on her. But he would gladly buy her fish and chips if it would only shut her up for five minutes. She hadn't stopped talking since they had left the cinema. Bob silently counted to ten as he always did in difficult situations, then he grabbed hold of Dolly's arm and firmly escorted her out of the pub, hardly noticing that it was beginning to rain.

'Ooee! We must do this again some time, it's been such fun!' Dolly's voice could only be described as a high-pitched squeal as she wove her way along the pavement. She barely avoided the other pedestrians as she ate her chips from the bag that was tucked inside a large newspaper. She had tried to link her arm through Bob's until she realized she couldn't eat and walk like that at the same time. But she didn't seem to notice that Bob was trying to distance himself as she kept burping out the most enormous hiccups.

Bob had to admit that the fish and chips were good, but by the time they reached Dolly's bus stop he was feeling slightly nauseous and he threw away what was left in his bag. He started to reckon up in his head how much the day had cost him and he was sorry that he had. Vera had never been so expensive, nor had she ever been so much trouble; how could he have thought of replacing her? He had been led astray by his mates and he now wondered what he had ever seen in Dolly. He was sorry that he had let her think he was made of money. He had learned a rather expensive lesson, only a part of which he might have to tell his friends, but he was thankful at least that Vera would never have to find out.

It began to rain even harder at the bus stop and Bob made one last attempt to salvage his pride. As they stood aside to allow the alighting passengers to get off the bus, he put his arms round Dolly and, squeezing her to him, gave her as long and lingering a kiss as he could bear. He was concentrating so hard that he took no real satisfaction from it and he didn't notice the first couple to step down from the platform onto the pavement, so he didn't see Martha Longhurst, her arm linked through that of her long-suffering husband Percy, staring at him in disbelief.

Chapter 30

'How the heck should I know Ena Sharples' daughter's intended? Ena's your friend not mine,' Percy Longhurst said crossly. 'And what difference would it make anyway?' They were making their way towards Deansgate where they could catch a direct bus to Weatherfield, heads down against the driving rain that must have started while they'd been in the Regal cinema on Oxford Road. Martha let out an exasperated sigh.

'The difference is that you'd understand what I'm saying for once!' Martha snapped. 'Here's poor Vera thinking she's going to get married and yet, while she's away serving her country, here's Bob Lomax necking, snogging or whatever it is they call it these days, kissing like there's no tomorrow, with another girl! And not a

Weatherfield one. It's no wonder Ena never liked him. She took against him right from the start. She always said she could see right through him, I'll give her that. Wait till I tell her this.' Martha giggled. 'I'll tell her she can get that Eric out of mothballs like she's been itching to do for a while since. Let's see what Vera makes of that.'

'Eric? Bob? I don't know,' Percy said. 'I can't keep up with our Lily's shenanigans, let alone Vera's. How am I supposed to know who any of these people are?'

'It might be nice if you took an interest in other folk from time to time, then you'd know what I was talking about. I hope you would care if it was our Lily's intended.'

'But it isn't, is it? She's a long way away and not trapped in any long engagement nonsense with someone nobody approves of, so don't talk such rubbish.'

Martha stopped and turned to stare at him.

'She's no further away than Vera.' Martha sounded incredulous. 'In fact, she's probably with Vera at this very minute.'

'I wonder what they're getting up to then?' Percy muttered. 'Nothing good, I shouldn't wonder.'

Irritated, Martha shook her arm free as they walked across Albert Square in silence.

'I tell you what,' Percy said with a tolerant smile, looping her arm through his again, 'when we get home why don't you go round to the Rovers and then you can gossip about these people to your heart's content?'

'Don't worry, I will,' Martha shot back. 'I'm sure Ena will be very interested in what I've got to say, even if you aren't.'

Martha was disappointed that neither Ena nor Minnie was there when she arrived at the Rovers Return but it wasn't long before Ena came in, waving the letter she'd received that day from Vera.

'I hope she's having a good time,' Martha said, a rather smug expression on her face.

'She most certainly is. They had some fancy party at the weekend up at the big house she's always banging on about,' Ena said not without pride.

'Good. I'm glad to hear it,' Martha said, trying desperately to get the most out of an element of surprise, 'because that so-called fiancé of hers is certainly enjoying himself in her absence.'

Martha sat back as she delivered the news. She tried to hold Ena's gaze as she laid down her trump card but she had to look away as she saw her friend's brows come together, her eyes clouding with anger.

'How do you mean?' Ena's voice was strained. 'What's he been up to then?'

Martha related what she had seen with a few embellishments and without explaining that the whole scene had only taken a matter of seconds. 'All I can say is, you should have seen them.' She had to look away for a moment as she was feeling intimidated by the strength of Ena's anger but that didn't stop her trying to make the most of her few minutes of glory. 'All over each other they were,' she said. 'Like two ferrets in a sack. He couldn't get enough of her.' She took a sup from her glass while she let the news sink in, though she did become a little concerned when she saw Ena's face actually turn from red to puce.

'What did I always say?' Ena barked out eventually. 'You can't deny it. I said no good would ever come of it and I've been proved right.'

'What are you going to do, Ena?' Martha's voice sounded soft, almost timid compared to her friend's.

'Do?' Ena said. She pitched her voice low now and that made it actually sound more dangerous. 'I shall challenge that little worm, that's what I'll do. Find out what he thinks he's doing, playing fast and loose with my daughter's feelings. But even before that I shall be round at the Bowmans, suggesting that now might be a good time for Eric to write to Vera again.'

'Oh, Ena! Do you really think he can?' Martha giggled behind her hand and the words were out before she could stop them.

'What do you mean? Of course he can. He went to school, didn't he?'

'Well I suppose he must have,' Martha said apologetically, 'but from what I've heard . . .'

'What have you heard?' Ena snapped. 'A load of idle gossip put about by them as are jealous?'

'Jealous of what?' Martha felt she had to interrupt.

'Jealous of the fact that Eric Bowman, possibly an heir to a sizeable fortune, doesn't fancy their daughters.' Ena sat back with some satisfaction, gratified by the reaction to her revelation. 'Oh, yes.' She nodded her head, unconcerned about what she might be doing to her own reputation. 'He's worth a bob or two, you know, is Eric Bowman.' She gave an enigmatic smile. 'When his father goes . . .'

'Oh, Ena, he's not that old!' Martha looked aghast.

'No, well, I'm not saying that he is, what I'm trying to tell you is that there's no shame in rag-and-bone. In fact, there's money in it.' And she buried her face in her glass.

'So are you going to tell Vera then?' Martha tried once more to reclaim the limelight. 'About Bob.'

'I can't write to her fast enough, Martha, believe you me!'

'Here, let me get you another drink,' Martha said with a satisfied smile and she took their empty glasses back to the bar.

Minnie Caldwell had just arrived and was buying her own drink and Martha took the opportunity to bring their friend up to date. Indeed, as the landlady, Annie Walker, saw to the drinks, Martha took pleasure in relating the story again in fine detail. She hadn't noticed that Elsie Tanner was sitting in one of the recesses at the other end of the bar . . .

Elsie stepped forward out of the shadows as Martha and Minnie disappeared into the snug and for once the pub's landlady gave her a smile. Elsie tapped the side of her nose and grinned back.

'Sounds like Mrs Sharple's is going to have her hands full with one very upset daughter when she finally comes home,' Annie said and Elsie looked at her in surprise. It was more words than the landlady had spoken to her for a long time but she was not one to miss an opportunity for some gossip.

'Do you know this Bob Lomax, then?' Annie asked.

'I've met him once or twice,' Elsie said. 'He's been in here. He's a good enough lad, and I know for a fact that Vera's really sweet on him.'

'Hmm . . .' Annie nodded her head. 'Then I reckon they're both in for a shock.'

'I wonder if he knows? Happen I should warn him that he's been rumbled,' Elsie said, more to herself than to Annie.

'You could be doing everyone a favour,' Annie said.

Chapter 31

Vera lay back on the hay in the corner of the barn and thought, not for the first time, how much she missed her Italian friend. She had grown used to his company during the long working days if they were assigned to the same task. She most enjoyed their talks when they relaxed at the end of the day and she needed a chance to unwind before going in for supper. She would tell him about any problems that had arisen between the girls, any worries about her work. They would talk things through and somehow he would make her see them from a different point of view. After a chat with Pietro, things never seemed quite so bad.

Today the work had been even harder than usual and her hands were blistered. She was tired and feeling miserable, but this time she had no one to talk to. It had been a particularly heavy morning, with the horses hard at work in the fields when one of the team had gone lame and she had had to quickly harness up a replacement.

She had then been ordered to the fields where there were beets and turnips to be gathered and she had worked until she felt as if her back would bend no more. It was getting colder as the winter was drawing in and it was more difficult to use her freezing fingers to gather in the sprouts or to keep the circulation going in her feet. But she was at least thankful that the ever-earlier darkness meant that much of the outdoor work came to a halt early. She'd completed the jobs required in the dairy, having to crack the ice in the washing bowls before she could clean out the storage jars and, once she had rehoused the chickens for the night and checked the food supplies and water levels for all the other animals, she slipped away to the barn where she was now determined to grab a quiet moment before the evening meal.

There was no one else there and she didn't have the energy to climb the ladder to her mattress. Instead, she threw herself down onto the comforting pile of hay in the corner. She took the two letters Mrs Temple had given her that morning out of her pocket and peered at them in the dim light, then, sitting up, she pulled out her torch. Two in one day; that was unusual and she wondered who they were from. The first one she could easily see was from her mother and she put it to one side; but the other was from someone whose childlike scrawl she didn't recognize. She slit the top open cautiously and turned immediately to the end of the single page to read the signature. The name ERIC BOWDON was written in the same childish capital letters she remembered from last time and Vera looked at it in disgust. What was he doing, writing to her again? This had to be her mother's doing. Furious, she tore the letter up without reading it. Was she never going to be free of her mother's interfering?

She was feeling so angry she almost didn't read her mother's letter either, but in the end she ripped it open and peered inside. The two sheets of paper filled with Ena's tightly cramped handwriting made Vera think of her mother's lips when they clamped together to form a distinct thin line of disapproval, but for once she was drawn to read them.

There was no return address, no greeting at the top, the letter went straight into, *I'm sorry to have to upset you but you can't say I didn't warn you. It seems your Bob has been playing around.* Vera caught her breath and she read the words again. They were penned so boldly there was no question that they might have been written in error. According to Ena, and a bit of detective work, Bob had been seen seen, caught in the act, kissing a girl called Dolly at a bus stop in town. *He must have thought a lot of her . . . Ena wrote. Not that it matters, but I have since found out that he took her to the Regal cinema and then they had fish and chips on the way home. I don't remember him treating you so generously!*

It was at that point that the words started to swim and Vera had to stop reading, her mind in turmoil. It was no wonder Bob hadn't written to her lately. Who was this girl called Dolly? How could Bob betray her like that? Vera was heartbroken. She looked at the words again in case she had made some mistake but when she saw how her mother had ended the letter she knew there was no room for misunderstandings.

He obviously had no intentions of marrying you so there's no point in getting too upset over him. You can forget the ring and the so-called engagement. He's a rotter and there's an end to it. By the way, don't be surprised if you hear from Eric – you remember Eric Bowdon? He still talks of you very fondly and I thought you might want to consider giving him another chance. I happen to know he's very keen. At that, Vera began to sob. How could her mother do that to her? Didn't Ena know how Vera would feel about losing Bob? Or did she really not care? Vera scrunched the letter into her pocket and curled her body into a tight ball.

And that was how Lily found her, her arm curved protectively over her head, her face almost lost in the hay.

'Vera?' Lily touched her friend tentatively and at first Vera didn't move. 'Vera, what's up?' Lily said. Then she paused before calling again, 'Vera!' and this time her tone changed when Vera didn't stir, for now she was getting concerned. But then suddenly Vera sat up and Lily could see that her eyes were red-rimmed and her cheeks streaked with grimed ruts of dried tears. 'Vera, are you all right? What's happened? Is there anything I can do?' She put her hand gently on Vera's shoulder. 'You've missed supper, you know. But here, I wrapped up a little bit of meat into a sandwich for you.'

'That's very kind but I'm not hungry,' Vera said.

'We've all been worried. Even Mr Grayling commented,' Lily said. 'But what are you doing here?'

Vera stared at Lily, as if not really seeing her, then reached into the pocket of her dungarees and pulled out Ena's two handwritten pages.

'What's this?' Lily said, not sure whether she should touch the flimsy looking paper.

'Read it. Then you'll know as much as I do,' Vera invited.

Lily picked up the letter and began to scan it, gasping as she read the opening few lines.

'Oh Vera, I'm so sorry,' Lily said. 'You had no idea?'

'None. Why would I?'

Lily thought for a moment. 'Things often have a funny way of working out. Do you think this could possibly be for the best?' she asked.

331

'What makes you say that?' Vera snapped.

'Only that Bob never did get you that ring. Is it possible that he's not the one? Maybe you need someone stronger, someone who can stand up to your mother.'

Vera began to sob again. 'You're dead right that she's the cause of all the problems,' Vera cried. 'If only she'd left us alone we'd have been perfectly happy and I'd never have had to go all this way to get away from her.'

Lily didn't say any more. She'd only been trying to help but there was a certain logic to what Vera said and she could see her friend was upset. She passed a clean piece of cotton material across to Vera to use as a handkerchief and Vera blew her nose loudly.

'I can't even tell Pietro what's happened,' she said and began to sob once more. 'He might have been able to help me to understand what made Bob do it. After all, he's got his own fiancée. I wonder if he's ever wanted to cheat on her?' Vera paused and, after a moment, looked at Lily seriously. 'I tell you what, if you really want to help, why don't you go to the rabbit hutches at the old tennis courts.'

Lily looked surprised. 'What do you mean? What for?'

'Pietro and I, we have an arrangement and that's where I leave him parcels of extra food each night. We don't actually meet because we're not allowed to, but he'll worry if there's no food there and I don't feel in a fit state to go there tonight. But you could go and leave this.' She picked up the sandwich Lily had brought for her. 'He'll like that and at least he won't worry.'

'Are you sure that's a good idea?' Lily looked doubtful.

'I've been dropping stuff off there almost every night since we were banned from seeing each other after the party and nobody has found us out, so you should be all right. No one will even suspect anything if it's you dropping the stuff off,' Vera said. 'Will you do it?'

Lily giggled. 'Yes, of course I will.'

'And if you should bump into him and have a chance to say anything, tell him about Bob and ask him what he thinks I should do.'

'Do?' Lily looked alarmed. 'What *can* you do?'

Vera shrugged. 'Should I write to Bob, tell him how he's broken my heart? Or should I ignore him and forget he ever existed?'

Lily put her hand over Vera's and looked into her friend's sad eyes. 'If we're being realistic, it's unlikely that I'll see Pietro,' she said, 'but if I do I'll ask him.'

At that moment Margaret and Jenny burst into the barn, astonished when they saw Vera. 'What's up? Where on earth have you been?' They spoke almost in unison but Vera didn't answer. It was Lily who said, 'I'm just going out and I'll leave Vera to explain where I'm off to and why.'

Chapter 32

It seemed to Bob like a long time since he'd been to the Rovers Return in Weatherfield; it felt strange entering the pub's trademark green doors without Vera and he was not looking forward to facing her mother there on his own. He had no idea why she had asked him to come, or why he'd felt so compelled to jump at her command when she'd offered no explanation. Her note had been curt, spelling out the time and the place where she wished to meet with him, but there had been nothing in the way of niceties and he'd realized, on reflection, that it wasn't so much a request as a summons.

It was late when he arrived after completing his fire watching duties for the night and the main bar was unusually crowded. He glanced around and he couldn't see Ena, but the landlady spoke to him from behind the bar.

'If you're here to see Mrs Sharples,' Annie Walker said, 'she's in the snug, through there.' He was surprised she had recognized him. Nodding his thanks he ordered a pint to take with him for courage and he followed the direction of her pointing finger. The snug too was crowded and he didn't immediately see Ena. The first person he did see was Elsie Tanner, sitting with one of her American airmen friends. She waved to him as he stood by the door and he waved back, then she indicated a table behind her where he could see Ena sitting with Martha Longhurst.

'So, you thought you could hide your little bit on the side.'

He was rocked by the loudness and directness of Ena's immediate attack as he stepped towards her. Nevertheless he couldn't find the voice to respond immediately and he put his pint down while he took a moment to reply.

'Don't pretend with me, lad. If there's one thing you should have learned about me by now it's that I can see right through you and there's nothing that you can put past me, even if you can pull the wool over my poor Vera's eyes. Fancy, you've been seeing someone else all the while you're supposed to be engaged to my daughter! That's what I call cheating.' She shook her head. 'Vera's far too trusting for her own good. I've always had to look out for her and probably always will.'

Bob had removed his fire watcher's helmet and now he held it awkwardly, shifting it from one hand to the other. 'I think there's been some grave misunderstanding here, Mrs Sharples,' he said eventually. 'I don't know what you've told her or where you've got your information from but when I explain the truth to Vera I know she'll understand.'

'Pah!' Ena said in disgust. 'You can forget all your fancy stories and explanations.' She waved her hand dismissively. 'I've had a letter from her only this morning, saying that she's heartbroken. In fact, she's so upset she never wants to see you again.' Ena stared at him directly so that she could see the force of her lies hit the mark. 'Besides, there's someone else in the running now and when she comes back to Weatherfield, I fully expect them to announce their engagement,' she continued, trying to put the final boot in while she was ahead. 'Unlike you, he really wants to marry her and he has a ring already lined up and waiting.'

Bob was still standing awkwardly at Ena's table; he hadn't been invited to sit down, and he could see out of the corner of his eye that Elsie and her friend were preparing to leave. They came over to Ena's table and Elsie stood back and regarded her adversary.

'I must say I feel sorry for you and Vera, Bob. I know that we've each got to fight our own battles, but this is one battle that you shouldn't have to be fighting.' She turned to Ena. 'I don't know why, for once in your life, you can't belt up and stop interfering in other people's lives, especially that of your own daughter.'

Ena gave an almost manic laugh. 'Sounds a bit like pots and kettles to me,' Ena said, 'butting your nose in where it's not wanted, Elsie Tanner.'

Elsie laughed but otherwise ignored Ena's comment. She pulled Bob away and whispered in his ear, 'You don't want to be believing everything she tells you. The best thing you can do to prove this one wrong, lad,' and she jerked her thumb in Ena's direction, 'is to stick with Vera. Give her what she wants and find a way out of this mess.'

Bob looked at her quizzically.

'Never mind Ena trying to get you replaced by some dozy devil Vera can't bear, you show Vera you're man enough to stand up to her mother and give her what she really wants.'

Bob still looked puzzled. 'How do you mean?' he asked.

'She's made it quite clear in the past that what she wants is you, lad. Am I right? You and a proper ring so that you can announce your engagement.'

Bob looked confused. 'But Vera's said . . .'

'And I'm telling you that's all lies,' Elsie said. 'I've also heard from Vera – and my advice to you is to give her a ring for her finger and set the wedding date. That'll stop this one,' she pointed at Ena again, 'trying to ruin your life because she'll have nothing left to batter you with.'

With that, Elsie squeezed his shoulder and walked out of the snug, leaving Ena with nothing to glare at but her back. Bob too stared after her but there was nothing but admiration on his face.

'Well!' Ena said when Elsie had gone. 'It's no wonder she's got the reputation she has round here.' But Bob had been bolstered up by Elsie's words. They gave him the confidence to see through Ena's bluster. He could never admit it but he did feel mean for having cheated on Vera, no matter how briefly, although now he believed he could write to Vera to explain. Elsie had given him new heart.

Chapter 33

Vera felt as if the heart had been punched out of her. She hated that she had heard the news from her mother and she wished that Bob had had the courage to tell her himself, but even as she longed for some sort of explanation, as time went on she gave up hope of hearing from him. There were times when she wondered how she would manage to keep going, but fortunately on most days she was able to get lost in her work.

She never ceased to be amazed at how much there was to do on a farm in order to keep the animals healthy and to make sure the plants in the gardens and the crops in the fields were in their best possible shape. At least the hard physical work kept her so busy during the day that she had no difficulty sleeping at night.

There were hidden benefits also from working with the animals who relied on her for their food and wellbeing. She found herself talking to them, particularly the dogs and the horses. She had begun to tell them her troubles since she and Pietro were forbidden to meet and she told them how much she missed him. Now she told them about her heartbreak over Bob and they didn't seem to mind if she made their noses wet with her tears. Sometimes she could swear the shire horses were pricking up their ears and nodding their heads in sympathy as if they understood.

Margaret and Jenny, as well as Lily, were sympathetic to her situation and they all offered to help in any way they could.

'I'm afraid there's nothing much you can do, thanks all the same.' Vera appreciated their offer. 'It's something I've got to get through,'

'And be thankful you weren't actually married,' Jenny said. 'I imagine that could have been ten times worse.'

'Listen to Job's comforter,' Margaret mocked. 'Don't mind her, Vera. But we are here if you need us to deliver food to Pietro or something, or to get a message to him,' she added. 'At least that's something practical we can do.'

Vera's and Bob's personal problems quickly receded in importance after what came to be known as 'the day of the bomb'. No one ever knew whether it was dropped by accident by a lost straggler plane or if it had been deliberate, an attack on a farm that would hinder food supplies, for it fell when they were least expecting it and did more damage than it might have done as it caught them all by surprise. They were used to planes flying back and forth in daylight and, unless the air-raid siren sounded, no one looked up every time there was a plane in the sky, so on that morning, when the major concern was for everyone to make it on time for break-fast, no one was immediately aware of any imminent danger.

Lily, almost at the house, noticed a problem of a different nature when she saw Tucker crouching behind the water pump on the other side of the courtyard, being sick. Her first reaction was one of shock as it reminded her of the last time she herself had been so sick in the early morning, during her brief pregnancy. She was shaken, thinking back to the night of the party and what she now thought of as her narrow escape. She wondered if the young maidservant had been smart enough to take precautions or whether she might indeed be in the same predicament Lily had once been in.

She was pondering whether she should let Tucker know that she had seen her, but she had no time to dwell on the question as, within seconds, she became aware of a high-pitched whining sound, followed by several moments of eerie silence. Then came the tremor of the ground she was walking on, the way she imagined an earthquake might feel, and the sound of an explosion at the same time. Lily was knocked off her feet and she noticed Tucker had been too. She only paused long enough to see Tucker pick herself up and then they both ran as fast as they could to the kitchen.

Vera, halfway across the yard, heard the explosion before she saw anything and then she was suddenly aware of the sound of smashing glass as windows were shattered in most of the buildings near to her and she saw clouds of black smoke coming from the direction of the barn and stable block. She knew she had been the last person to leave the barn, so her first thought was for the horses penned up in the stables, as she knew they were terrified of fire. Somehow she managed to remain on her feet and, guided through the smoke by the pitiful neighing, she made her way as quickly as she could back across the courtyard. She shouted to Margaret, who was already on the scene, that she should move the rabbits and round up as many chickens as possible as they had scattered about the old tennis courts while she put her best efforts into rescuing the horses.

What happened next remained mostly a blur. She remembered running into the stables where the horses were rearing and kicking, doing their best to knock down the walls of their individual stalls. Vera screamed for help to the men who had begun to run out of the Summer Wing, yelling to them to fetch water buckets

344

and hoses, then she quickly opened up the horses' stalls and, throwing blankets over their heads, something Pietro had told her should be done when confronted by fire, she spoke to them softly as she began to lead them to safety.

At one point she was convinced that Pietro had appeared at her side and that he was helping her round up the horses. She remembered thinking that she would like to hug him, knowing he cared about them as much as she did and she remembered moving towards him, but in the mist and smoke she couldn't be sure that it was actually him. It all seemed like a bad dream. Suddenly she looked up and when she saw one of the roof timbers catch alight and shift its position she knew that it was really happening. She screamed with whatever air was left in her lungs and, with all her strength, tried to push Pietro out of harm's way although she couldn't be sure in the billowing smoke that she had succeeded.

Somehow the horses were dragged clear of the stable yard and Vera managed to lead them through the archway and onto the lawns in front of the house where she removed the blankets that had acted as blindfolds. There Ken Abbott was loosely lassoing them together and tethering them to makeshift poles. Much later, when her prompt actions were commended and she was praised for her bravery in saving the horses' lives, Vera realized that she had acted instinctively. She couldn't remember much of what she had done, even as Mrs Temple dressed the minor wounds on her arms, but she knew that it was mainly thanks to the help of Pietro and several other of the POWs that she had been able to manage so well.

It wasn't until she heard the clanging of the ambulance bell that had been called to take him to the local hospital that Vera found out the extent of Pietro's injuries. She was told that the flaming beam had caught him as it had crashed down, badly burning his right arm and side, his injuries so extensive they didn't know at first whether he would survive.

Several of the farmworkers were also taken to the hospital, with less severe injuries, but it was some time before it was confirmed, to everyone's relief, that no one had actually died.

When it was clear that all the fires had been extinguished and they were eventually able to check the extent of the damage, everyone seemed to gravitate naturally towards the kitchen which became the centre for the latest news. Mrs Temple provided endless cups of weak Camp coffee and, at Lady Edgefield's request, even dug into some of the precious tea rations. People were milling about, no one sure what they should be doing or where they should be going when Mr Abbott appeared. He raised his hand for silence.

'I know you're all exhausted and would probably like to go back to bed to start this unfortunate day again,' he began, 'but I'm afraid that won't be possible for many of you.' There was a low buzz of muttered reaction to this news, then silence prevailed once more.

'Fortunately, there weren't too many casualties, the worst being one of the Italian POWs, though we are hoping that he'll pull through. As far as the farm goes, thanks to people's prompt actions we've managed to save a large part of the structure of the outbuildings, even though much of the content has been destroyed. Thankfully there were only minimal casualties among the livestock. So if you'll please report to wherever it is that you normally work, you'll soon see what needs to be done to patch things up temporarily. But you must make the animals your top priority. By tonight, hopefully, we might begin to have a bigger picture.' He paused, as if expecting interruptions, but when no one said anything he went on, 'Sadly, the land girls' sleeping quarters have been damaged beyond repair so we will let you know a little later about the necessary emergency arrangements.'

Chapter 34

Life settled back into some sort of routine after the fire but it had changed. The land girls still worked as hard during the day, sometimes working even longer hours so that they could have more leisure time at the weekends because there was more on offer now, different ways in which they could spend their spare time.

The main outer structure of the barn was quickly resurrected but the fixtures and fittings that had been destroyed were not replaced. This meant that the large downstairs area was ideal for hosting a series of social events. These were significantly smaller than the 'Social' they had enjoyed several weeks earlier in the main house, but these smaller occasions were held more frequently and were free from the restraints of the drawing room.

The land girls, airmen, locals and farmworkers and the POWs were now regularly invited to take part in sing-songs or to dance to the gramophone records that could be played on the old wind-up gramophone. These get-togethers were held as often as they could be arranged and occasionally the more technically-minded airmen hired a cine projector and showed films on a large white sheet. Then rations would be pooled to provide some cinema-style snacks and refreshments.

The sleeping area of the barn had been too badly damaged to be restored so it was decided that the land girls should be accommodated in the old servants' quarters of the main house. Vera thought it felt strange to be sleeping in a proper bed, albeit a narrow one, but it stood more than a foot off the ground and had its own individual mattress. She had been allocated to share a room with Lily and the two enjoyed being able to chat together before they fell into an exhausted sleep. What they hadn't realized was that they were in Tucker's old room and they weren't told for several days that she had been dismissed.

Lily was not so surprised. 'I told you she had early morning sickness,' she said to Vera, 'and you know what that means.' She tried hard to keep the triumphant note out of her voice. 'All I can say is, I'm extremely thankful that it wasn't me this time.' Lily shivered. 'That young marquis has a lot to answer for.'

Vera looked shocked. 'Do you really think . . .?'

'At least I'm presuming it was him,' Lily said quickly, 'although that's strictly between you and me,' and she actually shuddered thinking of her own near miss. 'I do feel sorry for her, though. I like to think I've grown up a bit since my . . . little problem. I'm a lot smarter now and I know something about protection at least and how not to get caught.'

'Doesn't sound like you're ready to think of settling down,' Vera said.

'Goodness, no,' Lily said. 'I'm far too young.' And she smiled, thinking about some of the good times she'd been having recently with some of the young airmen she'd met since they'd been at the manor. She hated to think of them flying off so soon and that so many of them would not be coming back, but she liked to think she had been able to help some of them to enjoy life while they could. It had been a silly, childish dream to even think of getting tangled up with someone like Duncan Edgefield.

'Are you ready to go back home, yet?' Vera asked. 'I know that we can't until the war is over, but wouldn't it be nice to see people we know?'

Lily thought for a moment. 'No, I don't think I am, ready to go home, not even for a visit! I've enjoyed these last few months and I'm happy to be a land girl until Herr Hitler is sorted. I wonder if I'll be ready to go back to Weatherfield even then. There's certainly no one I want to settle down with there!'

Vera's eyes suddenly filled. 'There was for me . . .' she said despondently.

'Oops, sorry,' Lily said and she went over and put her arm round her friend.

Vera felt unsettled and miserable after the fire because all her regular routines had been disrupted. She liked having a proper bed in the big house and she enjoyed sharing the room with Lily, but she still found it too painful to think of Bob and how he had humiliated her and she wondered if she'd ever be able to forgive him. There had been an unopened letter from him that had gone up in the flames but she didn't imagine it had said anything new.

She also badly missed Pietro, for he was still in the hospital, and especially she missed trying to sneak time to talk to him. She was greatly relieved to hear that he was making good progress and the thought struck her that she might be able to visit him in the hospital and so one morning when she was alone with Mrs Temple in the kitchen she plucked up the courage to ask.

To her surprise, Mrs Temple did not dismiss the idea out of hand. 'I could have a word with Lady Edgefield,' she offered and when Vera unwittingly raised her eyebrows, added with a laugh, 'She's not a total dragon, you know.'

'I never thought she was,' Vera said hastily and then involuntarily she burst into tears.

'Come and see me tomorrow morning and we'll see what she says.' Mrs Temple patted Vera's arm. 'And whether the hospital will allow it.'

Vera was so delighted to see Pietro that all she wanted to do was to throw her arms around him and squeeze him tight, but the pain that was etched onto his face when he made the slightest movement made her realize how impossible that would be. Instead, she brought a chair up to his bedside and they talked quietly with no attempt at making any kind of physical contact.

'It's wonderful to see you looking so well,' Vera said.

Pietro smiled weakly, as if sharing a joke. 'Good to see you,' he said. 'How long you stay?'

'We don't have long, I believe the hospital rules are very strict,' Vera said. 'Besides, Mr Abbott's taking the marquis back to his regiment – he had leave to see the bomb damage – and he'll pick me up on his way home. But I'm so pleased to see you for however little time we've got,' she said. 'How are you feeling?' she asked and she couldn't stop smiling.

'Wonderful to see you, everybody so kind.' Pietro tried to smile back though his lips were strained and grey. He glanced over to the top of the little cupboard that was beside his bed and with his eyes indicated a letter with an Italian postmark.

'My Sophia,' he said with a different kind of smile. 'I get letter from her through Red Cross. She never get letter from me so she worry. She tell me she is waiting for me. I tell her I am OK. The nurse, she write for me in Italian. And you, dear Vera? The fire hurt you?'

She shook her head. 'No, thankfully. Not much.' She indicated the small bandage on her right arm. 'You and me, and some of your fellow POWs managed between us to save all the horses.'

'Very good.' Pietro looked pleased. 'And Bob, he know? He worry about you?' Pietro asked.

Vera had never had a chance to tell him about Bob's betrayal and she hadn't intended to tell him now, but suddenly she found the whole sorry story about her mother's letter and the heartbreaking end of her engagement was pouring out.

Pietro listened carefully and, when she had finished, said, 'And you, my poor Vera? How you feel?' She suddenly felt uncomfortable at the way he was looking so directly at her.

'How do you mean?'

'I hear about feelings of your mother, but what about your feelings and feelings of Bob?'

Vera skipped the first part of his question. 'I don't know about Bob's feelings,' she said. 'I haven't heard from him.' She thought guiltily of the letter she had never read that had been swallowed by the fire.

'Then how he break engagement?'

'It was me. I broke it off as soon as I received the letter from my mother.'

Pietro looked shocked, though it seemed to pain him to frown so hard. 'You not talk to him but you do that? Remember what I tell you? How you know what is in his heart?' He painfully clutched at his chest with his good hand. 'He need chance to explain.'

'Explain what? My mother said—'

'You marry your mother? Or Bob?' Pietro actually looked angry and Vera was shocked.

'You believe everything your mother say?' he asked, his voice still sounding cross.

Vera stopped. 'N-no, I don't,' she said.

'Then stop talking of mother now. Instead, think,' he said, gesturing to his forehead. 'You learn very important lesson. You go home to Weatherfield soon, yes? You talk to Bob.'

Vera squirmed uncomfortably. 'I don't know. Since the fire we've been told at the manor that we can go home on leave if we want, but what will I be going back to? Bob won't want me.'

'And you? You want him?'

'I . . . I don't know. He cheated on me.'

'I know. But you away a long time. Like me. But me? Can't wait to get home to my Sophia.' He winced as he moved his heavily bandaged arm and he closed his eyes as if in prayer. 'Maybe they send me back to Italy soon . . .'

'And what would you do if you found out Sophia had been cheating on you?' Vera asked, though she felt mean for even suggesting it because he was obviously so much in love.

'I love her enough to forgive her – and we have been apart very long time,' he said simply. 'I still have dream. Many children, my own vineyard. We must learn to forgive.' He sank back onto his pillows.

'I think I'd better leave you now, Pietro,' Vera said sadly.

'Goodbye, my dear friend. One day you come and visit me and Sophia in Italy. You and Bob.' He smiled at her and then closed his eyes, falling instantly into a calm sleep.

Vera sat for several more minutes, thinking of her own dreams that had once been focussed on Bob and she suddenly felt a stab of guilt as she began to wonder about what it was that she felt for this humble Italian man. Who was she to sit in judgement of Bob? Hadn't she, in her mind at least, often betrayed her fiancé? When she felt the tears drip slowly onto her cheeks she kissed his forehead and left, casting a look back at the dear Italian man she felt so fondly for now.

Vera felt disturbed the whole of the next week after her visit to Pietro, for he had certainly made her stop and think. She felt she had grown up since becoming a land girl and she had welcomed the freedom it had given her to live without being under the constant scrutiny of her mother. But despite what she had said to Lily, she wasn't sure she was ready to face the prospect of going back to Weatherfield, even for a visit. But she knew for certain that she wasn't prepared for a life with the likes of Eric Bowman – or any other young man her mother might try to foist on her. She and Lily discussed it often and Lily was adamant she was not ready to go back on the leave they were being offered, but Vera really couldn't decide what to do.

One afternoon she was mucking out the temporary stalls that had been rigged up to house the horses until the new stable block was built, when, to her astonishment, Lady Edgefield appeared, whip in hand, wearing highly polished leather riding boots and a smart navy velvet jacket with matching cap over her khaki jodhpurs.

'It's Vera, isn't it?' she said, coming into the provisional stables.

'Yes, it is ma'am,' Vera said, feeling bemused and wondering if she should drop a curtsy. But the family dogs had followed their mistress into the yard and were yapping excitedly around Vera's legs so that it felt more natural to drop down and give them a stroke and a hug.

'I've come to see if I can get out for a ride this afternoon,' she said, 'while the rain holds off. Perhaps you could harness up Nellie for me?' Lady Edgefield gave a tinkly sort of laugh as she held out her hand full of carrots to her favourite horse. 'And then you might want to get up to the house. You have a visitor.' She looked down at Vera's muddy gumboots. 'I directed him to the kitchen, I thought it best if you meet him there,' she said.

'Yes, of course I can – and thank you!' Vera said, wondering how Pietro had made such a quick recovery from the time she had seen him in the hospital. 'It won't take long to get Nellie ready then I'll go up to the kitchen straightaway.'

'I thought it would be good for the dogs to have a lengthy run; they need the exercise as much as I do, although from the looks of it they might prefer to go with you,' Lady Edgefield said and she laughed. But when Vera had saddled up Nellie the dogs seemed to have changed their minds and went tearing off after the young horse as she cantered away.

Vera practically ran back to the courtyard, looking for Pietro, and remembered just in time to remove her muddy boots before she entered the kitchen. But as she went inside she was astonished to see that the only person sitting on one of the benches at the table was Bob! He had already taken off his cap and he stood up as she entered, awkwardly shifting from foot to foot.

'Surprised to see me?' he said.

'Yes, of course I am. I didn't expect you. You never said anything, you didn't write,' Vera said, her feelings in turmoil.

'Well, after you didn't reply to my last letter, I wasn't sure what to do,' Bob said.

Vera quickly explained.

'So we both have things to apologize for . . .' he said. 'That letter was an apology.'

Vera could feel her cheeks reddening but she didn't say anything.

'I had to get special leave to come here from the fire-watch crew.' Bob eventually spoke into the silence.

'That's very good of them to give you time off. How are things at home?'

'Everyone's well,' he said.

'What did my mother say when she knew you were coming?' Vera was curious.

'Nothing. She doesn't know I'm here,' he said. 'I thought it best not to tell her.'

Vera gave a guffaw. 'I'd love to see her face when she finds out.'

'Me too,' he said. 'I was hoping perhaps that we might be able to tell her together.'

Vera stared at him and frowned. 'How do you mean?'

'Well, about all that Dolly stuff.' He waved his arms in the air. 'I think your mother made more of a meal of that whole episode than was fair. After all, I didn't mean to hurt you. Dolly meant nothing to me. It was really the fault of the lads at the Field. It was stupid, I admit and I should never have gone along with it, but it was a sort of a dare . . .'

'The fact was you did hurt me, Bob,' Vera said quietly. 'I'm sure Mam was only trying to protect me.'

'Of course, I realize that now, and that's why I've come to apologize. And to promise never to do anything like that again.'

He sounded so sincere that Vera suddenly felt overcome and had to blink hard.

'I realized, part way through that whole sorry day with her, what a stupid mistake I'd made,' Bob said. 'She meant nothing to me.' He paused and looked down into his lap as he said, 'Not like you. I knew then that I really loved you, Vera, and that I'd made a terrible mistake.' He looked up once more and, as the tone of his voice changed, Vera examined his face carefully. 'I wish you could come home, Vera,' he said. 'I'm no good on my own. As you can see, I get into real trouble without you there to keep me steady. But it would be so much easier if we were officially engaged and you were wearing my ring . . .'

And he put his hand into his jacket and from the inside pocket pulled out a small leather box. When he opened it, Vera gasped. Inside was a small gold ring with a ruby-coloured stone in the centre, surrounded by gold petals and tiny pearls.

'Oh, Bob! It's lovely,' Vera exclaimed.

'Try it on. It's the real thing, so they can alter it if it doesn't fit,' he said.

'*You* put it on.' Vera suddenly became diffident and

she held out her hand as she had practised so often. Bob slipped the dainty ring on the appropriate finger and she held her hand up as she had always longed to do to show it off.

'It fits perfectly,' she announced.

'So there's no need for you to take it off,' Bob said. 'Ever.'

In that moment Vera thought of Pietro, thinking of his wise words and she knew that she could find it in her heart to forgive Bob in the same way her Italian friend would forgive his Sophia.

It was too easy to waste one's life, she decided, misinterpreting or misunderstanding. Far better for everybody that she should be willing to give Bob the benefit of the doubt and always forgive him.

Epilogue

December 1943

Vera thought that it was fitting that their engagement party should be held not only in Weatherfield, but at Coronation Street's Rovers Return. She was surprised, however, when Annie Walker offered to collect ration coupons so that she could put on a little spread for all the neighbours from the Street, for that was more than her own mother was prepared to do.

Ena had dismissed the whole idea of holding an engagement party as foolish and ill-advised as the wedding was never likely to take place, and she had frequently said so whenever she was in the Rovers. But, almost as if to spite her, there was a good turnout on the night of the party and even Ena's reputation for spitefulness and meanness didn't prevent the neighbours of Coronation Street from wanting to wish Vera and Bob well and to drink the couple's health.

The Lomax family were also grudging in their recognition of the event, but as it was being held well away from the Mission they were willing to attend. Vera was not surprised when Ena arrived late. She was only glad to see her at all and she was immensely relieved that her mother hadn't invited Eric Bowman or his rag-and-bone father to join them.

Martha and Percy Longhurst were there too, welcomed by Vera and Bob despite Martha's role in their temporary split, and Lily had travelled up especially for the weekend from Kent and she had swapped her land girl's uniform for a particularly pretty blue dress with a full skirt and fashionably enlarged shoulders. Vera couldn't help smiling when she saw her friend chatting up Elsie Tanner's airmen friends as they all stood together at the bar. It was a shame, Vera thought that neither Margaret nor Jenny had been able to join them for the party though they had sent their good wishes.

As the evening wore on, Ena seemed to recede into the shadows and showed no sign of proposing a toast to the young couple. Eventually Elsie stood up and tapped her glass for silence.

'Bob and Vera, might I say how happy you look

tonight?' Elsie began. 'Vera, you look radiant in your lovely pale pink that looks like it was made for you.'

'It was,' Vera laughed and nodded towards Martha.

'Then let me say that you couldn't look prettier or happier if it was your wedding day,' Elsie said. 'I'm sure we all want to welcome you back home to Weatherfield, however briefly, and to drink to your engagement and I know I'm speaking on behalf of everyone here when I say may the engagement rings quickly turn into wedding bells.' She lifted up her half-filled glass. 'Ladies and gentlemen, friends and neighbours, please raise your glasses and drink a toast to Bob and Vera.'

'To Bob and Vera!' the general shout went up as Elsie lifted her glass once more and noted, with some satisfaction, that even Ena deigned to raise a glass of sherry to the happy couple.

THE END

Violet Carson

The force of nature behind Ena Sharples

*'If you've owt to say, spit it out before it flamin'
well chokes yer'*

Violet Helen Carson OBE, who brought the character
of Ena Sharples to life in the 1960s in ITV's soap opera
Coronation Street, was herself born in the 19th Century
on September 1st, 1898. She was born in Ancoats,
Manchester to a Scottish father who ran a flour mill
and a mother who was an amateur singer.

As *Coronation Street* developed in the 1960s and 70s,
Ena Sharples' legendary piano playing and hymn singing
were much mocked by her Weatherfield neighbours but
maybe it is not surprising that Violet Carson began her
show business career as a singer and pianist herself and
that her musical ability and voice had already established

her as a radio star. She was much-loved particularly in the North where she frequently appeared, her repertoire ranging from comic Music Hall-style songs to light operatic arias. Initially, she worked mainly on the radio, later adding much-acclaimed stage and television performances to her curriculum vitae.

She began performing with her younger sister Nellie as The Carson Sisters, then in 1913 Violet became a cinema pianist providing the musical accompaniment for silent films. In 1935 she joined the BBC in Manchester where she became well known to listeners. Most notably she appeared in *Songs at the Piano*, but she was also a regular contributor to *Children's Hour* and became the star of *Nursery Sing Song*. During the Second World War she worked with the Council for the Encouragement of Music and the Arts. In addition she spent five years presenting and interviewing on *Woman's Hour*, six years as the resident pianist for the perennially popular Mabel and Wilfred Pickles radio show *Have A Go*, and made regular appearances on the hymn programme *Stars on Sunday*. She also acted in numerous radio and stage dramas.

In 1926 Violet married George Peploe but sadly he died three years later. They had no children and she never remarried.

Violet continued to enjoy radio stardom where her cut-glass accent and perfect 'received pronunciation' was a world away from the gruff, Northern vowels she later adopted in *Coronation Street*. It wasn't until the latter two decades of her life that she became a television star when she brought to life the razor-tongued martinet and gossip Ena Sharples. Ena was the widowed caretaker of the Glad Tidings Mission Hall and mother of Vera and Madge. Her straight-talking and caustic character, complete with her ever-present hairnet and double-breasted overcoat, quickly became a national treasure. She and her old school friends Martha Longhurst (Lynne Carol) and Minnie Caldwell (Margot Bryant) invariably sat drinking milk stout in the snug of the Rovers Return, criticising Coronation Street's residents and squaring up to Ena's long-standing nemesis, Elsie Tanner (Pat Phoenix). From the airing of the first episode of the soap opera on Granada Television in December 1960, Ena Sharples became a firm favourite with viewers and the character who was meant to appear for only thirteen weeks became a stalwart for twenty years. Violet had mixed feelings about the part and said, 'Violet Carson was destroyed the day Ena Sharples first appeared in *Coronation Street*' feeling that it had overshadowed all her previous achievements. However Violet immediately inhabited the role, saying of Ena, 'I've known this woman all my life.'

Wherever she went she was stopped by someone asking her if she was 'the lady that's on t'telly?' Violet, an accomplished actor and performer through and through, had much in common with the formidable busybody, Ena. 'I'm like her in that neither of us suffer fools gladly.' The series creator Tony Warren had worked with her as a child actor and remembered her as an imperious figure. It is reported that she once introduced herself to a new director on the show with the words, 'My name is Violet Carson and my train leaves at five o'clock.'

Despite Violet's grumblings, Ena Sharples came to embody the show and presenter Melvyn Bragg said of her, 'She was the rock on which *Coronation Street* was built.'

In 1962 Violet Carson was named ITV Personality of the Year. In 1964 she had a salmon-pink rose named after her and in 1965 she was awarded the OBE.

The character of Ena Sharples was firmly established in the 1960s though she appeared less frequently during the 1970s as Violet's health declined and in April 1980 Ena had to be written out of the script though with an option enabling her to return. Sadly, Violet's health did not permit it and she died on Boxing Day in 1983 in Blackpool at the age of 85. Ena Sharples may have slipped quietly out of *Coronation Street*, but she will always remain one of its best-known characters – the sharp-tongued harridan who viewers loved to hate.

Maggie Sullivan

Acknowledgements

When I first began writing this book, Covid-19 was not in my vocabulary and no one wore a face mask except at Halloween. And yet, this is the second book I have completed while being confined by varying degrees of constraint and lockdown. My thanks, therefore, go to all of those who have helped it come to fruition despite the difficult circumstances under which we have all been working. Special thanks go to those who have adjusted their work schedules and modus operandi so that through the use of modern technology, the book writing process has been able to continue. Who would have believed we would be holding meetings in the comfort of our own homes and producing books without the writers and members of the production team ever having to meet face to face?

To all those who have facilitated the birth of *The Land Girls of Coronation Street* through this newly evolving process, colleagues, friends, family and supporters, I would like to say a huge thank you. To Kate Bradley, Editorial Director at HarperCollins, for her help and guidance throughout every step of the process; to my ever supportive agent Kate Nash for her belief and encouragement at this difficult time; to my fellow authors and Zoom colleagues for taking time out from their own busy writing schedules to offer support and to share experiences; to Sheila Creighton (author Daisy Tate) for her assistance regarding farming issues; to Sue Moorcroft for her help with military matters, and for her and Pia Fenton's (author Christina Courtenay) weekly support chats; to Jannet Wright who was always available at the end of a WhatsApp chat; to Ann Parker, who deserves to be awarded shares in BT and to all my family and friends, in particular the Finlay family, who have provided more support than the word 'bubble' could ever suggest.

As ever, grateful thanks to Dominic Khouri and Shirley Patton from ITV for their endless knowledge and advice regarding *Coronation Street*.

Maggie Sullivan

If you loved this book, turn the page
to discover all of Maggie's previous titles,
available now.

Christmas on

·CORONATION ST.·

Can the nation's favourite street
keep calm and carry on?

MAGGIE SULLIVAN

Mother's Day on

•CORONATION ST.•

Someone's about to get
a surprise on the nation's
favourite street...

MAGGIE SULLIVAN

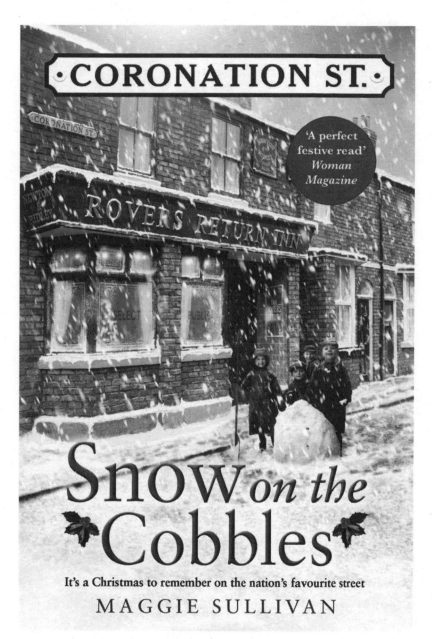

·CORONATION ST.·

'A perfect
festive read'
*Woman
Magazine*

Snow *on the* ❦Cobbles❦

It's a Christmas to remember on the nation's favourite street

MAGGIE SULLIVAN

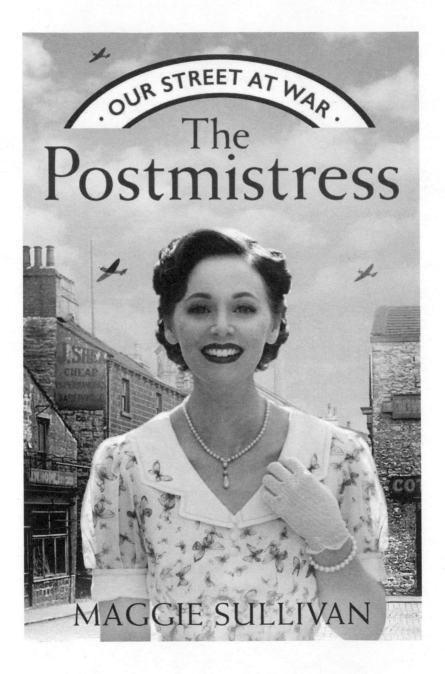

OUR STREET AT WAR

The
Postmistress

MAGGIE SULLIVAN